the

NAUGHTY
BITS

Edited and Introduced by
JACK MURNIGHAN

Also by Jack Murnighan
Full Frontal Fiction:
The Best of Nerve.com

C.2

the

NAUGHTY BITS

The Steamiest

(and most scandalous)

Sex Scenes

from the World's

Greatest Books

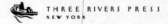

THREE RIVERS PRESS
NEW YORK

Translations © Jack Murnighan unless otherwise noted. Credits appear on p. 235.

Published by Three Rivers Press, New York, New York. Member of the Crown Publishing Group.

Random House, Inc. New York, Toronto, London, Sydney, Auckland
www.randomhouse.com

THREE RIVERS PRESS is a registered trademark and the Three Rivers Press colophon is a trademark of Random House, Inc.

Most material in this book was previously published on the website Nerve.com.

Printed in the United States of America

Design by Elina D. Nudelman

Library of Congress Cataloging-in-Publication Data
Murnighan, Jack.
    The naughty bits: the steamiest (and most scandalous) sex scenes from the world's greatest books / by Jack Murnighan.
    1. Sex—Literary collections. I. Title.
PN6071.S416 M87   2001
808.8'03538—dc21   00—047963

ISBN 0-609-80660-2

10   9   8   7   6   5   4   3   2   1

FIRST EDITION

To my grandparents, whose decades of industry have allowed me to spend my life reading and to turn the poets' pages with uncallused hands.

Contents

Do you ask why I fill all my books with wanton poems? I do it to repel dull grammarians. If I sang the warlike exploits of magnanimous Caesar, or the pious deeds of holy men, what a load of notes, what corrections of the text, I should have to endure! What a torment I should become for little boys! But now that moist kisses are my theme, and the lusty blood tingles at my prurient verses, let me be read by the youth who hopes to please his virgin mistress, by the gentle girl who longs to please her new-made spouse, and by every sprightly brother poet who loves voluptuous ease and mirth. But stand aloof from these frolic joys, ye sour pedants, and keep off your injurious hands, that no boy, whipped and crying on account of my amorous fancies, may wish the earth to press hard upon my bones.

—JOHANNES SECUNDUS, *BASIA*, 16TH CENTURY

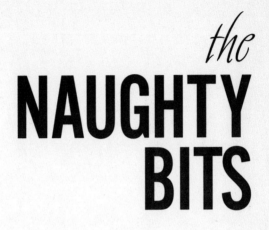

the
NAUGHTY
BITS

Introduction

Three and a half years ago, my best friend Rufus told me he and his girlfriend were going to start a smart sex magazine on the Internet. They were calling it *Nerve*, and it was supposed to appeal to men and women and pick up where *Playboy* left off. I was in the middle of doing a Ph.D. in medieval literature and was steadily getting as moldy as most of my books. Rufus wanted to hire me and offered to triple my salary. I had been making a whopping four digits at that point and thought it high time to break five. I packed my suitcase.

My first assignment was to do an article on banned books and to compile some sexy excerpts from banned classics. Putting together the predictable Boccaccio, Henry Miller, James Joyce, Leopold von Sacher-Masoch, and the Marquis de Sade, I jokingly argued that book banning was a *good* thing; it confirms the power of the books banned and gives people a decent idea of what to read. It also gave me another idea: namely, that there was a lot of sex in the history of literature and a lot in places you wouldn't expect. I suggested doing a weekly column on the steamiest scenes from books past. *The Naughty Bits* was born.

Every Monday since then, I've introduced and excerpted everything from Greek myths to Japanese cult novels, Sanskrit lyrics to New York slam. I wanted to include books from the entirety of world literature, but I knew that there was no way I could be exhaustive—or even include all the most famous passages. But in a sense, that's not what I was after. Alongside all the usual suspects, I wanted to feature writers and works that most people would be unlikely to associate with sex. Anaïs Nin, sure. Chaucer, of course. But Dante on erotica? Joyce on rim jobs?

So, although it might have been nice to call this book *The Best Sex Scenes from the History of Literature*, that's not what it is. Such a thing cannot really exist. Sex is too varied, personal, and intricate to qualify for Bests; what works at one point for one person doesn't necessarily work for someone else, or even for that same person at a different time. I also realized that the column would be a lot more interesting if I included scenes that reflected the truth and diversity of sex, not just idealized fantasies. Cormac McCarthy writing about necrophilia, a medieval poem equating homosexuality to bad grammar: these are not what you'd expect to find in your basic erotica anthology, and I'm happy about that. *The Naughty Bits* is ultimately less a book *of* sex in literature as much as a book *about* sex in literature. If you come looking for brief and steamy diversions, you'll find them, but if you are looking for the ecstasy, agony, absurdity, and poignancy of sex, you'll find that too.

Although I'm often asked if I'm close to exhausting all the naughty bits out there, I've found that the more I read, the more it's clear that sex has permeated literature to such an extent that I could probably collect naughty bits for the rest of my life. Sex is everywhere in writing, but it's not always there in the form we think it's going to take. And not all authors are up to the challenge. I often joke that half the sex scenes in the history of literature consist of only one word: afterwards. And it's almost true. You get all the buildup, perhaps even some heavy breathing and the taking off of shoes, and then "Afterwards, Gary and Bunny picked up their fallen clothes and . . ." Yeah, yeah. Cop-outs we have known.

The Naughty Bits is a celebration of all the writers who decided that a single word wasn't enough, that something in the knocking together of the bodies, the mixing of memory and desire, the slip of skin and sweat on skin and sweat was an integral part of the human experience—something vital to their characters and thus their stories, not to be missed.

Of course, not everyone agrees. Some people believe that sex is better left behind closed doors and that to bring it out for public scrutiny somehow demystifies it, strips it of its magic. To me, all human experience shimmers with the luster of miracles, if we can bring ourselves to see it. Poets and fiction writers do their best to point it out; in those rare moments that they succeed, they are really creating art. Yes, sex is full of mystery, but it would take a lot of monkeys sitting at a lot of typewriters for a lot of eternities to begin to capture any of that magic on paper. When we are examining what's worthy of spilled ink, we should be less concerned with robbing something of its mystery as catching some measure of it. It's doubtful that any art, even photographs, steals the soul of the subject; the bigger question is whether, when the negatives are tweezed out of the fixer, any soul is visible on the film. We have to hope there is. And if sex is so likely to be divested of its gravity by writing about it, then what of love? And what of death?

The irony, of course, is that the accomplished sex writer, not unlike the capable psychiatrist, neurosurgeon, or relief worker, undoes the need for his or her labor in the very act of doing it. You write well about sex and your readers close the book—to move on to the real thing. That's why the most archetypal of all naughty bits in the history of literature is also my favorite: Dante's story of Paolo and Francesca in the *Inferno*. Banished to Hell for adultery, Francesca tells how it was a book that did them in. They were reading the tale of Lancelot when things got a bit steamy. Paolo looked at her, they kissed, and the book fell to the floor. Now that I've got the best of the naughty bits together in one volume, I hope you find ample occasion to drop it too.

FROM *The Inferno* by Dante

. . . There is no greater pain
Than to remember happy days in days
Of sadness . . .

But if to know the first root of our love
You have so strong a desire,
I'll tell you as one who weeps while she speaks.

One day, for pleasure simply, we were reading
Of Lancelot, and how love overpowered him;
Alone we were, and free from all suspicions.

Often that reading caused our eyes to meet,
And often the color from our faces went,
But it was a single passage that overcame us:

When we read how the desired smile was
Kissed by so true a lover as he, this one,
Who from me never will be taken,

Kissed me, his body all trembling, on the mouth.
. . . And no more did we read that day.

—*translated by Jack Murnighan*

from Lady Chatterley's Lover

D. H. LAWRENCE

Lawrence delivers. No book in any public library is likely to be as dog-eared from furtive bathroom reading as *Lady Chatterley's Lover*. Sure old D. H. had some dubious politics—no small number of sexist and classist remarks suppurate forth from his books—but the man could write a sex scene. First published privately in Italy in 1928, *Chatterley* caused the predicted uproar and was banned in the United States until the late 1950s. Finally, an American judge approved it as the classic it surely is. The first sentence gets us going ("Ours is essentially a tragic age, so we refuse to take it tragically"), and it doesn't lose steam thereafter. Readers who fast-forward a hundred pages to get to the raunch lose out on Chatterley's nuanced social critique. But don't worry, that's just what we'll do.

What fascinates me about *Lady Chatterley's Lover* is that it manages to present some of the more piquant sex that you'll find in English literature yet also one of the most brutal dissections of the act that I've ever read. Which opens some interesting questions: Did Lawrence like sex? If not, how could he write such arousing scenes? Does not liking sex facilitate writing about it, or was he just honest and saw sex, warts and all, for what it is? I occasionally have the experience of listening to a Caruso aria, then suddenly hearing it as if I was someone who had never listened to opera. Stepping out of the inside of experience, the ordinary, even the beautiful, can become absurd. This is what happens in Lawrence's description of Lady Chatterley losing sync with her lover: "She lay with her hands inert on his striving body, and do what she might, her spirit seemed to look on from the top of her head, and the butting of his haunches seemed ridiculous to her, and the sort of anxiety of his penis to come to its little evacuating crisis seemed farcical. Yes, this was love."

It goes on in the same damning vein, but you get the point. And this from a woman who, as you will see in the scene below, had supped at lust's table, and greedily. It is a curious dichotomy—sex from the inside, sex from the outside—and Lawrence is savvy to present it. If there is a moral, and whether it's intended or incidental, it is to live from within. Writers, perhaps, have to write from without, but let the rest of us just be there doing it.

●••

He led her through the wall of prickly trees that were difficult to come through to a place where there was a little space and a pile of dead boughs. He threw one or two dry ones down, put his coat and waistcoat over them, and she had to lie down there under the boughs of the tree, like an animal, while he waited, standing there in his shirt and breeches, watching her with haunted eyes. But still he was provident—he made her lie properly, properly. Yet he broke the band of her underclothes, for she did not help him, only lay inert.

He too had bared the front part of his body and she felt his naked flesh against her as he came into her. For a moment he was still inside her, turgid there and quivering. Then, as he began to move, in the sudden helpless orgasm, there awoke in her new strange thrills rippling insider her. Rippling, rippling, rippling, like a flapping overlapping of soft flames, soft as feathers, running to points of brilliance, exquisite, exquisite and melting her all molten inside. It was like bells rippling up and up to a culmination. She lay unconscious of the wild little cries she uttered at the last. But it was over too soon, too soon, and she could no longer force her own conclusion with the activity. This was different, different. She could do nothing. She could no longer harden and grip for her own satisfaction upon him. She could only wait, wait and moan in spirit as she felt him withdrawing, withdrawing and contracting, coming to the terrible moment when he would slip out of her and be gone. Whilst all her womb was soft and open, and softly clamoring, like a sea anemone under the tide, clamoring for him to come in again and make a fulfillment for her. She clung to him unconscious in passion, and he never quite slipped from her, and she felt the soft bud of him within her stirring, and strange rhythms flushing up in to her with a strange rhythmic growing motion, swelling and swelling till it filled all her cleaving consciousness, and then began again the unspeakable motion that was not really motion, but pure deepening whirlpools of sensation swirling deeper and deeper through all her tissue and consciousness, till she was one perfect concentric fluid of feeling, and she lay there crying in unconscious inarticulate cries.

from Portnoy's Complaint

PHILIP ROTH

If there's a place where Catholics and Jews are in complete accord, it's in their sovereign deployment of guilt. My childhood home was ostensibly atheist, but the mere fact that Irish Catholic blood flows in half of my veins seems to have consigned me, phylogenetically, to the full complement of nookie neuroses. Had I been Jewish it seems I would have gone through the same issues, at least if one believes Philip Roth. The protagonist of *Portnoy's Complaint*'s agonized confrontations with his sexuality are meant to be a case study in the effects of Jewish Mother Syndrome on a randy adolescent, but they remind me strongly of my own agnostic fits. As such, Portnoy stands as a larger allegory on the pain and humor of a potently sexual individual scraping against a culture of repression. It's an old tune, certainly, but few sing it as well as Roth.

So what do frustrated teenagers do to release all their pent-up urges? They masturbate, of course, and Portnoy is a pro. He starts by doing it in hiding, though he gets more and more public as the years pass. He does it in the family bathroom, pretending to have the runs; he does it on the bus sitting next to a sleeping archetypal shiksa; he does it in movie theaters; he does it in the woods; he does it in the beef liver his family had reserved for dinner; and he does it in his baseball mitt, having snuck into the burlesque. It's this last that I've selected to excerpt, for here, more than anywhere else in the novel, Roth spells out the material stuff of Portnoy's fantasy. And it's a scream. Earlier in the novel Portnoy's dream women (and milk bottles and cored apples and his sister's brassieres) called him "Big Boy" and asked him to give them all he's got; here he adopts the quaint moniker "Fuckface" and gets it on with a chorus girl. In the best book on masturbation, this might well be the finest scene.

What if later, after the show, that one over there with the enormous boobies, what if . . . In sixty seconds I have imagined a full and wonderful life of utter degradation that we lead together on a chenille spread in a shabby hotel room, me (the enemy of America First) and Thereal McCoy, which is the name I attach to the sluttiest-looking slut in the chorus line. And what a life it is too, under our bare bulb (HOTEL flashing just outside our window). She pushes Drake's Daredevil cupcakes (chocolate with a white creamy center) down over my cock and then eats them off of me, flake by flake. She pours maple syrup out of the Log Cabin can and then licks it from my tender balls until they're clean again as a little boy's. Her favorite line of English prose is a masterpiece: "Fuck my pussy, Fuckface, till I faint." When I fart in the bathtub, she kneels naked on the tile floor, leans all the way over, and kisses the bubbles. She sits on my cock as I take a shit, plunging into my mouth a nipple the size of a tollhouse cookie, and all the while whispering every filthy word she knows viciously in my ear. She puts ice cubes in her mouth until her tongue and lips are freezing, then sucks me off—then switches to hot tea! Everything, everything I have ever thought of, she has thought of too, and will do. The biggest whore (rhymes in Newark with "poor") there ever was. And she's mine! "Oh Thereal, I'm coming, I'm coming, you fucking whore," and so become the only person ever to ejaculate into the pocket of a baseball mitt at the Empire Burlesque house in Newark.

from "Roman Elegy 5"

JOHANN WOLFGANG VON GOETHE

You have found a magic lantern and a few rubs brought forth its occupant. He's kind of a bottom-drawer djinn so you're only entitled to one wish and not even one of your own devising. But he's not all bad, so he asks you, "Whaddaya want, Love or Art?" And which do you pick, the consummate romantic relationship or the great Work, suspecting that having one pretty much negates the chance of the other? Love or Art—that's how it's normally presented, and most of us don't question the dichotomy.

But why should they have to be mutually exclusive? Does every artist need to be tortured and loveless? Must every great lover be consumed by passion to the exclusion of all else? We imagine both artists and lovers as addicts: the artist is Picasso, surrounded by women but loving only himself and his work; the lover is—yes, who is the lover? How would we have heard of him? Each day spent in a rhapsody of sexual bliss—who would have time to paint or write, or even buy milk? I once arbitrated a dispute between a couple over how much sex they should have: she was arguing for four times a day; he said once every other day. Her reasoning was obvious—the more the merrier. His? That he was only able to work because of the sadness of his life. His artistic fuel derived from discontent; having sex every day would make that discontent go away, and with it all his ambition. I advised for once every other day, with marathon weekend supplements.

My own humble life has been an attempt to reconcile impulses in both directions. There are those rare people who seem to have balanced their seduction and career schedules (Wilt Chamberlain, for example, scoring at will in both sex and hoops), but when I want real inspiration, I look to literature. Specifically, to an elegy of Goethe's. Germany's greatest writer was a lifelong student of the erotic arts and wrote a number of scurrilous verses. He also had an enormous collection of penis-centric art and curios from around the world, and I suspect he was something of a perv. Yet his *Roman Elegies* reveal his most romantic side, none more than the Fifth (which I've translated below). Its theme is not the separation of Love and Art, but how the former can be used to facilitate the latter. And I ask you, if it's possible, is there a greater synthesis?

● ●·

I find myself now on classical ground, filled with joy and
    inspiration;
Voices from past and present speak loudly to me, all full of charm.
I turn the pages of the Ancients and follow their counsel;
My hand doesn't tire, and each day I find a new delight.
But when the night comes, love occupies me otherwise.
And if the result is that I'm only half as learned, I am still doubly
    happy.
But then, is it not a kind of learning when the lovely curve of her
    bosom
I admire, and let my hand slide down her hips?
Then I can truly understand a marble sculpture; I conjure and
    compare,
I see with a feeling eye, feel with a seeing hand.
And if, being with my beloved, I am deprived of some daylight
    hours
She makes amends by giving me all the night's hours in return.
What's more, we're not always kissing, but often speak with reason;
And when she falls to sleep, I lie beside her and think a good deal.
And frequently while in her arms I have composed beautiful
    poems,
Softly measuring the beat of the hexameters, tapping my finger
Along her naked back. She breathes softly in a gentle slumber,
And her breath glows through me, to the depths of my chest,
While Cupid stokes the fire . . .

—*translated by Jack Murnighan*

from **Beloved**

TONI MORRISON

Hard-bought, wisdom. Take something away from a man, then he'll understand. Heidegger says you don't know the tool-ness of a tool until it breaks. And the heart? I wonder how much we can hurt, how much we can know. I'm listening to some music now, pretending not to be alive, looking down at a book I have read many times, trying to figure out how to describe that feeling you get when something strikes the deepest tuning fork you've got in the hollow case in your chest. I'm not always sure I can go on living, but that's when I think I'm doing it for real. Feeling the accumulated weight of silent tragedy, drunk with how beautiful beauty can be. It seems I have to go on, but feeling this much feeling head-on I don't know how I ever will.

This is what happens when I reread *Beloved*. Pure, lucid knowledge that I'm brushing against the true. Wondering how I could ever manage not to break beneath the weight. How any of us do. Morrison's achievement is among the handful of books that take us to the love-ravaged, love-saved heart of human experience. And remind us that we've been there all along.

●••

[Note: Sethe and Paul D are in bed, thinking back on how Sethe lost her virginity to Halle in a cornfield, while Paul D, Sixo and others looked on.]

Both Halle and Sethe were under the impression that they were hidden. Scrunched down among the stalks they couldn't see anything, including the corn tops waving over their heads and visible to everyone else.

Sethe smiled at her and Halle's stupidity. Even the crows knew and came to look. Uncrossing her ankles, she managed not to laugh aloud.

The jump, thought Paul D, from a calf to a girl wasn't all that mighty. Not the leap Halle believed it would be. And taking her in the corn rather than her quarters, a yard away from the cabins of the others who had lost out, was a gesture of tenderness. Halle wanted privacy for her and got public display. Who could miss a ripple in a cornfield on a quiet cloudless day? He, Sixo, and both of the Pauls sat under Brother pouring water from a gourd over their heads, and through eyes streaming with well water, they watched the confusion of tassels in the field below. It had been hard, hard, hard sitting there erect as dogs, watching corn stalks dance at noon. The water running over their heads made it worse.

Paul D sighed and turned over. Sethe took the opportunity afforded by his movement to shift as well. Looking at Paul D's back, she remembered that some of the corn stalks broke, folded down over Halle's back, and among the things her fingers clutched were husk and cornsilk hair.

How loose the silk. How jailed down the juice.

The jealous admiration of the watching men melted with the feast of new corn they allowed themselves that night. Plucked from the broken stalks that Mr. Garner could not doubt was the fault of a raccoon. Paul F wanted his roasted; Paul A wanted his boiled and now Paul D couldn't remember how finally they cooked those ears too young to eat. What he did remember was parting the hair to get to the tip, the edge of his fingernail just under, so as not to graze a single kernel.

The pulling down of the tight sheath, the ripping sound always convinced her it hurt.

As soon as one strip of husk was down, the rest obeyed and the ear yielded up to him its shy rows, exposed at last. How loose the silk. How quick the jailed-up flavor ran free.

No matter what all your teeth and wet fingers anticipated, there was no accounting for the way that simple joy could shake you.

How loose the silk. How fine and loose and free.

from **Hopscotch**

JULIO CORTÁZAR

It's a standby among parlor-room
conundrums: If you had to be
deprived of all your senses save
one, which would you keep?
Taste, perhaps, if you were
Paul Prudhomme and lived
down the block from La
Tour d'Argent; or smell, if Carolina wisteria bloomed outside your bay
windows; some would say hearing, transfixed by the rapture of
Beethoven or Bessie Smith; but most people would cling to sight, "the
prime work of God" (as Milton called it after he lost his), and hope to
fight back the haunting darkness.

Not I. For my money, if I could only retain one means of interacting
with the world, it would be touch. Touch, soft like the powder on a
moth's wing, the cool parabola of a slow-traced finger along my brow. I
imagine myself blind as Borges, reading the Braille dots that circle a nipple or stroking the soft harp strings of down on my lover's belly. Deaf as
the desert amid the seesaw scissoring of body on body, hearing through
contact the syllables of joint and sinew, learning through movement the
grammar of friction. My brain is full of visual images I won't soon forget;
the jukebox of the mind contains innumerable tracks; I can recall the
smell and taste of my favorite things almost at will; but of touch I require
a constant transfusion. Something about touch defies memory—it is dif-
fuse, complex, and difficult to render in language. Aristotle was probably
right that we receive all our knowledge through our senses, but touch is
the only one I trust, and sex the language in which I'm least willing to lie.
Fingers working like self-aware brushes on the electrified canvas of skin,
a hundred million nerve endings in constant communion with the
brain—that is the source of touch's appeal.

We've all temporarily experienced what it would be like to have only
one sense (at least under ideal circumstances): headphones on and eyes
closed, surrendering to the tweeter and woof, or full-mouthed and chew-

ing, head thrown back in communion with the flavor of a morel. With porn, especially, we limit ourselves to a one-sense experience, even if more would be merrier. Internet smut is the worst: sitting unfeelingly in a desk chair, gazing through the blue flicker to unreachably distant, odorless, 2-D bodies gathering themselves in their pixels for our delight, the crotch and the eye connected by a single, throbbing nerve—not how I prefer my arousal. I don't think I'm alone in this opinion. Among allies in the cult of contact I can number the great Argentine writer Julio Cortázar. Cortázar's chef d'oeuvre, the avant-garde novel *Hopscotch*, contains one of my favorite love scenes in modern literature. He paints it in a few hundred words, and in all five senses, but it's clear that touch is sovereign. Two eyes, two ears, one tongue, one nose, ten fingers. See what I mean? Reach out.

●••

I touch your mouth, I touch the edge of your mouth with my finger, I am drawing it as if it were something my hand was sketching, as if for the first time your mouth opened a little, and all I have to do is close my eyes to erase it and start all over again, every time I can make the mouth I want appear, the mouth which my hand chooses and sketches on your face, and which by some chance that I do not seek to understand coincides exactly with your mouth which smiles beneath the one my hand is sketching on you.

You look at me, from close up you look at me, closer and closer and then we play cyclops, we look closer and closer at one another and our eyes get larger, they come closer, they merge into one and the two cyclopses look at each other, blending as they breathe, our mouths touch and struggle in gentle warmth. . . . Then my hands go to sink into your hair, to cherish slowly the depth of your hair while we kiss as if our mouths were filled with flowers or with fish, with lively movements and dark fragrance. And if we bite each other the pain is sweet, and if we smother each other in a brief and terrible sucking in together of our breaths, that momentary death is beautiful. And there is but one saliva and one flavor of ripe fruit, and I feel you tremble against me like a moon on the water.

—*translated by Gregory Rabassa*

from **Falconer**

JOHN CHEEVER

Some fiction, seeking to shock, asks you to visualize the most extreme acts of human behavior. Other, more confident narratives demonstrate that the extreme doesn't reside at the margins but at the center of who we all are, not in monstrous aberrations of humanity but in the unknown, perhaps best unexplored, innermost natures of each of us. We see tapes of wartime atrocities and can't help wonder what made it possible for ordinary men to become concentration camp guards. Could it happen to you? Of what are we capable? Few of us want to know. But it's not only the possibility of evil that we are afraid of; more personal questions can be almost as daunting. Would you drink urine in the desert? Or eat human flesh if starving? We never know for sure what capacities we have inside us—or what desires. How perverse are we at heart? Would you be able, or under certain circumstances even want, to have sex with an animal, a child, a corpse? It seems unlikely, but how would you know? All these questions can be speculated on, but we'll never really be certain. The possibility can't be denied, and that's what creates fear. For many men, the threat of homosexuality creates just such an anxiety. In a bunker, in prison, in an orgy, could you take pleasure from another man? Would you succumb to temptation, to desperation? And if so, would you find yourself liking it? John Cheever's great prison novel, *Falconer,* dives unflinchingly into the heart of these questions. At every turn, Falconer acknowledges, without glorification, the sexuality that permeates the men's prison. Whereas writers like Genet portray prison sex like scenes out of *Tom of Finland,* Cheever is as gentle as Tom's of Maine. He's at his best, and most subtle, when he depicts how homosexual encounters occur among men who the rest of the time act straight. The waspy married protagonist Farragut has an extended affair with a fellow inmate; there is a urinal trough where the men line up side by side to masturbate (which includes one of the most ample descriptions of the range of human penises anywhere); and, in the scene below, the little-liked candy-fat Cuckold tells his story of the first time he crossed over. His response is a poignant combination of resistance and resignation, a slow—and eventually happy—acceptance of what lies within.

●••

"I scored with a man," said the Cuckold. "That was after I had left my wife. That time I found her screwing this kid on the floor of the front hall. My thing with this man began in a Chinese restaurant. In those days I was the kind of lonely man you see eating in Chinese restaurants. You know? . . . The place, this Chinese restaurant, is about half full. At a table is this young man. That's about it. He's good-looking, but that's because he's young. He'll look like the rest of the world in ten years. But he keeps looking at me and smiling. I honestly don't know what he's after. So then when I get my pineapple chunks, each one with a toothpick, and my fortune cookie, he comes over to my table and asks me what my fortune is. So I tell him I can't read my fortune without my glasses and I don't have my glasses and so he takes this scrap of paper and he reads or pretends to read that my fortune is I am going to have a beautiful adventure within the next hour. So I ask him what his fortune is and he says it's the same thing. He goes on smiling. He speaks real nicely but you could tell he was poor. You could tell that speaking nicely was something he learned. So when I go out he goes out with me. He asks where I'm staying at and I say I'm staying at this motel which is attached to the restaurant. Then he asks if I have anything to drink in my room and I say yes, would he like a drink, and he says he'd love a drink and he puts his arm around my shoulder, very buddy-buddy, and we go to my room. So then he says he can make the drinks and I say sure and I tell him where the whiskey and the ice is and he makes some nice drinks and sits beside me and begins to kiss me on the face. Now, the idea of men kissing one another doesn't go down with me at all, although it gave me no pain. I mean a man kissing a woman is a plus and minus situation, but a man kissing a man except maybe in France is a very worthless two of a kind. I mean if someone took a picture of this fellow kissing me it would be for me a very strange and unnatural picture, but why should my cock have begun to put on weight if it was all so strange and unnatural? So then I thought what could be more strange and unnatural than a man eating baked beans alone in a Chinese restaurant in the Middle West—this was something I didn't invent—and when he felt for my cock, nicely and gently, and went on kissing me, my cock put on its maximum weight and began pouring out juice and when I felt of him he was half-way there.

"So then he made some more drinks and asked me why I didn't take off my clothes and I said what about him and he dropped his pants displaying a very beautiful cock and I took off my clothes and we sat bare-ass on the sofa drinking our drinks. He made a lot of drinks. Now and then he would take my cock in his mouth and this was the first time in my life that I ever had a mouth around my cock. I thought this would look like hell in a newsreel or on the front page of the newspaper, but evidently my cock hadn't ever seen a newspaper because it was going crazy. So then he suggested that we get into bed and we did and the next thing I knew the telephone was ringing and it was morning."

A twelfth-century French poem by Thibaut de Champagne asks an important and difficult question: When alighting on your beloved's doorstep, what should you kiss first, her lips or her feet?

Although the question seems a little dated by the last eight hundred years of sexual relations, the issue of how best to express devotion is not yet cut and dried. Devotion is a dicey thing; different women require different kinds of signs, and anybody who wants a fast and steady rule might as well stay home memorizing it; it ain't gonna be worth much in the real world.

For a long time, I was obsessed with a not dissimilar question: which should you kiss first, a woman's breasts or between her legs? Now conventional wisdom tells you that one kisses the breasts before—in Monty Python's fine phrasing—"stampeding toward the clitoris." But it was precisely that conventionality that irritated me back in those years when I thought the bedroom a fine site for personal politics. So I made it my one-man mission to invert the conventional kissing narrative and refuse to kiss the breasts before crossing the Mason-Dixon. This form of political resistance met with no small confusion from the women so implicated, you can be sure. As we were all in college, my partners were a bit too young to know to say something along the lines of "Son, what in the bejesus are you up to muff-diving me before you give my sweet rack the slightest consideration?" But that's really what I needed to hear. Because, and I say this to would-be iconoclasts everywhere, sexual conventions evolved that way for a reason. A bit of prepping goes a long way, and gentle/rough breast attention—however anticipated—is still welcomed by most women. Although I thought that my partners would think of me as a truly independent-minded lover, unfettered by everyone else's precedents, Lewis-and-Clarking my way up the proverbial flood, no, they just thought I was a twit who didn't know what the hell he was doing. And they were right.

One thing I want to ask you, Baudoin:
If a true, loyal lover
Who has loved his woman a long time
And long prayed that she'd take pity on him
Is written to and told to come to her
In order to finally do what he wishes,
What should he do first to please her
When she says, "Welcome, my love,"
Kiss her on the mouth or the feet?

Sir, I believe that first one kisses her on the mouth
As such a kiss makes descend
To the heart a sweetness which embodies
The great desire they have for each other.
A joy lights her heart
That no lover can conceal or suppress
So he will thus make himself happy
When he kisses the mouth of his love.

Look, Baudoin, I won't lie to you,
Whoever wants first to kiss his woman
On the mouth does not love from the heart—
For that is how you'd kiss a shepherd's daughter.
I think it better to kiss her feet and thank her
Than to do something so outrageous.
You have to believe your lady is wise,
And good sense tells us that humility
Will help to make you better loved.

But sir, I've heard many times that
Humility helps the lover along,
But when the lover—through humility—

Is enough advanced that she gives him his reward,
And he has what he loves and holds dear,
Then I'd say he'd be foolish
Not to pay his homage on her mouth,
For I have also heard, and you know well,
To bypass the mouth for the feet is a bit precious.

Baudoin, look, I'm not saying
That one should neglect the mouth for the feet,
Only that I want to kiss her feet right away
And then, when I'm ready, I'll kiss her mouth
And her beautiful body, which should never be in the dark,
And her beautiful eyes and face
And her blond head, next to which spun gold is nothing.
But you are brash and mix everything up;
It's pretty clear you know little of love.

Sir, you'd have to be both cowardly and lax
Having been allowed to kiss and enjoy
The sweet solace of a long, plump body
To remain nonchalant near the mouth's sweetness
In order to kiss the feet; it makes no sense.
God only wants us to do whatever
One must to win a lady's grace,
And it is a thousand times better to savor
Her mouth than her feet!

Baudoin, whoever keeps up the chase until he gets
What he wants, errs if he does not fall at her feet;
I say he's a devil who does not.

Sir, a man who is bound up in love can't help but forget
Given the room to realize all that he wishes
All about the feet in favor of the mouth.

—*translated by Jack Murnighan*

from **"The Rape of Lucrece"**

WILLIAM SHAKESPEARE

The most explicit sex in the writings of Shakespeare takes place in his most conventionally moralizing work: "The Rape of Lucrece." This is hardly surprising. To be didactic, literature relies on the seductiveness of evil: first it needs to entice readers in order then to be able to scold them for their impurity. Milton's *Paradise Lost* is the crowning achievement of this technique: Generations of readers were sold on the allure of Satan, but the perspicacious realized later that they'd fallen for a siren song. Like Eve, you're supposed to resist the viper; if you are unable, then you open yourself up to moral coaching.

The story of "The Rape of Lucrece" works in a similar fashion. Told and retold by Livy, Ovid, Chaucer, and Shakespeare, it is a classic Trojan horse, wrapping sex appeal in a cloak of moral propriety and political history. Ostensibly recounting the central events that caused the Romans to banish the Tarquin kings and elect public consuls, "The Rape of Lucrece" clearly remained popular more for its sexual narrative than its historical one. (A similar situation took place with the movie *The Accused,* where droves of cretins went to the cinema just to see Jodie Foster get raped.)

I say this as if I was immune to the poem's power, but the sad truth is that it's hard not to get aroused by the representation of rape. One doesn't need to believe in the Freudian id or the Jungian shadow to know that we all have a dark side, and violence often creeps up in our fantasies no matter how far it is from our daily lives.

Which leads to a difficult question: does literature encourage rape by portraying it in a titillating way, or does the fact that the representations are fictional allow one's violent impulses a safe and victimless outlet? I've found myself persuaded by both sides of this debate, and I think it's very hard to say. It is true that over time my sexual fantasies have gotten more involved and elaborate—as has my waking sex life—but this doesn't seem to have brought me closer to trying to merge the most extreme discrepancies between the two. I hope the same is true for other men, though I fear it is not always so.

Another difficult question, then, is whether literature like "The Rape of Lucrece" is actually didactic or whether the ersatz morality is but a front to permit a lot of licentious versifying. I have to think the latter. The moral that one takes away from Shakespeare's poem is so banal and obvious it would hardly be informative to anyone. And if you wanted to recount the fall of Tarquin, you could simply say he was a rapist and a murderer and eventually the people got fed up. The details are unnecessary to the story and seem to be there just to please the reader.

But how explicit is "The Rape of Lucrece"? Both more and less than one might expect. To maintain the veil of propriety, the physicality of the rape itself had to be underplayed, but that only directed Shakespeare's descriptive efforts elsewhere. It's the setup that creates the excitement, drawing itself out by a long series of stanzas dedicated to Lucrece's beauty, in extended internal monologues by Tarquin on the lust and will that drive him forward, and, finally, in a long debate between Lucrece and Tarquin over whether or not he would rape her. I have often noted how suspense seems relatively underutilized as a device in premodern literature; here is the reverse: an early modern example of plot sequencing at its most nail biting.

Not innocently or guiltlessly do I excerpt the lines below—the most physically explicit part of the poem. They concern Lucrece's breasts, which Tarquin sees and gropes while Lucrece is sleeping. In doing so he wakes her but also wakes a certainty that he will carry out his treacherous plan. My selection is not an endorsement; it is a chronicle. And if you find it arousing, let it remind you of the twin-edged power of the pen and the need to retain separation between reality and the outer corners of the imaginable.

●●•

Her breasts, like ivory globes circled with blue,
A pair of maiden worlds unconquered,
Save of their lord no bearing yoke they knew,
And him by oath they truly honoured.
These worlds in Tarquin new ambition bred;
Who, like a foul ursurper, went about
From this fair throne to heave the owner out.

. . .

His drumming heart cheers up his burning eye,
His eye commends the leading to his hand;
His hand, as proud of such a dignity,
Smoking with pride, march'd on to make his stand
On her bare breast, the heart of all her land;
Whose ranks of blue veins, as his hand did scale,
Left there round turrets destitute and pale.

They, mustering to the quiet cabinet
Where their dear governess and lady lies,
Do tell her she is dreadfully beset,
And fright her with confusion of their cries:
She, much amazed, breaks ope her lock'd-up eyes,
Who, peeping forth this tumult to behold,
Are by his flaming torch dimm'd and controll'd.

Imagine her as one in dead of night
From forth dull sleep by dreadful fancy waking,
That thinks she hath beheld some ghastly sprite,
Whose grim aspect sets every joint a-shaking;
What terror or 'tis! but she, in worser taking,
From sleep disturbed, heedfully doth view
The sight which makes supposed terror true.

. . .

His hand, that yet remains upon her breast,—
Rude ram, to batter such an ivory wall!—
May feel her heart-poor citizen!—distress'd,
Wounding itself to death, rise up and fall,
Beating her bulk, that his hand shakes withal.
This moves in him more rage and lesser pity,
To make the breach and enter this sweet city.

from Roughhouse

THADDEUS RUTKOWSKI

Although I normally find no ethical compromise in taking elitist pot-shots at all but the most rarefied of literary production, I can be won over by things outside the *Norton Anthology*. The stray song lyric strikes a chord (Cream's "I'll soon be with you my love / And give you my dawn surprise," for example); once a blue moon I'm taken with something I read in a 'zine (*Bust* has always been a favorite); and every odd year I find myself capable of taking in a little Charles Bukowski and the like. But most of the time, being an editor, I think that writers need an editor. And in some cases the editorlessness is all too pronounced.

But perhaps it's confession time. My virulence against mediocre writing is clearly backlash against the embarrassment I feel at my own earliest attempts. Truth be told, freshman year I arrived at my college dorm and, with a black indelible marker, proceeded to cover the walls in poems. And yes, Houston, they were bad. Real bad. Real good-god-does-anyone-still-remember bad. If memory allows me to dredge the floors of the great seas of shame, I believe that most of them were unapologetically Pink Floyd—inspired—as damning an epithet as could be attributed to any production of the pen. Had my roommate only been there to read them in advance, to help me see with an eye other than my own, then maybe I would have realized the error of my ways, capped the Mr. Marks-a-Lot and put up a few Vanilla Ice posters like everyone else.

All this was running through my mind when a friend suggested I go see S/M slam poet Thad Rutkowski. My first thought: slam poetry, S/M slam poetry—now there's a subgenre. And a subgenre it is, but not without bright spots. Rutkowski live was quite compelling, so I got my hands on his novel, *Roughhouse*. And though it's clear that he, like Eliot, could have used a Pound to tighten up his wasteland, *Roughhouse* definitely has its moments. My favorite was the crafted jewel that follows, as

tight and nuanced a 123-word story as you're likely to find anywhere—
even in the *Norton Anthology.*

● ● ●

I went with a girl to a lake. We walked on boulders that lined the shore. She stood on a rock a few feet above the water, put her hands behind her back and said, "If my hands were tied, you could push me in."

I looked at her hands for a moment, then took off a sneaker lace and wrapped it around her wrists.

"You can untie me now," she said.

I made no move to release her.

"I'm going to ask my mother if this is normal," she said.

I took off my other lace and wrapped it around her ankles.

"No," she said, then said my name.

As time passed, her voice got louder. I did not push her in.

from **Pan**

KNUT HAMSUN

It is customary to think of madness as a desert, where solitude, isolation, and monomania join forces to turn the mind away from the world and into itself. Madness might also be thought of as a wood, where the constant hum and rustle of multiplicitous forest life intrudes on the sanctity of thinking, denying it peace, preventing rest. What would happen if the hum of the everyday suddenly became a bit louder? The continual hum of passersby, the buzz of the refrigerator, the dull rumble of each and every thing is normally audible only if you think about it. But if you started to think about it, weren't able not to think about it, it would drive you crazy within a day. A day, then madness.

Consciousness is all about creating filters, sieves to reduce the too much of which we are ultimately given too little. Fine grit to polish down the edges of the too rough, the too raw, the too direct. I think of all this when I think of the writers who've gone mad, of those who've turned to suicide or alcohol. In the film *Barton Fink,* the aging, Faulkner-based character explains: "Writing is peace"; otherwise drink. Later in the film his lover elaborates, "We all need to be understood."

Among memorable chronicles of the onset of madness—Poe's "Tell-Tale Heart," Shakespeare's *Troilus and Cressida*, Nietzsche's *Ecce Homo*—Knut Hamsun's fin-de-siècle *Pan* is the most environmental. The dark, living woods of northernmost Norway mirror the teeming fullness of the mind of Glahn, the solitary hunter. Having grown accustomed to his hermitage, he suddenly finds himself falling in love with the daughter of his only neighbor. And he begins to slip. He attends parties at her father's house across the lake, and his animal nature both intrigues and grates against the society she represents. Then one night, he takes her shoe and hurls it into the lake. It is an unexplainable act, patently absurd. He is lost.

In the passage that follows, Glahn, in his loneliness, imagines a sexual encounter with mythic forest-goers Diderik and Iselin. Immediately after, he is found by a village girl who, having heard rumor of the barbarity in his eyes, wants to know what's behind them. Glahn, losing the superego, becomes a primal enactment of the id.

●••

A few days passed as best they might; my only friend was the forest and the great solitude. Dear God, I had never known such solitude as on the first of these days. It was full Spring; I found wintergreen and yarrow in the fields, and the chaffinches had arrived; I knew all the birds. Sometimes I took a couple of coins from my pocket and chinked them together to break the solitude. I thought: what if Diderik and Iselin came along!

Soon there began to be no night; the sun barely dipped his face into the sea and then came up again, red, refreshed, as if he had been down to drink. How strangely affected I was sometimes these nights; no man would believe it. Was Pan sitting in a tree watching to see how I would act? And was his belly open; and was he crouching so that he seemed to sit and drink from his own belly? But all this he did just to keep one eye cocked on me; and the whole tree shook with his silent laughter when he saw all my thoughts running away with me. In the forest there was rustling everywhere; animals snuffled, birds called to each other, their whirring mingled with that of the moths so that there was a sound as of whispering back and forth all over the forest. How much there was to hear! For three nights I did not sleep, I thought of Diderik and Iselin.

See, I thought, they might come. And Iselin would lure Diderik over to a tree and say: "Stand here, Diderik, and watch, keep guard over Iselin; that hunter shall tie my shoelace."

And I am that hunter and she will sign to me with her eyes so that I may understand. And when she comes, my heart understands all and it no longer beats, it booms. And she is naked under her dress from head to foot and I place my hand on her.

"Tie my shoelace!" she says with flaming cheeks. And in a little while she whispers against my mouth, against my lips: "Oh, you are not tying my shoelace, you my dearest heart, you are not tying . . . not tying my . . ."

But the sun dips his face into the sea and comes up again, red, refreshed, as if he had been down to drink. And the air is filled with whispers.

An hour later she says against my mouth: "Now I must leave you."

And she waves back to me as she goes and her face is still flaming, her face is tender and ecstatic. Again she turns to me and waves.

But Diderik steps forth from the tree and says: "Iselin, what were you doing? I saw you."

She answers: "Diderik, did you see? I did nothing."

"Iselin, I saw you do it," he says again. "I saw."

Then her loud and happy laughter sounds through the forest and she walks away with him, exulting and sinful from head to foot. And where does she go? To the next one, a hunter in the forest.

It was midnight. [My dog] Aesop had broken loose and was out hunting on his own; I heard him baying up in the hills and when I finally had him again it was one o'clock. A goatherd girl came along; she was knitting a stocking and humming and looking about her. But where was her flock? And what was she doing there in the forest at midnight? Nothing, nothing. Perhaps she was restive, perhaps just glad to be alive, what does it matter? I thought: she has heard Aesop barking and knows I am out in the forest.

When she came, I stood up and looked at her and saw how young and slender she was. Aesop also stood and looked at her.

"Where are you from?" I asked her.

"From the mill," she answered.

But what could she have been doing in the mill so late at night?

"How is it that you dare to walk here in the forest so late at night," I said, "you who are so young and slender?"

She laughed and answered: "I am not so young, I am nineteen."

But she could not have been nineteen, I am convinced that she was lying and was only seventeen. But why did she lie and pretend to be older?

"Sit down," I said, "and tell me what they call you."

And, blushing, she sat down by my side and said she was called Henriette.

I asked: "Have you a sweetheart, Henriette, and has he ever embraced you?"

"Yes," she answered with an embarrassed laugh.

"How many times already?"

She remains silent.

"How many times?" I repeated.

"Twice," she said softly.

—translated by James W. McFarlane

from Elegy XIX: "To His Mistress Going to Bed"

JOHN DONNE

Let us praise Eve. Without her impertinent nibble, we'd never have had the joy of undressing or of being undressed. Nudity is nice—I am wont to walk the beach un-thonged, slide between the sheets pajama-less, and once I attended a party where the requisite costume was none —but naked skin requires a having been clothed–ness to actualize its full appeal. A world without clothes would display its nudity like scenes from *National Geographic,* or, worse still, like the aging hippie leftovers in the nudist colonies of Goa on the western coast of India. And nude beach paddle ball is not a pretty sight. The oft-sublime French literary critic Roland Barthes makes a big deal of disclosure in the context of concealment, of the need for covering to make exposure. He's right, of course. Have you ever met someone who says they have no secrets? When they tell you something personal, it's like it doesn't matter. Lovers, like literature, are best when they're a dance of a thousand veils, ever concealing, ever revealing, keeping you guessing, keeping you piqued.

Early Western literature, despite its infrequent use of narrative suspense, tended to take a staggered approach to the unconcealing of the body. The Song of Solomon made famous the literary device the blazon, where each component of the body was described singly and in turn: your hair is like such and such, your eyes like . . . , your cheeks like . . . , your neck like, your breasts . . . This is, in effect, a kind of narrative strip tease, presenting to the reader's eye one morsel at a time, allowing each to be visualized and processed before moving on to the next. In the Song the descriptions are outlandish, and only occasionally sexy; subsequent literature would raise the ante, culminating in the seventeenth century with John Donne's justly famous "To His Mistress Going to Bed." Here Donne describes both raiment and remainder, what he wants her to take off and what he knows lies beneath. No poet ever crafted images as opalescent as Donne's, and no subject, to my eye, is as worthy as the human body. Here is the highest beauty given its deserved due.

● ●·

Come, madam, come, all rest my powers defy,
Until I labor, I in labor lie.
The foe oft-times having the foe in sight,
Is tired with standing though he never fight.
Off with that girdle, like heaven's zone glistering,
But a far fairer world encompassing.
Unpin that spangled breastplate which you wear,
That th' eyes of busy fools may be stopped there.
Unlace yourself, for that harmonious chime
Tells me from you that now it is bed time.
Off with that happy busk, which I envy,
That still can be, and still can stand so nigh.
Your gown, going off, such beauteous state reveals,
As when from flowry meads th' hill's shadow steals.
Off with that wiry coronet and show
The hairy diadem which on you doth grow:
Now off with those shoes, and then safely tread
In this love's hallowed temple, this soft bed.
In such white robes, heaven's angels used to be
Received by men; thou, Angel, bring'st with thee
A heaven like Mahomet's Paradise; and though
Ill spirits walk in white, we easily know
By this these angels from an evil sprite:
Those set our hairs on end, but these our flesh upright.
License my roving hands, and let them go
Before, behind, between, above, below.
O my America! my new-found-land,
My kingdom, safeliest when with one man manned,
My mine of precious stones, my empery,
How blest am I in this discovering thee!
To enter in these bonds is to be free;

Then where my hand is set, my seal shall be.
Full nakedness! All joys are due to thee,
As souls unbodied, bodies unclothed must be
To taste whole joys. Gems which you women use
Are like Atalanta's balls, cast in men's views,
That when a fool's eye lighteth on a gem,
His earthly soul may covet theirs, not them.
Like pictures, or like books' gay coverings made
For lay-men, are all women thus arrayed;
Themselves are mystic books, which only we
(Whom their imputed grace will dignify)
Must see revealed. Then, since that I may know,
As liberally as to a midwife, show
Thyself: cast all, yea, this white linen hence,
There is no penance due to innocence.
To teach thee, I am naked first; why then,
What needst thou have more covering than a man?

from **Le morte d'Arthur**

THOMAS MALORY

When most people think of
medieval literature, they think of
knights and damsels, shining
armor and battles on horseback.
It would probably surprise
them to hear that for centuries there was more litera-
ture written about penitential sacraments than about King Arthur and
the knights of the Round Table. The French tradition has the most chivalric lit, from its appropriately famous *chansons de geste* to Chrétien de
Troyes to the prose Lancelot and beyond. Together, these tales are the
Rambos of the Middle Ages, centered around bad-ass heroes who ride
around and off a lot of chumps. In England things were a little tamer. No
chivalric cycle was penned in English until Malory's *Le morte d'Arthur* in
the fifteenth century, and even that has a French name (meaning "the
death of Arthur"). Our association of knights and England probably has
as much to do with Monty Python as with the actual literary tradition.

Le morte d'Arthur is, nonetheless, among the finest presentations of
the medieval concept of chivalry (in its twilight). Knighthood in Malory's
Arthuriad is based on three principles: fighting well, speaking well, and
being good to women. If you've got those down, you're pretty much
in business. Lancelot is the *über*-stud in all these categories, not only
kicking everybody's butt (all the time) but also cuckolding Arthur with
Queen Guinevere ("Lancelot . . . wente to bedde with the quene . . . and
toke hys plesaunce and hys lykynge untyll hit was the dawning of the
day"). Which is all well and good, but the real sex in *Le morte d'Arthur*
happens in the pavilions (tents), set up here and there in the forests
where the knights ride. And it rarely happens with the intended person.
Somehow, by quirk of fate, lighting, or narrative necessity, the errant
knights stumble into pavilions where someone happens to be waiting for
a midnight tryst. The knights bed down, a little hanky gets pankied, they
realize the mistaken identity, and end up falling in love.

Sometimes. Not, as it turns out, if the bedmates are the same sex. Finding a beard on your unseen smoochee is a bit of a problem for these long-lanced cavaliers. And if the cavalier is Lancelot, look out. In the original French version of this tale, Lancelot confuses his bedmate for a woman. A fight ensues and he kills the would-be amorist. Oops. In Malory's version the error is discovered more quickly, and it ends more comically than tragically. The moral to the story? Look before you lip.

●··

Then within an hour there came to the pavilion the knight who owned it. He thought that his mistress would be lying in the bed, so he lay himself down alongside Sir Lancelot and took him in his arms and began to kiss him. When Lancelot felt a rough beard kissing him, he jumped quickly out of bed, and the other knight did the same. Both of them grabbed their swords, the first knight ran out of the pavilion and Lancelot followed him. And there by a little valley Lancelot wounded him right close to death. And so the knight surrendered to Lancelot, who accepted, so that he could tell him why he had come into the bed.

"Sir," said the knight, "the tent is mine. And I had asked my mistress to have slept with me here tonight, and now instead I am likely to die of this wound."

"Ah, yes. Sorry about that."

—modernized by Jack Murnighan

I never got to meet any members of the Circle Jerks, so I never got to ask them a question that has long mystified me. Modern literature is speckled with scenes of adolescent boys getting together to pull their puds en masse, but how widespread is the phenomenon? I, having had no childhood friends, am in a less authoritative position to say than most other people. The fact that I was never invited to one only means that they are no more common than birthday parties or trips to the roller rink. Nor, however, have any of the adult friends I've spoken to had the peculiar experience of wanking alongside a troupe of his classmates. Were we just the weird kids, left out of a truly common cultural event, or is the circle jerk something of an urban myth, exaggerated from its infrequent occurrence into apparent ultranormalcy? I have no idea, and I doubt I ever will.

I do keep reading about them, however—most recently in *Cat and Mouse*, the second novel of Nobel Prize–winner Günter Grass. When you debut with a novel as prodigious as *The Tin Drum*, you set yourself up for a pretty nasty sophomore slump. But Grass was wise; he scaled back his ambitions (and his page count—*Cat and Mouse* is barely more than a novella) and succeeded in creating a laugh-a-page character study of a mythic wartime teen, Joachim Mahlke. Most of *Cat and Mouse* is staged around a half-submerged minesweeper in the Baltic off of Gdansk (then Danzig). A cadre of underachieving boys sits around picking gull droppings off the protruding hull (and eating them—yuck!) and occasionally diving into the black water, trying to salvage what they can from the ship. And Mahlke is their hero; only he makes it into the interior chambers of the vessel; only he dredges up lucre of any value; only he wears a screwdriver on a cord around his neck to aid in his liberations.

And only he bears two other peculiar traits: an enormous Adam's apple that bobs constantly (the mouse of the title), and a similarly oversized, similarly bobbing southerly analog, the principal of the following passage. If circle jerks don't happen in life, they still make great literature.

● ● ·

She always found some good-natured fool who would get to work even if he wasn't at all in the mood, just to give her something to goggle at. The only one who wouldn't give until Tulla found the right words of encouragement—and that is why I am narrating these heroic deeds—was the great swimmer and diver Joachim Mahlke . . .

"Won't you? Aw, do it just once. Or can't you? Don't you want to? Or aren't you allowed to?"

Mahlke stepped half out of the shadow and slapped Tulla's compressed little face left right with his palm and the back of his hand. His mouse went wild. So did the screwdriver . . . "Okay. Just so you'll shut your yap."

Tulla came out of her contortion and squatted down normally with her legs folded under her, as Mahlke stripped his trunks down to his knees. The children at the Punch-and-Judy show gaped in amazement: a few deft movements emanating from his right wrist, and his pecker loomed so large that the tip emerged from the shadow of the pilothouse and the sun fell on it . . .

"Measure it!" cried Jürgen Kupka. Tulla spread the fingers of her left hand. One full span and another almost. Somebody and then somebody else whispered: "At least twelve inches!" That was an exaggeration of course. Schilling, who otherwise had the longest, had to take his out, make it stand up, and hold it beside Mahlke's: Mahlke's was first of all a size thicker, second a matchbox longer, and third looked much more grownup, dangerous and worthy to be worshipped . . . Strangely enough, the length of his sexual part made up for the otherwise shocking protuberance of his Adam's apple, lending his body an odd, but in its way perfect, harmony.

No sooner had Mahlke finished squirting the first load over the rail than he started in all over again. Winter timed him with his waterproof wrist watch; Mahlke's performance continued for approximately as many seconds as it took the torpedo boat to pass from the tip of the breakwater to the buoy; then, while the torpedo boat was rounding the buoy, he unloaded the same amount again; the foaming bubbles lurched in the smooth, only occasionally rippling swell, and we laughed for joy as the gulls swooped down, screaming for more.

—*translated by Ralph Manheim*

from **Moby Dick**

HERMAN MELVILLE

To know one thing truly is to know all things. I suspect that this sentiment, which I've long believed, is the underpinning of many an aphorism now lost to my bourbon-addled memory. The logic behind the conceit presumes that, like Andrew Marvell's famous drop of dew, each entity in this world reflects the entirety of the universe of which it is part. The truth of any one thing stands in direct analogy to the truth of all others. Vico claimed that man, seeing things through a human brain, could only understand man; cosmology is reduced to history. I see the reverse; as we can only know through our own selves, each perceivable thing becomes a mirror or a canvas for painting our souls.

One is thus given the choice to arrive at the particular through the general or the general through the particular. The former is encyclopedism, the latter anatomism, but the difference lies only in method. Literature has mimicked both forms: Flaubert's comic and unfinished *Bouvard et Pecuchet* is the most literal embodiment of the encyclopedic impulse. On the other side, Burton's great *Anatomy of Melancholy* can easily be understood as an encyclopedia of a single thing. Nicholson Baker's *The Mezzanine* falls somewhere in between, retelling an escalator trip at such length and precision as to appear both anatomistic and encyclopedic. But nowhere is encyclopedism more sustained, more methodical and staggering than Melville's singular, monolithic *Moby Dick*. It is said that the Babelites used bricks of stone to build their tower toward God; Melville uses the lore of whaling to build his. Nor will it be toppled. God, apparently, is letting <u>The Whale</u> stand, testament though it is to human industry. And what industry! Compiling everything there is to know about whales, whaling, and whiteness, Melville creates a symbolic tapestry as intricate as anything in the world on land. Seeking only to sketch a portrait of a now-dying industry, Melville rendered the bulk of human experience, seen through the salt-crusted lens of a collapsible eyeglass.

So, although I might have excerpted from Ishmael's curious night in Nantucket with the savage Queequeg, I opt instead for the passage on Moby's big one. For if all things are analogous to one another, Melville's great book sits, like Willy's willy in the Pequod's scuppers, dauntingly on the foredecks of world literature.

●••

Had you stepped on board the Pequod at a certain juncture of this post-mortemizing of the whale; and had you strolled forward nigh the windlass, pretty sure am I that you would have scanned with no small curiosity a very strange, enigmatical object, which you would have seen there, lying along lengthwise in the lee scuppers. Not the wondrous cistern in the whale's huge head, not the prodigy of his unhinged lower jaw; not the miracle of his symmetrical tail; none of these would so surprise you as half a glimpse of that unaccountable cone—longer than a Kentuckian is tall, nigh a foot in diameter at the base, and jet-black as Yojo, the ebony idol of Queequeg. And an idol, indeed, it is; or rather, in old times, its likeness was. Such an idol as that found in the secret groves of Queen Maachah in Judea; and for worshipping which, King Asa, her son, did depose her, and destroyed the idol, and burnt it for an abomination at brook Kedron, as darkly set forth in the fifteenth chapter of the First Book of Kings.

Look at the sailor, called the mincer, who now comes along, and assisted by two allies, heavily backs the grandissimus, as the mariners call it, and with bowed shoulders, staggers off with it as if he were a grenadier carrying a dead comrade from the field. Extending it upon the forecastle deck, he now proceeds cylindrically to remove its dark pelt, as an African hunter the pelt of a boa. This done he turns the pelt inside out, like a pantaloon leg, gives it a good stretching, so as almost to double its diameter; and at last hangs it, well spread, in the rigging, to dry. Ere long, it is taken down; when removing some three feet of it, towards the pointed extremity, and then cutting two slits for arm-holes at the other end, he lengthwise slips himself bodily into it. The mincer now stands before you invested in the full canonicals of his calling. Immemorial to all his order, this investiture alone will adequately protect him, while employed in the peculiar functions of his office.

That office consists in mincing the horse-pieces of blubber for the pots; an operation which is conducted at a curious wooden horse, planted endwise against the bulwarks, and with a capacious tub beneath it, into which the minced pieces drop, fast as the sheets from a rapt orator's desk. Arrayed in decent black; occupying a conspicuous pulpit; intent on bible leaves; what a candidate for an archbishopric, what a lad for a Pope were this mincer!

from **The Floating Opera**

JOHN BARTH

A lovely word, now out of fashion, permitted poets of the seventeenth century to denigrate
rivals whose verse achievements
were not quite up to snuff:
poetaster. Ben Jonson
addressed one of his poems
"To Poetaster"; you won't be surprised when I tell you it's not nice.
Sadly, there is no comparable term for fiction writers. "Scribbler" lacks
precision, "hack" has a blunt edge and "novelistaster" is an abomination.
Nor does it exist, though that is really what I am after—some way of
dismissing the epigones and the claimants, the muddlers, the half talents,
and the stone-footed who would drink at the muses' fount. We don't
need novels; we need novelists, writers whose very names would daunt
the occasional ink dippers from ever scratching out a single clause. I have
written of Gabriel García Márquez as being one such writer and Cormac
McCarthy another (*Blood Meridian* is like something released from the
fist of an angry god); there are few others who qualify. But having read
in the last few weeks an armload of John Barth, I can happily name him
among them.

Three things, in my opinion, make for worthwhile novels: wisdom,
style, and imagination. Possessing any one, you're likely to get published;
two, you'll write a damn good book; possess all three and you're truly
great. In books like *Giles Goat-Boy, The Sot-Weed Factor,* and *Chimera,*
Barth shows a range of styles and, even more, a scope of imagination
barely rivaled in American fiction. But even in his first novel, *The Floating Opera* (written in his mid-twenties), he displays a human wisdom
and sensitivity that remains consistent through the rest of his work. As
far-fetched as his experiments can be, Barth's fictions remain true to the
truest truths, and this is what gives them meaning.

In *The Floating Opera*, protagonist Todd Andrews has his first fateful
encounter with the wife of his best friend. It begins a love triangle that

sets into motion much of the plot of the book (an extended recounting of why Todd doesn't commit suicide, having decided one day to do so), but the triangle doesn't come off without a hitch. Cast within the following five hundred words is the unsugared reality of the quick male trigger—a hard topic, harder still to sketch with grace and humor. Barth shows us how.

•••

Needless to say, I dreamed of Jane. The absence of Harrison—the first time he'd left Jane and me alone together, as it happened, because of my supposed shyness—was embarrassingly obvious, and on my way to sleep I was acutely conscious of her presence on the opposite side of the plywood partition between us. I fell asleep imagining her cool brown thighs—they must be cool!—brushing each other, perhaps, as she walked about the kitchen; the scarcely visible gold down on her upper arms; the salt-and-sunshine smell of her. The sun was glaring in through a small window at the foot of the bed; the cottage smelled of heat and resinous pine. I was quite tired from swimming, and sleepy from beer. My dream was lecherous and violent—and unfinished. Embarrassingly so. For suddenly I felt a cool, shiveringly cool, hand caress my stomach. It might have been ice, so violently did all my insides contract; I fairly exploded awake, and wrenched up into a sitting position. I believe it was "Good Lord!" that I croaked. I croaked something, anyhow, and with both arms instantly grabbed Jane, who sat nude—unbelievable!—on the edge of the bed; buried my face in her, so excruciatingly startled was I; pulled her down with me, that electrifying skin against mine; and *mirabile dictu!* at the sheer enormous lust of it I did indeed explode, so wholly that I was certain liver, spleen, guts, lungs, heart, head, and all had blown from me, and I lay a hollow shell without sense or strength.

Damned dream, to leave me helpless! I was choked with desire, and with fury at my impotency. Jane was terribly nervous; after the first approach, to make which must have required all her courage, she collapsed on her back beside me and scarcely dared open her eyes.

The room was dazzlingly bright! I was so shocked by the unexpectedness of it that I very nearly wept. Incredible smooth, tight, perfect skin! I pressed my face into her; I couldn't leave her untouched for the barest sliver of an instant. I quiver even now, twenty-two years later, to write of it, and why my poor heart failed to burst I'm unable even to wonder.

Well, it was no use, and if I'd had a knife handy then, I'd have unmanned myself. I fell beside her, maddened at my impotency and mortified at the mess I'd made. That, it turned out, was the right thing to do: my self-castigation renewed Jane's courage, gave her the upper hand again.

"Don't curse yourself, Toddy," she soothed, and kissed me—sweetness!—and stroked my face.

"No use," I muttered into her breast.

"We'll see," she said lightly, entirely self-possessed now that I seemed shy again: I resolved to behave timidly for the rest of my life. "Don't worry about it, honey; I can fix it."

"No you can't," I moaned, as strickenly as I could.

"Yes I can," she whispered, kissing my ear and sitting up beside me.

Merciful heavens, reader! If you must marry, marry from Ruxton and Gibson Island, I charge you! Such a magnificent, subtle, versatile, imaginative, athletic, informed, delightful, exuberant mistress no man ever had, I swear.

from **A Moveable Feast**

ERNEST HEMINGWAY

Penis size: a topic for the ages. Few will go to the grave not having discussed it, though only two opinions seem to have emerged: bigger is better, or it's not.

Maybe it's not that surprising —other equally binary topics have merited similar scrutiny (Does God exist?)—but I for one remain fascinated with our fascination. Breasts, though seeming to have considerable size-based cultural import, don't elicit the same mystery. Although many or most women obsess about the size of their breasts, there is little or no ambiguity to the matter. They get ranked with cup size, they can be pushed up or bound back or surgically augmented, but it's pretty much a scientific process. Not so with penises, apparently. I myself have gone through the gamut of perceptions of my Johnson: it's little, it's big, it's normal, it's weird, I don't really know, I couldn't care less, I couldn't care more. As the apparatus itself never really changed, these opinions obviously have more to do with my sense of self and my relationship to my own sexuality than anything you could measure in inches. To that extent, then, the penis for a man might less be the fleshy appurtenance dangling between his legs and more a consolidation of his sexuality as a whole. No wonder we worry.

Commonplace as penis questioning is, it, like pooping, does not have a strong literary history. The exceptions are noted: Joyce advanced modern literature by putting Bloom on the can; Hemingway advanced modern biography by making public Scott Fitzgerald's concerns about his ability to satisfy women. I can't say that I list Hemingway among my favorite authors; his baby-step sentences never jazzed me the way those of more self-conscious stylists do. But, old Hem loosens his belt a little bit when he's writing autobiographically, even permitting himself the odd comma. And nowhere is he funnier than in *A Moveable Feast,* the account of his time in that hunger-inducing expat haven, Paris. His tales of trying to negotiate the arrondissements without passing a single restaurant (to keep from teasing his underattended-to stomach) reminded me of my own Gallic misadventures, but his escapades with Fitz and Zelda are even better. We don't often get to go behind the scenes of a writer working up to and through his masterpiece; Hem's account of Fitz is a rare portrait of an artist. Here is the most intimate detail.

He said he had something very important to ask me that meant more than anything in the world to him and that I must answer absolutely truly. I said that I would do the best I could . . .

"You know I never slept with anyone except Zelda."

"No, I didn't."

"I thought I had told you."

"No." . . .

"Zelda said that the way I was built I could never make any woman happy . . . She said it was a matter of measurements. I have never felt the same since she said that and I have to know truly."

"Come out to the office," I said.

"Where is the office?"

"Le water," I said.

We came back into the room and sat down at the table.

"You're perfectly fine . . . There's nothing wrong with you. You look at yourself from above and you look foreshortened. Go over to the Louvre and look at the people in the statues and then go home and look at yourself in the mirror in profile."

"Those statues may not be accurate."

"They are pretty good. Most people would settle for them."

"But why would she say it?"

"To put you out of business. That's the oldest way in the world of putting people out of business" . . .

We went over to the Louvre and he looked at the statues but still he was doubtful about himself.

"It's not basically a question of the size in repose," I said. "It is the size that it becomes."

from **My Secret Life**

ANONYMOUS

I remember a discussion I had with some friends in college about how far we had traveled to have sex. The general consensus: far, quite far. We had all cashed in frequent flier miles or student vouchers, driven long hours, and even, in my case, taken two-day bus trips just to get some nook. I regret none of it. Nor, truth be told, do I regret vast amounts of time expended for less tangible erotic results: watching discolored and unshaped images on the scrambled Playboy channel, flipping through my mom's nursing books for good line drawings and the occasional photo (preferably without venereal disease), sneaking onto my roof in the middle of the night to try to catch my neighbor undressing, watching countless hours of late night Cinemax with the sound off hoping just to see a boob. Practices such as these would be really pathetic if they weren't so universal. We are amateur pornographers, all of us, in the most amateurish ways—at least at certain points in our lives. And if we grow up and gain the right simply to go to the local adult bookstore and purchase a video, it is not without a certain diminishment of the joys of what we find. As Augustine says about reading the Bible, it's the work that makes it interesting.

All this is why, of the twelve volumes of the anonymous Victorian diary, *My Secret Life,* the most interesting are the first few, in which Walter (the diarist) recounts his various endeavors to see quim. Walter is a randy little man, and he spends a lot of time trying to get an eyeful. His first chance comes with his cousin when they catch his mother and aunts peeing. Later they get the most out of keyholes, of lifting the petticoats of the servants, and of hiding under street grates. The grates provide the best viewing, as the following excerpt demonstrates. Good things come to those who wait.

Another night we heard two pairs of feet above us, one was the heavy footstep of a man. "Don't be foolish, he won't know," said a man in a very low tone. "Oh! no—no, I dare not," said a female voice, and the feet with a little rustling moved to another grating. Henry and I moved on also. "You shall, no one comes here, no one can see us," said the man in a still lower tone. "Oh! I am so frightened," said the female. A little gentle scuffling now took place, and then all seemed quiet but a slight movement of the feet. "Are they there?" whispered Henry from the vault. I nudged him to be quiet, and putting the light as high up as I could, pushed aside the slide a little only.

We were well rewarded. Just above our heads were two pair of feet, one pair wide apart, and hanging only partly down at her back the garments of a female, in front the trousers of a man, with the knees projecting slightly forward between the female's legs, and higher up a bag of balls were hanging down hiding nearly the belly and channel, which the prick was taking. The distended legs between which the balls moved, enabled us however to get a glimpse of the arsehole end of a cunt. The movement of the ballocks showed the vigor with which the man was fucking, but there must have been some inequality in height, and either he was very tall, or she very short, for his knees and feet moved out at times into different positions. He then ceased for an instant his shoving, as if to arrange himself in a fresh and more convenient posture, and then the lunges recommenced. He must have had his hands on her naked rump, from the way her clothes hung, showing her legs up to her belly, or to where his breeches hid it, or where the clothes fell down which were over his arm.

Once, I imagine, the lady's clothes were in his way, for there was a pause, his prick came quite out, her feet moved, her legs opened wider. He did not need his fingers to find his mark again, his long, stiff, red-tipped article had slidden in the direction of her bumhole, but no sooner had they readjusted their legs than it moved backwards, and again it was hidden from sight in her cunt. The balls wagged more vigorously than ever, quicker, quicker, the lady's legs seemed to shake, we heard a sort of mixed cry, like a short groan and cry together, and the female voice say, "Oh! Don't make such a noise," then a quiver and a shiver of the legs, and all seemed quiet.

When I first had removed the slide, I did so in a small degree, fearing they might look below and see it, but if the sun had shone from below, I believe now they must have been in that state of excitement that they would not have noticed it. To see better I opened the slide more, and gradually held the lantern higher and higher, until the chimney through which the light issued was near to the grating. I was holding it by the bottom at arms length, and naturally, so as to best see myself. Henry could not see as well, although standing close to me, and our heads nearly touching. "Hold it more this way," said he in an excited whisper. I did not. Just then the lady said, "Oh! Make haste now, I am so frightened." Out slipped the prick—I saw it. At the very instant, Henry pulled my hand to get the lantern placed so as to enable him to see better. I was holding it between the very tips of my fingers, just below the feet of the copulating couple. His jerk pulled it over, and down it went with a smash . . . A huge prick as it seemed to me drew out, and flopped down, a hand grasped it, the petticoats were falling round the legs, when the crash of the lantern came. With a loud shriek from the lady, off the couple moved, and I dare say it was many a day before she had her privates moistened up against a wall again, and over a grating.

from **"A Rapture"**

THOMAS CAREW

Censorship works. Much as I like to point out the contrary voices that have peeped out of the history of repression, we still have a radically skewed idea of centuries past because so many of their great works are kept from our eyes. Until recently, few people would know, for example, the number of women who were writing in the Middle Ages and the massive contributions they made to the culture of the West—including such breakthroughs as the first autobiography written in English (by Margery Kempe), the first Christian plays (by Hrotsvita of Gandersheim), or the first biography (of Charles V, by Christine de Pisan). Nor, thanks to other censorship agendas, do most people realize that Elizabethan drama contains as much bisexuality as Greek and Roman literature or that Victorian England was a hotbed for pornography. We imagine times past as but stepping-stones to the liberal triumph of today, but to think that ours is the most progressive period in history is to know little of the cultures that precede us. Time and again, by ignorance or purposeful exclusion, by selective canonization, bowdlerizing translations, or exclusionary syllabus creation, the history of literature, like so many other so-called histories, is bound and recast in a conservative package that fails to represent the actuality of what was.

So, given the sterility of most literature textbooks, one would not expect to find, browsing through an anthology of seventeenth-century poetry, a consummate how-to guide to lovemaking. But Thomas Carew's "A Rapture" is just that. His detailed account of undressing, stroking, muff-diving, and out-and-out shtupping would rouge the cheeks of even the most licentious *Cosmopolitan* editor—and, truth be told, those of this editor too. "A Rapture" is not, I am warning you, a poem to read at your desk, unless you have a *Flashdance*-style cold shower chain you can pull. Score the point: poets, 1; censors, 0.

Come, then, and mounted on the wings of Love
We'll cut the flitting air, and soar above
The monster's head, and in the noblest seats
Of those blest shades quench and renew our heats.
There shall the Queen of Love, and Innocence,
Beauty, and Nature, banish all offence
From our close ivy-twines; there I'll behold
Thy baréd snow and thy unbraided gold;
There my enfranchised hand on every side
Shall o'er thy naked polished ivory slide.
No curtain there, though of transparent lawn,
Shall be before thy virgin-treasure drawn;
But the rich mine, to the inquiring eye
Exposed, shall ready still for mintage lie,
And we will coin young Cupids. There a bed
Of roses and fresh myrtles shall be spread
Under the cooler shade of cypress groves;
Our pillows, of the down of Venus' doves,
Whereupon our panting limbs we'll gently lay,
In the faint respites of our active play;
That so our slumbers may in dreams have leisure
To tell the nimble fancy our past pleasure,
And so our souls that cannot be embraced
Shall the embraces of our bodies taste.
Meanwhile the bubbling stream shall court the shore,
Th' enamoured chirping wood-choir shall adore
In varied tunes the deity of love;
The gentle blasts of western winds shall move
The trembling leaves, and through their close boughs breathe
Still music, whilst we rest ourselves beneath
Their dancing shade; till a soft murmur, sent
From souls entranced in amorous languishment,
Rouse us, and shoot into our veins fresh fire,
Till we in their sweet ecstasy expire.

Then, as the empty bee, that lately bore
Into the common treasure all her store,
Flies 'bout the painted field with nimble wing,
Deflow'ring the fresh virgins of the spring,
So will I rifle all the sweets that dwell
In my delicious paradise, and swell
My bag with honey, drawn forth by the power
Of fervent kisses, from each spicy flower.
I'll seize the rosebuds in their perfumed bed,
The violet knots, like curious mazes spread
O'er all the garden, taste the ripened cherry,
The warm, firm apple, tipped with coral berry;
Then will I visit with a wand'ring kiss
The vale of lilies and the bower of bliss;
And where the beauteous region doth divide
Into two milky ways, my lips shall slide
Down those smooth alleys, wearing as I go
A tract for lovers on the printed snow;
Thence climbing o'er the swelling Apennine,
Retire into thy grove of eglantine,
Where I will all those ravished sweets distill
Through love's alembic, and with chemic skill
From the mixed mass one sovereign balm derive,
Then bring that great elixir to thy hive.

Now in more subtle wreaths I will entwine
My sinewy thighs, my legs and arms with thine;
Thou like a sea of milk shalt lie displayed,
Whilst I the smooth, calm ocean invade
With such a tempest, as when Jove of old
Fell down on Danaë in a storm of gold;
Yet my tall pine shall in the Cyprian strait
Ride safe at anchor, and unlade her freight;
My rudder, with thy bold hand, like a tried
And skillful pilot, thou shall steer, and guide
My bark into love's channel, where it shall

Dance, as the bounding waves do rise or fall.
Then shall thy circling arms embrace and clip
My willing body, and thy balmy lip
Bathe me in juice of kisses, whose perfume
Like a religious incense shall consume,
And send up holy vapors to those powers
That bless our loves, and crown our sportful hours,
That with such halcyon calmness fix our souls
In steadfast pace, as no affright controls.
There no rude sounds shake us with sudden starts;
No jealous ears, when we unrip our hearts,
Suck our discourse in; no observing spies
This blush, that glance traduce; no envious eyes
Watch our close meetings; nor are we betrayed
To rivals by the bribéd chambermaid.
No wedlock bonds unwreathe our twisted loves;
We seek no midnight arbor, no dark groves
To hide our kisses: there the hated name
Of husband, wife, lust, modest, chaste, or shame,
Are vain and empty words, whose very sound
Was never heard in the Elysian ground.
All things are lawful there that may delight
Nature or unrestrainéd appetite;
Like and enjoy, to will and act is one:
We only sin when Love's rites are not done . . .

Come then, my Celia, we'll no more forbear
To taste our joys, struck with a panic fear,
But will dispose from his imperious sway
This proud usurper, and walk free as they,
With necks unyoked; nor is it just that he
Should fetter your soft sex with chastity,
Which Nature made unapt for abstinence;
When yet this false imposter can dispense
With human justice and with sacred right,
And, maugre both their laws, command me fight

With rivals, or with emulous loves, that dare
Equal with thine their mistress' eyes or hair.
If thou complain of wrong, and call my sword
To carve out thy revenge, upon that word
He bids me fight and kill, or else he brands
With marks of infamy my coward hands,
And yet religion bids from bloodshed fly,
And damns me for that act. Then tell my why
This goblin Honor, which the word adores,
Should make men atheists, and not women whores.

from **Serve It Forth**

M. F. K. FISHER

How gentle can a touch be? How delicate? Fine questions, in my opinion, for though I've heard that eros can be delivered in boxes and blows, it can also be communicated through spiderweb tracings of skin on skin. Euphues, the title character of England's most popular book of the sixteenth century, expressed a desire to "dine with the Epicures and fast with the Stoics." This is my sentiment regarding most things: embrace both ends of the spectrum, straddle every divide, be yourself and not-yourself as best you can. And so with touching, to know force and control, yet to manage delicacy and precision. To touch or be touched with pure certainty in a way that negotiates the razor-line limen between contact and noncontact: that, to me, is sexy as hell.

It's hard not to think of delicacy and eroticism when reading the prose of M. F. K. Fisher. The preeminent American food writer treats her topic as Melville did whales: till it expands to include the very universe. With a Ginsu wit worthy of Dorothy Parker, Fisher writes of snails and spuds, soufflés and schnapps. She also manages, in deft flicks of her pen, to pillory first her taste-blind countrymen, then her back-biting adopted French neighbors, and, finally, everyone in between. And still more enticingly, there is a saffron tinge of sexuality that runs through her work and infuses everything, leaving you hungry, aroused, and completely in love. This is why, by way of introduction, I spoke of the gentlest touch, for the delicate precision of Fisher's writing beckons and beguiles, never making the analogy of food to sex explicit, but letting it slowly seep into you like the smell of garlic roasting. Where *Tampopo* trumpets, Fisher whispers.

●●·

Almost every person has something secret he likes to eat . . . I remember that Al looked at me very strangely when he first saw the little sections lying on the radiator. That February in Strasbourg was too cold for us. Out on the Boulevard de l'Orangerie, in a cramped dirty apartment across from the sad zoo half full of animals and birds frozen too stiff even to make smells, we grew quite morbid.

Finally we counted all our money, decided we could not possibly afford to move, and next day went bag and baggage to the most expensive pension in the city.

It was wonderful—big room, windows, clean white billows of curtain, central heating. We basked like lizards. Finally Al went back to work, but I could not bear to walk into the bitter blowing streets from our warm room.

It was then that I discovered how to eat little dried sections of tangerine. My pleasure in them is subtle and voluptuous and quite inexplicable. I can only write how they are prepared.

In the morning, in the soft sultry chamber, sit in the window peeling tangerines, three or four. Peel them gently; do not bruise them, as you watch soldiers pour past and past the corner and over the canal towards the watched Rhine. Separate each plump little pregnant crescent. If you find the Kiss, the secret section, save it for Al.

Listen to the chambermaid thumping up the pillows, and murmur encouragement to her thick Alsatian tales of *l'intérieur*. That is Paris, the interior, Paris or anywhere west of Strasbourg or maybe the Vosges. While she mutters of seduction and French bicyclists who ride more than wheels, tear delicately from the soft pile of sections each velvet string. You know those white pulpy strings that hold tangerines into their skins? Tear them off. Be careful.

Take yesterday's paper . . . and spread it on top of the radiator . . . After you have put the pieces of tangerine on the paper on the hot radiator, it is best to forget about them. Al comes home, you go to a long noon dinner in the brown dining room, afterwards maybe you have a little nip of quetsch from the bottle on the armoire. Finally he goes. Of course you are sorry, but—

On the radiator the sections of tangerine have grown even plumper, hot and full. You carry them to the window, pull it open, and leave them for a few minutes on the packed snow of the sill. They are ready.

All afternoon you can sit, then, looking down on the corner. Afternoon papers are delivered to the kiosk. Children come home from school just as three lovely whores mince smartly into the pension's chic tearoom. A basketful of Dutch tulips stations itself by the tram-stop, ready to tempt tired clerks at six o'clock. Finally the soldiers stump back from the Rhine. It is dark.

The sections of tangerine are gone, and I cannot tell you why they are so magical. Perhaps it is that little shell, thin as one layer of enamel on a Chinese bowl, that crackles so tinily, so ultimately under your teeth. Or the rush of cold pulp just after it. Or the perfume. I cannot tell.

There must be someone, though, who knows what I mean. Probably everyone does, because of his own eatings.

from Ironweed

WILLIAM KENNEDY

Let this be said: I have tasted many of the joys under heaven and found none more reliably luscious than the kiss. Fragile yet potent, combustible, tangy, push-pull, and eminently expressive, the kiss has all the upsides of sex and none of the mess. The kiss is a Trojan horse of intimacy, so seemingly innocent, so licit, yet so gut wrenching, soul speaking, and endorphin firing at the same time. I am a kiss junkie; I love to kiss, I kiss to love, I'm constantly trying to steal women away from conversations to secret them into back bedrooms for some serious necking. And every once in a while, it actually works.

My first real kiss came behind the storage sheds next to the junior high school football field. A year or two later, I got one from a popular girl; it was shocking both because I was the most loathed kid in the school and because her mouth was large enough to encircle mine completely. I mentioned this fact to a "friend," and he told two friends, and they told two friends, and soon she was cursing me through the halls of the school, lowering my social status even further. A more felicitous early kiss came in high school, at the behest of the costume designer for the school play, whose lips had the incomparable collapsing effect of a Ziplocked bag of pudding. (Where are you now, darling? Where are you?) The most bittersweet was a single, slow-planted dream smooch from an angelic beauty who, when I asked her some days later if it was a fluke, said that it most assuredly was. She died in her teens, and that one kiss was all I knew, yet I will never forget her.

Later life has not ceased to provide me still more astonishing meetings of lips, and many lessons to learn from them. Some women kiss you because that's as far as they'll go; others kiss you to decide if they'll go further. An experienced friend laughed at me when I told her I still occasionally have bad sex, saying that I should know from the first kiss how it will work out. She's right, of course, so now I try to kiss, dance with, and see the SATs of all prospective girlfriends before things get serious. The kissing, ultimately, is the most important indicator, for kisses are the vehicle for the joy of fresh infatuation, yet remain a reservoir of warmth as even the oldest loves grow older. And in their ultimate role, kisses can provide indelible proof of love itself. That is the theme of the excerpt below, from William Kennedy's Pulitzer Prize–winning novel, *Ironweed*.

But then you get [a kiss] like that first whizzer on Kibbee's lumber pile, one that comes out of the brain and the heart and the crotch, and out of the hands on your hair, and out of those breasts that weren't all the way blown up yet, and out of the clutch them arms give you, and out of time itself, which keeps track of how long it can go on without you gettin' even slightly bored the way you got bored years later with kissin' almost anybody but Helen, and out of fingers (Katrina had fingers like that) that run themselves around and over your face and down your neck, and out of the grip you take on her shoulders, especially on them bones that come out of the middle of her back like angel wings, and out of them eyes that keep openin' and closin' to make sure that this is still goin' and still real and not just stuff you dream about and when you know it's real it's okay to close 'em again, and outa that tongue, holy shit, that tongue, you gotta ask where she learned that because nobody ever did that except Katrina who was married with a kid and had a right to know, but Annie, goddamn, Annie, where'd you pick that up, or maybe you been gidzeyin' heavy on this lumber pile regular (No, no, no, I know you never, I always knew you never), and so it is natural with a woman like Annie that the kiss come out of every part of her body and more, outa that mouth . . . and he sees well beyond the mouth into a primal location in this woman's being, a location that evokes in him not only the memory of years but decades and even more, the memory of epochs, aeons, so that he is sure that no matter where he might have sat with a woman and felt this way, whether it was in some ancient cave or some bogside shanty, or on a North Albany lumber pile, he and she would both know that there was something in each of them that had to stop being one and become two, that had to swear that forever after there would never be another (and there never has been, quite), and that there would be allegiance and sovereignty and fidelity and other such tomfool horseshit that people destroy their heads with when what they are saying has nothing to do with time's forevers but everything to do with the simultaneous recognition of an eternal twain, well sir, then both of them, Francis and Annie, or the Francises and Annies of any age, would both know in that same instant that there was something between them that had to stop being two and become one.

Such was the significance of that kiss.

from Sexing the Cherry

JEANETTE WINTERSON

With its live-in livestock, death carts in the streets, and manor lords who could sleep with your betrothed and tax you as much as they felt like, the Middle Ages was a hell of a time to live. But as history moved along, things got a little better: the blanket was invented (what took them so long?), peasants could start owning land, and a lighter form of literature emerged to go alongside all the religious poems and heroic epics—comedy. Comedy had existed in Greece and Rome, but it didn't flourish again until the Dark Ages had brightened and Europe approached its eventual Renaissance.

What comedy did obtain in the later Middle Ages jibed well with the culture of the time. Oft I have written of the medieval sense of humor, of its excesses and exaggerations, its vulgarity, its sense of the absurd. Where in today's culture we have *Dumb and Dumber,* the Middle Ages had gross and grosser, with Boccaccio, Chaucer, and Rabelais outdoing one another with tales of the scatalogical and obscene. When their characters weren't having their asses rammed with red-hot pokers, they were falling into full latrines or standing beneath rivers of urine.

But what has become of comic saturnalia in the literature of our own hygienic times? T. C. Boyle's raucous novel, *Water Music,* evokes the roguery and raunch that survived the Middle Ages into England's eighteenth century; John Kennedy Toole's bloated Ignatius J. Reilly is a self-conscious throwback to the medieval in a variety of unappetizing senses; but nowhere do we find a character more truly Rabelaisian in proportion than the Dog Woman of Jeanette Winterson's *Sexing the Cherry.* Set in England in the years leading up to and just after the Restoration, *Cherry* is a nice tale of a boy and his mother—and what a mother! The Dog Woman proves to be larger than an elephant, louder than a thunderclap, keeper of fifty-plus hounds, and beholden to none but them and her son. She is an architectonic force, and never more than in her disastrous encounters with the less fair sex. The excerpt below is her account of a man's attempt at pleasuring her. Confronted with her not-negligible womanhood, he finds himself not quite up to the task. Sounds like he would have been happier reading theology.

●●•

Whilst Jordan was away I discovered from time in the brothel that men's members, if bitten off or otherwise severed, do not grow again. This seems a great mistake on the part of nature, since men are so careless with their members and will put them anywhere without thinking. I believe they would force them in a hole in the wall if no better could be found.

I did mate with a man, but cannot say that I felt anything at all, though I had him jammed up to the hilt. As for him, spread on top of me with his face buried beneath my breasts, he complained that he could not find the sides of my cunt and felt like a tadpole in a pot. He was an educated man and urged me to try to squeeze in my muscles, and so perhaps bring me closer to his prong. I took a great breath and squeezed with all my might and heard something like a rush of air through a tunnel, and when I strained up on my elbows and looked down I saw I had pulled him in, balls and every-thing. He was stuck. I had the presence of mind to ring the bell and my friend came in with her sisters, and with the aid of a crow-bar they prised him out and refreshed him with mulled wine while I sang him a little song about the fortitude of spawning salmon. He was a gallant gentleman and offered a different way of pleasuring me, since I was the first woman he said he had failed. Accordingly, he burrowed down the way ferrets do and tried to take me in his mouth. I was very comfortable about this, having nothing to be bitten off. But in a moment he thrust up his head and eyed me wearily.

"Madam," he said, "I am sorry, I beg your pardon but I cannot."

"Cannot?"

"Cannot. I cannot take that orange in my mouth. It will not fit. Neither can I run my tongue over it. You are too big, madam."

I did not know what part of me he was describing, but I felt pity for him and offered him more wine and some pleasant chat.

When he had gone I squatted backwards on a pillow and parted my bush hair to see what it was that had confounded him so. It seemed all in proportion to me. These gentlemen are very timid.

from **Portable People**

PAUL WEST

There's a phrase bandied about in philosophy classrooms that gives me enormous pleasure: the problem of other minds. Much as I would like these words to refer to the irremovable thorn-in-the-side fact that other people have ideas and opinions of their own (Why? I ask, why?), the phrase is actually used to talk about the fact that neither Descartes nor Russell nor anybody else has been able to prove with certainty that there are intelligences beyond their own. The upshot is that the only consciousness you can attest to is yours, and all else could be a hallucination, an error, a fabrication. (To this, however, my response was always, If I was cooking this whole thing up, there would be a lot more free parking.)

In writing, of course, the phrase could be adapted quite readily to speak to the difficulty of creating characters that aren't mere extensions of the author. Not surprisingly, the protagonists in my early stories were chaps rather like myself—lonely, emotionally stunted ne'er-do-wells who talked a lot better than they listened. Only later did I even dare to try to generate characters from my own imagination. And even those, as it turned out, tended to be drawn from some distant corner of my self. We bear a lot of people within us, and to be a decent fiction writer you end up seeking out even the Rhode Island delegates from the Congress of Identity.

It is the mark of a truly gifted writer to be able to go beyond this. Not only must they enter into the minds of others, they also have to make the minds themselves. Paul West takes this challenge to an extreme in his "novel" *Portable People,* a collection of channeled voices from the living and the long and recently dead, with characters as diverse as Imelda Marcos and Lord Byron's doctor. West's gift is dazzling: No two sound alike (beyond suspiciously prodigious vocabularies), and, what's more, no two seem to share a philosophical or ethical position. Each is a discrete human writ large on three pages or less. So the scandal of a crotchety and mischievous Rodin in the excerpt that follows is counterbalanced elsewhere by the proud and surgical Edith Sitwell or the consummately disdainful Hermann Goering. West speaks more voices than the whispering winds.

○ ●●·

Auguste Rodin

God's dong, if such a thing can be, is a velvet hammer made of love that thumps the stars home, where they belong, in the moist pleat of the empyrean. Surely He needs no goading on, unlike myself, finger-dipping each and every cleft of every model, and all that a mere preliminary to what goes on after the day's work is done, and we twist the big key clockwise. That is when I get my girls to tongue one another before my very eyes. It is almost as if the sculpting is mere prelude to the venery. By midnight, they are all going their ways, about their business, with Rodin syrup dribbling from them as they walk, like molten marble. Those who pose for me must taste my will, upended like ducks on a pond.

When my Balzac, now, strides forth with upright phallus in his fist, from behind he must be read as a giant lingam marching to India. I mean these burly semblances to stun, my Lord, as when, for Becque and sundry appreciative madams, I turn actor and behead with a sword the plaster statues arranged in front of me. Those who cry out, in abuse, "Rodin is a great big prick" are right. I am always and ever the policeman's son, neither peasant nor poet.

I receive on Sundays, as my copy of *The Guide to the Pleasures of Paris* says, married to that carthorse, Rose, who gave me a son with a broken brain, abandoned by Camille, who once adored me and now in the asylum murmurs, "So this is what I get for all I did." At least she, unlike my Yankee heiress Claire, fat and daubed and drunk, never kept leaving the dinner table to go and throw up, as now, or play her creaky gramophone while my public sits around me, hearing me tell them yet again that it was indeed I who stove in

Isadora Duncan, pommeling that little ear-like hole between her lively legs, and it was also I who, like the milkman delivering, brought her weekly orgasm to little sad Gwen John in her rented room. I snapped her like a wineglass stem, but made her coo all the same.

When I get Upstairs, His Nibs and I are going to go on such a masterful rampage the angels will cry to be raped, neuter as they are, and none shall contain us, we shall be so massive in our roistering, from the hand-gallop to the common swyve, with our hump-backed fists banged deep into the soft clay of eternity.

from **The Theogony**

HESIOD

So let's imagine you're thinking of
writing a book. What are you
going to write about? Your family
perhaps, your quirky friends,
some ex-lover who wronged
you (after having righted you
so nicely), the day-to-day liv-
ing tips you learned from your cat? Or maybe you're an ex-lawyer, ex–
navy SEAL, ex–secret agent, or ex–medical examiner whose insider
information will drive a nail-biter narrative. But how about this as a topic
for your first book? The origin of the gods and the history of the world.
Nice modest project, no? But that's what Hesiod, an eighth century B.C.
contemporary of Homer, opted for as the subject of his first book, the
Theogony—no small proof of how much Western literature has changed
in the last twenty-eight hundred years.

Now Hesiod probably didn't invent all his material (much of it he
could have taken from oral legends passed down or from written sources
that predate him), but it's still great to imagine him trying to pitch it to a
Hollywood producer: "Well, Mr. Coppola, it's kind of this classic tale of
birth and rebirth, of gods being created out of nothingness or out of the
side of each other's heads, of sons castrating their fathers and genitals
floating on the sea and turning into goddesses, that kind of thing."
Francis Ford would probably look him deep in the eye, put his hand on
his shoulder and say, "Best lay off that crack pipe, son."

But although much of the *Theogony* is decidedly distant to the modern sensibility, the one thing it shares with much modern literature,
sadly, is its leaning toward misogyny. In a book that otherwise makes
almost no reference to normal human reality, Hesiod pauses long enough
to take some gratuitous potshots at our mothers, wives, and sisters.
Women are the curse Zeus inflicted on mankind because his son Iapetos
stole fire and brought it to us, and apparently we haven't been forgiven.

Yet among the gods at least, it's not the females who cause trouble but the fathers and sons. Iapetos stole the fire from Zeus. Zeus, meanwhile, vanquished his father, Kronos, who had eaten all of his other children. And Kronos, as we will see in the following excerpt, also had a father to fear and, with the help of his mother, took matters into his own hands. Centuries before Sophocles and millennia before Freud, Oedipal myths were in full force, nowhere more clearly than in Hesiod.

● ●·

For of all the children that were born of Earth and Heaven, these were the most terrible, and they were hated by their own father [Heaven] from the first. And he used to hide them all away in a secret place of Earth as soon as each was born, and would not suffer them to come up into the light, and he rejoiced in his evil doing. But vast Earth groaned within, being strained, and she thought up a crafty, wicked plan. Quickly she made grey adamant and shaped a giant sickle and told her plan to her dear sons. And as she spoke, she was vexed in her heart:

"My children, gotten of a sinful father, if you will obey me, we should punish the vile outrage of your father, for he first began devising his shameful deeds."

Thus she spoke, but fear seized them all, and none uttered a word. But great Cronos the wily took courage, and answered his dear mother:

"Mother, I will undertake to do this deed, for I revere not our father of evil name, for he first thought to do the evil things."

So he said, and vast Earth rejoiced greatly in spirit, and set and hid him in an ambush, and put in his hands the jagged sickle, and revealed to him the whole plot.

And Heaven came, bringing on night and longing for love, and he lay about Earth spreading himself full upon her. Then the son from his ambush stretched forth his left hand and in his right took the great long sickle with jagged teeth and swiftly lopped off his father's members and cast them away to fall behind him. And not vainly did they fall from his hand, for all the bloody drops that gushed forth Earth received, and as the seasons moved round she bared the strong Erinyes and the great Giants with gleaming armor, holding long spears in their hands, and the Nymphs whom they call Meliae all over the boundless earth. And so soon as he had cut off the members with adamant and cast them from the land into the surging sea, they were swept away over the main a long time, and a white foam spread around them from the immortal flesh, and in it there grew a maiden. First she drew near holy Cythera, and from there, after, she came to Cyprus and came forth an awful, lovely goddess, and grass grew up beneath her shapely feet. And gods and men call her Aphrodite.

—*translated by Hugh G. Evelyn-White,*
modified by Jack Murnighan

from **Singular Pleasures**

HARRY MATHEWS

Come a little closer, I want to whisper something in your ear: I play Scrabble—alone. Frequently, joyfully, almost compulsively, I take out my dictionaries, set up the board, draw the tiles for one side (leaving the other side's tiles undrawn until I've played the first side's—so as not to "cheat"), and shift the letters in my mind until the near certainty that I've extracted as many points as humanly (or cybernetically) possible from the move tells me I can place the tiles out on the board. Then it's the competition's turn, and I do the same thing. An hour later the game is over. The score is astronomical; my mind is calm. And I've successfully kept for myself something that's supposed to be shared with another.

And that, in fact, was the crime of the biblical father of masturbation, Onan, who, when he was supposed to impregnate his brother's wife, pulled out instead and spilled his seed on the ground. So the word *onanism*—though it's come to mean masturbation—really just means wasting. Perhaps, then, the mental masturbation of abstruse art and writing is so named not because of the pleasure it gives the practitioner but instead because it breaks the promise of communication.

Harry Mathews has no such problem. The lone American member of the group of mathematicians and writers known as Oulipo (short, in French, for "workshop in potential literature"—they are dedicated to the creativity fostered by formal constraint), Mathews composed a book of sixty-one prose poems about masturbation. And though the collection is titled *Singular Pleasures*, it shares its gift most readily. Each poem presents a different scene, in a different locale, of a different person of varying age (from nine to eighty-one) masturbating in imaginative, telling, poignant, and playful ways. After reading the entirety of Math-

ews's collection, you begin to get a sense of the limitless possibilities—
and want to add new ones to his list. "There was a man of thirty in a
squalid walk-up in Little Italy, leaning naked over a Scrabble board . . ."

⬤ ● ·

A man of thirty-five is about to experience orgasm in one of the
better condominiums in Gaza. He is masturbating, but neither
hand nor object touches his taut penis: arranged in a circle, five
hairblowers direct their streams of warm air toward that focal point.
He has plugged his ears with wax balls.

⬤ ● ·

While the Aeolian String Quartet performs the final variation of
Haydn's "Emperor" Quartet in the smaller of Managua's two concert halls, a man of three score and four summers sits masturbating
in the last row of the orchestra, a coat on his lap. Thirty-three years
before, after relieving himself during the intermission of another
concert, he had returned to his seat with his fly unbuttoned.
Unconscious of his appearance, he had become erect during a scin-
tillating performance of the Schubert Octet and actually ejaculated
during the final chords. The house lights had come up to reveal his
disarray; he had fled; ever since, he has been laboring steadfastly to
recreate that momentary bliss.

⬤ ● ·

As he masturbates, a forty-five-year-old man in Pretoria is standing in front of a full-length mirror watching himself. On the far
side of the two-way mirror, a woman of eighty-one sits looking at
him, one hand busy beneath her skirts. The man ejaculates onto the
mirror: she mutters, "Too soon!"

⬤ ● ·

Inmates of the pensioners home in Constantia, Romania, four women (aged seventy-one, seventy-three, seventy-four, and seventy-six) and four men (seventy, seventy-two, seventy-five, seventy-eight) conceive and execute a plan for independent, simultaneous masturbation. Each agrees to aim for orgasm, in the privacy of bed, on the twelfth stroke of midnight every Saturday night, after the weekly bingo and dancing.—The director of the home will later be struck by the particular vivacity of these eight as it grows from week to week. They will refuse, however, to divulge the reason for their zest.

●••

Sitting on an overstuffed chair by his bed, a boy of nine is masturbating near Stamford, Connecticut. He does not ejaculate, but a pearl of sperm gathers at the point of his still-childish erection. He knows what's going on.

from **Poems**

CATULLUS

Recently, my friends have been indulging their lust for schaden-freude by telling me that the Latin language has grown unhip. How can this be? When people speak coarsely of the "dead" languages, I inquire, "Dead for whom?" Almost invariably they respond, "For everybody."

It is a sad state of affairs. With the demise of Latin, lost will be the poignancy of Augustine's plaintive cries for God's mercy; forgotten will be the singular nobility of Virgil's hexameter (his readers turned to swine by the Circe of modernity); erased will be the majesty of Cicero, whose rhetoric was considered so supreme that throughout the Renaissance many speakers would not use a word if it did not appear in the Ciceronian corpus, believing that if it was unnecessary to Cicero it was unnecessary to language in general.

But of these crimes, perhaps the greatest will be the fading of Catullus, whose two-thousand-year-old bawdy and satiric lyrics are some of history's wittiest barbs. If Latin is truly to die, much laughter will die with it.

XV

To you, Aurelius, I give you both my self and my young love,
and ask but one a small favor:
That if, in the depths of your heart, you have ever wished
The object of your desire to remain pure and unspoiled,
Then you'll protect my boy from lechery;

I speak not of the public—I don't fear those milling about the
    squares,
Entirely occupied in their own affairs;
It's you who scares me: you and your penis,
That menace to children both good and bad.
Use it wherever you wish, given whatever chance,
Excepting only my young friend. This, my modest request.
But should your wicked impulses or evil mind
Impel you, blackguard, to commit a crime
Of treachery against my person,
Ah, then you'll rue your miserable fate;
You'll have your legs bound
And your backdoor rammed with fish and radishes!

LXIX

Do not wonder, Rufus, why no woman
Wants to place her soft thighs under you,
Even when you give her rare fabrics
Or precious stones of perfect translucence.
Your problem is an unfortunate rumor
That you tend a mean goat in the armpit's valley,
Who scares all the women away.
No mystery: It's a nasty beast
No girl would want to sleep with.
So either kill off this scourge of the nostril,
Or stop wondering why they all run away.

XCVII

I had thought (so help me gods!) that it made no difference
Whether I smelled Amelius' mouth or asshole;
The one being no cleaner, the other no filthier.
But, in fact, his asshole is cleaner, and much preferable:
It has no teeth. The mouth has teeth a foot and a half long
And gums like an old wagon car. When it opens
It's like the cunt of a heatstruck donkey pissing.

And yet he fucks quite a bit and thinks himself a playboy—
Is he not afraid of any retribution?
But the women who touch him,
Would they not lick the asscrack of a hangman?

—*translated by Jack Murnighan*

from **Near to the Wild Heart**

CLARICE LISPECTOR

I've met people who remember the moment they became sexually aware, some early trigger like a tickle or a special itch that, when scratched, evoked a new kind of pleasure, perhaps mingled with a touch of shame. Of course, I too can remember early sexual moments: being dragged under a blanket-covered picnic table for a game of show-and-show with a neighbor girl when I was five (she was enthusiastic and I shy as hell); years later sharing backyard kisses with a future ballerina; later still my repeated and occasionally successful attempts to convince a friend's sister to striptease; and, finally, deep in junior high, finding my first true girlfriend, who was famous for palming guys from the front and whom I later lost to my best friend. But although these events represent symptoms of sexuality, they still don't help me recover, in good Proustian fashion, the precise awakening of my sexual self. That sudden flicker or steady trickle remains obscured.

Some of my favorite writers, however, have succeeded in capturing these most elusive moments. In Günter Grass's *The Tin Drum*, young Oscar first confronts the "hairy triangle"; in James Baldwin's *Giovanni's Room*, David discovers he's gay. The excerpt below, taken from Clarice Lispector's *Near to the Wild Heart*, describes the moment when Joana, a young girl taking a bath, discovers both her sexual identity and place in the universe. *Near to the Wild Heart* was published in 1944, when Lispector was only nineteen, and is a marvel of expressiveness. In this scene, as elsewhere, the young Lispector seems unwilling or unable to filter the raw truth, and her uniquely tactile language strikes a probing, poetic chord: a girl's recognition of her body and its isolation from the other bodies of the cosmos.

The girl laughs softly, rejoicing in her own body. Her smooth, slender legs, her tiny breasts emerge from the water. She scarcely knows herself, still not fully grown, still almost a child. She stretches out one leg, looks at her foot from a distance, moves it tenderly, slowly, like a fragile wing. She lifts her arms above her head, stretches them out towards the ceiling lost in the shadows, her eyes closed, without any feeling, only movement. Her body stretches and spreads out, the moisture on her skin glistening in the semi-darkness—her body tracing a tense, quivering line. When she drops her arms once more, she becomes compact, white and secure. She chuckles to herself, moves her long neck from one side to another, tilts her head backwards—the grass is always fresh, someone is about to kiss her, soft, tiny rabbits snuggle up against each other with their eyes shut. She starts laughing again, gentle murmurings like those of water. She strokes her waist, her hips, her life. She sinks into the bathtub as if it were the sea. A tepid world closes over her silently, quietly. Small bubbles slip away gently and vanish once they touch the enamel. The young girl feels the water weighing on her body, she pauses for a moment as if someone had tapped her lightly on the shoulder. Paying attention to what she is feeling, the invading tide. What has happened? She becomes a serious creature, with wide, deep eyes. She can scarcely breathe. What has happened? The open, silent eyes of things went on shining amidst the vapors. Over the same body that has divined happiness there is water—water. No, no . . .

I've discovered a miracle in the rain—Joana thought—a miracle splintered into dense, solemn, glittering stars, like a suspended warning: like a lighthouse. What are they trying to tell me? In those stars I can foretell the secret, their brilliance is the impassive mystery I can hear flowing inside me, weeping at length in tones of romantic despair. Dear God, at least bring me into contact with them, satisfy my longing to kiss them. To feel their light on my lips, to feel it glow inside my body, leaving it shining and transparent, fresh and moist like the minutes that come before dawn. Why do these strange longings possess me? Raindrops and stars, this dense and chilling fusion has roused me, opened the gates of my green and somber forest, of this forest smelling of an abyss where water flows. And harnessed it to night . . . Because no rain falls inside me, I wish to be a star. Purify me a little and I shall acquire the dimensions of those beings who take refuge behind the rain . . . And I am in the world, as free and lithe as a colt on the plain. I rise as gently as a puff of air . . . I sink only to emerge . . .

—*translated by Giovanni Pontiero*

from The Decameron

GIOVANNI BOCCACCIO

The intelligence of Plato, the humanity of Dante, the imagination of Shakespeare, the virtuosity of Donne, and the wit of Boccaccio: a decent set of wishes for an aspiring writer lucky enough to stumble on a pair of genie lamps. But to pick only one—and any one is certainly enough—that's a tough call. Unless, of course, it's not fame but fun that you're after, in which case Boccaccio is the only way to go. Boccaccio was the most spirited writer of the Middle Ages—and among the most spirited of any age—and he's still the unrivaled master of saucy plots and mischievous characters, guaranteed to please.

Boccaccio's most famous work, the *Decameron,* is a fourteenth-century collection of one hundred short tales, told by a group of nobles taking refuge in a villa. The stories are a panorama of medieval culture and wit, and they are, in turn, raucous, sinister, clever, and often, as in the excerpt that follows, quite racy (the Middle Ages were more fun than you'd think!). The *Decameron* is one of the great works of Italian literature and one of the first to tell stories about real people in real situations (often having real sex). But what ties the tales together is not so much this realism as Boccaccio's fabulous sense of the world: in virtually every story some clever trickster takes advantage of his thick or naïve dupes. Boccaccio's world is a meritocracy of ingenuity where the creative win at everyone else's expense. This is why I'd rather live in Boccaccio's world than any other, for intelligence works in the service of play, and morality means that the quick thinking get their just desserts. Take the following tale, for example, and see what a little imagination can do with an otherwise unpromising situation.

Dear Ladies, the deceits used by men towards your sex, but especially husbands, have been so great and many as when it hath sometime happened, or yet may, that husbands are repaid in the self-same manner, you need not find fault . . . but rather you should refer it to general publication so that immodest men may know . . . that women are in no way inferior to them. . . . Mine intent therefore is to tell you, what a woman (though but of mean quality) did to her husband all of a sudden, and in a moment for her own safety.

Not long ago, there lived in Naples an honest mean man, who did take to wife a fair and lusty young woman, being named Peronella. It came to pass that a certain young man, well observing the beauty and good parts of Peronella, became much addicted in affection towards her: and by his often and secret solicitations, which he found not to be unkindly entertained, his success proved answerable to his hope. . . .

Now, for their securer meeting, to stand clear from all matter of scandal or detection, they concluded in this order between themselves. Lazaro, for so was Peronella's husband named, was an early riser every morning. Poor Lazaro was no sooner gone, but [Peronella's lover] presently enters the house, which stood in a very solitary street. Many mornings had they thus met together, to their no small delight and contention, till one particular morning among the rest, when Lazaro was gone forth to work, and Striguario (so was the amorous young man named) visiting Peronella in the house. Upon a very urgent errand, Lazaro returned back again, quite contrary to his former wont, keeping forth all day, and never coming home till night.

Finding his door to be fast locked, and he having knocked softly once or twice, he spoke in this manner to himself: "Fortune I thank thee, for albeit thou hast made me poor, yet thou hast bestowed a better blessing on me, in matching me with so good, honest, and loving a wife. Behold, though I went early out of my house, her self hath risen in the cold to shut the door, to prevent the entrance of thieves, or any other that might offend us." Peronella having heard what her husband said, and knowing the manner of his knock, said fearfully to Striguario: "Alas, dear friend, what shall we do? I am a dead woman. For Lazaro my husband is come back again, and I know not what to do or say. He never returned in this manner before now, doubtless he saw when you entered the door. For the safety of your honor and mine, creep under this brewing pot, till I have opened the door and know the reason of his so soon returning."

Striguario made no delaying of the matter, but got himself closely under the pot, and Peronella opening the door for her husband's entrance, with a frowning countenance, spoke thus unto him: "What meaneth this so early returning home again this morning? It seemeth thou intends to do nothing today, having brought back thy tools in thy hands? If such be thine intent, how shall we live? Where shall we have bread to fill our bellies? Dost thou think that I will allow thee to pawn my gown and other poor garments, as heretofore thou hast done? I that card and spin both night and day till I have worn the flesh from my fingers will hardly find oil to maintain our lamp. Husband, husband, there is not one neighbor dwelling by us but makes a mockery of me, and tells me plainly, that I may be ashamed to drudge and toil as I do, wondering not a little how I am able to endure it; and thou returnest home with thy hands in thy hose, as if thou hadst no work at all to do this day."

Having thus spoken, she fell to weeping, and then thus began again: "Poor wretched woman as I am, in an unfortunate hour was I born, and in a much worse when I was made thy wife. I could have had a proper, handsome young man—one that would have maintained me brave and gallantly, but, beast as I was, to forgo my good and cast myself away on such a beggar as thou art, and whom none would have had, but such an ass as I. Other women live at heart's ease and in jollity, have their amorous friends and loving paramours, yea, one, two, three at once, making their husbands look like a moon crescent whereon they shine sun-like with amiable looks because they know not how to help it, when I, poor fool, live here at home a miserable life, not daring once to dream of such follies, an innocent soul, heartless and harmless."

"Many times, sitting and sighing to my self, 'Lord,' think I, 'of what metal am I made? Why should not I have a friend in a corner, as well as others have? I am flesh and blood as they are, not made of brass or iron, and therefore subject to women's frailty.' Would thou should know it husband, and I tell it thee in good earnest, that if I would do ill, I could quickly find a friend at a need. Gallants there are in good store, who, of my knowledge, love me dearly, and have made me very large and liberal promises, of gold, silver, jewels, and gay garments, if I would extend them the least favor. But my heart will not suffer me, I never was the daughter of such a mother, as had so much as a thought of such matters. No, I thank our blessed Lady, and Saint Friswid for it. And yet thou returnest home again, when thou shouldst be at work."

Lazaro, who stood all this while like a well-believing logger-head, demurely thus answered: "Alas good wife! I pray you be not so angry, I never had so much as an ill thought of you, but know well enough what you are, and have made good proof thereof this morning. Understand therefore patiently, sweet wife, that I went forth to my work as daily I use to do, little dreaming (as I think you do not) that it had been a holiday. Wife, this is the feast day of Saint Gale-one whereon we may in no ways work, and this is the reason of my so soon returning. Nevertheless, dear wife, I was not careless of our household provision, for, though we work not, yet we must have food, which I have provided for more than a month. Wife, I remembered the brewing pot, whereof we have little or no use at all, but rather it is a trouble to the house. I met with an honest friend, who is standing outside the door; to him I have sold the pot for five gigliatoes, and he is waiting to take it away with him.

"Husband, what do you mean?" replied Peronella, "Why now I am worse offended then before. Thou that art a man, walkest every where, and shouldst be experienced in worldly affairs: wouldst thou be so simple, as to sell such a brewing pot for five gigliatoes? Why, I that am a poor ignorant woman, a house dove, seldom going out of my door have sold it already for seven gigliatoes to a very honest man, who, even a little before thy coming home, came to me. We agreed on the bargain, and he is now underneath the pot, to see whether it be sound or no."

When credulous Lazaro heard this, he was better contented then ever, and went to him that tarried at the door, saying, "Good man, you may go your way, for, whereas you offered me but five gigliatoes for the pot, my loving wife hath sold it for seven, and I must maintain what she hath done." So the man departed, and the conflict ended.

Peronella then said to her husband, "Seeing thou art come home so luckily, help me to lift up the Pot, that the man may come forth, and then you two end the bargain together." Striguario, who though he was mewed up under the tub, had his ears open enough, and hearing the witty excuse of Peronella, [came out] from under the Pot, pretending as if he had heard nothing nor saw Lazaro, looking round about him, said, "Where is this good woman?" Lazaro stepping forth boldly like a man, replied, "Here am I, what would you have Sir?" "Thou?" quoth Striguario, "what art thou? I ask for the good wife, with whom I made my match for the pot." "Honest gentleman," answered Lazaro, "I am that honest woman's husband, for lack of a better, and I will maintain whatsoever my wife hath done."

"I ask your mercy Sir," replied Striguario, "I bargained with your wife for this brewing pot, which I find to be whole and sound: only it is unclean within, hard crusted with some dry soil upon it, which I know not well how to get off. If you will do the work of making it clean, I have the money here ready for it." "For that, sir," quoth Peronella, "do not worry. Though we had not agreed on it, what else is my husband good for, but to make it clean?" "Yes, forsooth Sir," answered silly Lazaro, "you shall have it neat and clean before you pay the money." So, stripping himself into his shirt, lighting a candle and taking tools fit for the purpose, the pot was placed over him, and he being within it, worked until he sweated with scraping and scrubbing. This way the lovers could finish that which earlier had been interrupted. And Peronella, looking in at the vent-hole where the liquor runneth forth for the meshing, seemed to instruct her husband in the business, as espying those parts where the pot was foulest, saying, "There, there Lazaro; tickle it there. The Gentleman pays well for it, and is worthy to have it. But see thou do thyself no harm good husband." "I warrant thee wife," answered Lazaro, "hurt not yourself with leaning your stomach on the pot, and leave the cleansing of it to me." To be brief, the brewing pot was neatly cleansed, Peronella and Striguario both well pleased, the money paid, and honest meaning Lazaro not discontented.

—translated by John Florio,
adapted and modernized by Jack Murnighan

from Giovanni's Room

JAMES BALDWIN

Perhaps it's my European wardrobe or the fact that I like to shake my money maker or that I try to be considerate of my women friends (always putting the seat down, for example), but I'm often asked if I am gay. Normally I respond that I don't think so, for I certainly don't seem aroused by male genitalia—but this answer doesn't seem to resolve the issue. I'd like to believe that I would know by now, that the truth 'twould have outed long ago, but the whole orientation thing is so complicated, so fraught with conflicting signs, that it's easy to doubt, to second-guess, and, finally, to third-guess the second-guesses and start the questioning over. If I say I'm gay, then clearly I'm gay, but if I deny it, I'm likely to be repressed (I grew up in the Midwest after all) and thus probably even more gay. Or so the vicious logic goes, thank you Dr. Freud.

You would think, then, that I could take some comfort in the notion that people's sexual preferences are said to fall on a continuum of 1 to 10, with the numbers at either end representing complete, unequivocal commitments to a single gender and the middle ones representing leanings either way. But for those of us who probably fall somewhere close to the equator, the continuum is a source of both relief and renewed suspicion. Relief because our sexuality doesn't seem deviant, suspicion because it's not clear where the truth might lie. Seven, three? Four, six? Five? God knows. How would I know? Ah . . . but wait. Some people do seem to know, and not only those at the far, unambiguous ends of the spectrum. Take, for example, James Baldwin's male protagonist in *Giovanni's Room,* who, early in the book, has his first sexual encounter— and it's with a boy. He realizes that he's gay but then tries to suppress it in the most painful account of unwelcome identity I've ever read. Baldwin's characters (both here and elsewhere) struggle mightily with their conflicted sexualities, bringing to the page the pain and anguish of living a lie, or a truth you are unwilling to accept. It's ironic that an author so adept at portraying the sexual identities of confused bisexual men would script the moment of realization with such lucidity and precision. But, sadly for Baldwin, that moment was the beginning, not the end, of the questioning.

●●●

I laughed and grabbed his head as I had done God knows how many times before, when I was playing with him or when he had annoyed me. But this time when I touched him something happened in him and in me which made this touch different from any touch either of us had ever known. And he did not resist, as he usually did, but lay where I had pulled him, against my chest. And I realized that my heart was beating in an awful way and that Joey was trembling against me and the light in the room was very bright and hot. I started to move and to make some kind of joke but Joey mumbled something and I put my head down to hear. Joey raised his head as I lowered mine and we kissed, as it were, by accident. Then, for the first time in my life, I was really aware of another person's body, of another person's smell. We had our arms around each other. It was like holding in my hand some rare, exhausted, nearly doomed bird which I had miraculously happened to find. I was very frightened, I am sure he was frightened too, and we shut our eyes. To remember it so clearly, so painfully tonight tells me that I have never for an instant truly forgotten it. I feel in myself now a faint, a dreadful stirring of what so overwhelmingly stirred in me then, great thirsty heat, and trembling, and tenderness so painful I thought my heart would burst. But out of this astounding, intolerable pain came joy, we gave each other joy that night. It seemed, then, that a lifetime would not be enough for me to act with Joey the act of love . . .

But Joey is a boy. I saw suddenly the power in his thighs, in his arms, and in his loosely curled fists. The power and the promise and the mystery of that body made me suddenly afraid. That body suddenly seemed the black opening of a cavern in which I would be tortured till madness came, in which I would lose my manhood. Precisely, I wanted to know that mystery and feel that power and have that promise fulfilled through me. The sweat on my back grew cold. I was ashamed. The very bed, in its sweet disorder, testified to vileness. I wondered what Joey's mother would say when she saw the sheets. Then I thought of my father, who had no one in the world but me, my mother having died when I was little. A cavern opened in my mind, black, full of rumor, suggestion, of half-heard, half-forgotten, half-understood stories, full of dirty words. I thought I saw my future in that cavern. I was afraid. I could have cried, cried for shame and terror, cried for not understanding how this could have happened to me, how this could have happened in me. And I made my decision . . .

from **Orlando Furioso**

LUDOVICO ARIOSTO

Ludovico Ariosto was the most popular Italian writer of the sixteenth century; when you read the passage that follows, you'll see why. Although the most popular book of the century in England, John Lyly's *Euphues,* mires you in its logorrheic cesspool, Ariosto's *Orlando Furioso* wins you over with high adventure, poetic charm, daring rescues, and dastardly wit. It's also pretty saucy, which elicited no small amount of blushing from its first English translators.

In this particular scene, one of the heroes, Ruggiero, comes to the castle of the evil witch Alcina, who disguises herself as a beautiful woman to seduce him. Romantic encounters are typical in the tradition of courtly literature, but, as with the Spenser excerpt on page 164, authors couldn't come right out with the sex and sexuality, but had to mute it within suggestive, though not explicit, descriptions. Spenser had his woman spill red wine on her lap; Ariosto resorts to other clever tactics. First breasts that hint at what lies beyond (there is always a veil, however transparent), then an ingenious explanation of why he can't describe the totality of their actions. It's a great rhetorical turn; would that pens could always be so pointed.

●••

[Alcina] was so well formed
that I can not describe her better without a painter's skill:
With long blond tresses tied in a knot;
Gold itself has no more luster.

Her delicate cheeks were spread
With the mixed color of roses and lilies;
Like polished ivory her serene brow;
and everything in perfect proportion . . .

Snow white was her neck; her breast white as milk;
her neck was slender, her breast broad and full.
Two sour apples, fashioned as from ivory,
Rose and fell like waves on the sea,
When the wind disturbs its peaceful calm.
Of her hidden parts, not even Argus
With his hundred eyes could see,
But one could judge that what lay beyond
Corresponded well to what was in view . . .

[Ruggiero] jumped from the bed and took her in his arms.
Nor could he wait for her to undress,
for she was wearing neither gown nor petticoat—
she had come in a light mantle put over a simple nightgown
white and of the finest texture.
As Ruggiero embraced her, her mantle slipped off,
leaving only the thin, transparent nightgown,
(which, before and behind, concealed no more than
a pane of glass would conceal a bouquet of flowers).

Never did ivy cling so tightly to the stem around which
it entwines than did these lovers cling together,
drawing from each other's lips so fragrant a succor
as not to be found in any flower grown on scented Indian sands.
But of the great pleasures this couple shared, it would be easier for
     them to say,
For often they each had more than one tongue in their mouth.

—translated by Jack Murnighan

from **Vox**

NICHOLSON BAKER

Okay, I don't know about you,
but the idea of being on a first
date with one of your coworkers
and sitting side by side on a
couch watching a porn video
and masturbating in unison
without touching one
another strikes me as somewhat improbable. Though very sexy. But this
is the scenario recounted by one of the protagonists in Nicholson Baker's
Vox, a novel consisting entirely of a conversation between a man and
woman having phone sex. There are other parts of the novel that are
sexy, but this particular narration was so goofy and curious and ultimately erotic that I had to take it for a Naughty Bit.

What's great about the passage is that Baker articulates the rudi-
ments of an erotics of restraint. Sure it's fun to hurtle headlong into the
sack, to run the Kama Sutra gamut first time around, to alpha and omega
sex like you're never going to get another chance, but there's also a delicacy, a precise, stinging frisson that accompanies not acting on desire.
Luring it, growing it, nurturing it—but not plucking. Perhaps sex benefits most from a combination of hot and cold: the yin of doing balanced
by the yang of deferral. Ah . . .

● ●·

[On the screen there were] two men with ties on are standing on
either side of [a woman] . . . and she's sucking one and then the
other. Emily whispered, "That's it." . . . We were both stroking
ourselves, and I could feel against the back of my hand the blanket
pulling with her little movements as I made mine. I sort of clamped
the blanket against the top of my cock with my thumb so that I'd stay

decent and yet have my left hand free, and I looked over at Emily's face, and watched her eyes traveling over those double-cock images, and I looked down at her breasts. I wanted to touch them, but I knew this would complicate things, it would have been a mistake. I could have come anytime. But suddenly the scene ended—one man suddenly comes on the woman's face and breasts, the other pulls out and comes on her bush, with strikingly white sperm. Emily wasn't fazed. She said, "Do you mind if I rewind a little?" . . . When it started playing, she said, kind of softly, "I think I want to come to this scene." I said, "Okay." But again the scene ended too quickly for her, and she had to rewind it a third time . . . She was flushed, her cheeks were shiny, she looked so transformed and sexual and elegant . . . and I said, "Can I touch your arm?" and she nodded, and I put my fingertips very lightly on the inside of her forearm, just above the wrist, and I felt her tendon going and going as she stroked herself, and this indirect feeling of being able to take the pulse of her masturbating was too much, I said, "I think I'm going to come," and I started to come into the blanket, and when the first guy in the movie came on the heroine, Emily closed her legs and started to come herself, and when the second guy came on the heroine, Emily was still coming, but not with any thrashing around, very focused, but I could hear the shaking of her legs slightly in her breathing.

from **A Man in Full**

TOM WOLFE

Though I grew up in a farming community, I can't say I've had much exposure to copulating animals. The closest I ever really came to living livestock was a comically disastrous attempt at cow tipping. (It was 3 A.M., but they were all wide awake and most un-tippable. We left with soiled boots as our only satisfaction.) There was, however, a kid on the next block who had supposedly boffed and thereby offed his pet kitty, but even at the time I doubted the veracity of the rumor. I've always been a firm believer that humans are the species to have sex with, at least if you're a human. But this much I am willing to confess: I did once write a prose poem about having seen rhinoceri having sex on TV. It was a very sordid affair. In effect, the lumbering male put his front legs up on the rump of the impassive female; then out came his enormous, candy-cane red, gnarled, pole-vault-pole-sized schlong (okay, not quite, but it seemed that way), and he started banging away. The female remained motionless. He kept it up, his head rolling around like he was at a Dead show, jerking his body back and forth and frothing madly, foam dripping down his chest. Finally, he shot (presumably) and rolled off her, falling heavily into the dust. She paused, reactionless, then slowly walked away without looking back. Sound familiar?

All these thoughts came back to me when a friend told me I should include an excerpt from Tom Wolfe's *A Man in Full*. The recommendation came with a caveat: the protagonists of the sex scene were not human but equine. But hey, a sex scene is a sex scene, and I'm no anthropo-centrist. To be precise, this scene is not so much hot as humorous (it's a prelude to the real horse smut that follows), and it is most, most infor-mative. So, here's everything you weren't sure you wanted to know about barnyard sex . . .

Snorting, highly agitated, the stallion walked into the stock and right up to the rear end of the mare. The mare began twitching and rolling her head and switching her furled-up tail. The stallion's penis was now a tremendous black shaft. Suddenly he extended his head and his long neck and pushed his nose into the mare's rear end, into her vulva. She tried to kick with her rear legs, but the hobble straps prevented it. She tried to bolt forward, but the walls of the stock hemmed her in, and the stable hands held her halter. The stallion kept twisting his head, rooting around in her vulva . . .

The deep voice of Lettie Withers: "Good Lord, Charlie, I thought this was the Bible Belt. That looks suspiciously like oral sex."

But no one laughed, and no one else said anything. The truth was, they were shocked.

All at once a gusher of yellowish liquid shot out the rear of the mare. The stallion pulled back. His lower jaw, throatlatch, and breast were dripping with it. It was urine, which continued to spew out. The stallion shook his head and whinnied and started back toward the mare, his penis fully erect, but two black handlers had him by the halter and were forcing him back, away from the stock . . .

"What's going on?" asked Howell Hendricks. "Why are they taking him away?" The other guests closed ranks in order to hear the answer.

"He's not the stud," said Charlie, "he's the teaser."

"The teaser?"

"Yep. You just use the teaser to get her aroused."

"And she urinates in his face?" said Howell.

"Yep. Always happens."

"That's about the size of it."

"Terrific," said Howell. "Reminds me of when I was in high school."

from "The Imperfect Enjoyment"

JOHN WILMOT, EARL OF ROCHESTER

The earl of Rochester (né John Wilmot) was the greatest lover of the seventeenth century and the naughtiest poet since Aretino. So famous were his charm and lovemaking, that Rochester-like characters appeared in plays on the English stage for over a century after his death. Ah, fame . . . and what better to be famous for?

But the MacDaddy of the Restoration did have a softer side, and by soft I mean not hard. Limp, detumescent, flaccid, droopy, withered, recently spent; in other words, not hard at all.

For even Rochester, apparently, was occasionally felled by that supremely male condition: the quick trigger, followed by the unwilling willie. Though we men rarely talk about it publicly (or even with one another), sometimes when the equipment is really needed, it's just not up for the task. And normally it happens right when it matters most, when the woman (or man) you adore is really hot to trot, on that dreamy night when it should have all worked out. Alas, such are the vagaries of the male beast. We are fragile things, and, loath as we are to admit it, we actually do have hang-ups. As Woody Allen demonstrated so beautifully in the last skit of *Everything You Always Wanted to Know About Sex,* the voices in the brain headquarters should be kept as far away as possible from the men working the turbines in the erection room. Too much desire means too much pressure means too much threat to the ego, and the whole house of cards can crumble under the weight. Not, of course, that it's ever happened to me . . .

Rochester's case is about as bad as it gets. A quick spurt and then . . . and then? This is his lover's question, and his body has no answer. Quite the pickle. But I'll let you read it for yourself, for the comic value is tops. And see if the earl's solution doesn't make you blush.

Naked she lay, clasped in my longing arms,
I filled with love, and she all over charms;
Both equally inspired with eager fire,
Melting through kindness, flaming in desire,
With arms, legs, lips close clinging to embrace,
She clips me to her breast, and sucks me to her face.
Her nimble tongue, Love's lesser lightning, played,
Within my mouth, and to my thoughts conveyed
Swift orders that I should prepare to throw
The all-dissolving thunderbolt below.
My fluttering soul, sprung with the pointed kiss,
Hangs hovering o'er her balmy brinks of bliss.
But whilst her busy hand would guide that part
Which should convey my soul up to her heart,
In liquid raptures I dissolve all o'er,
Melt into sperm, and spend at every pore.
A touch from any part of her had done 't:
Her hand, her foot, her very look's a cunt.
Smiling, she chides in a kind murmuring noise,
And from her body wipes the clammy joys,
When, with a thousand kisses wandering o'er
My panting bosom, "Is there then no more?"
She cries. "All this to love and rapture's due;
Must we not pay a debt to pleasure too?"
But I, the most forlorn, lost man alive,
To show my wished obedience vainly strive:
I sigh: alas! and kiss, but cannot swive.
Eager desires confound my first intent,
Succeeding shame does more success prevent,
And rage at last confirms me impotent.
Ev'n her fair hand, which might bid heat return
To frozen age, and make cold hermits burn,
Applied to my dead cinder, warms no more
Than fire to ashes could past flames restore.
Trembling, confused, despairing, limber, dry,

A wishing, weak, unmoving lump I lie.
This dart of love, whose piercing point oft tried,
With virgin blood ten thousand maids have dyed;
Which nature still directed with such art
That it through every cunt reached every heart—
Stiffly resolved, 'twould carelessly invade
Woman or man, nor ought its fury stayed:
Where'er it pierced, a cunt it found or made—
Now languid lies in this unhappy hour,
Shrunk up and sapless like a withered flower.
Thou treacherous, base deserter of my flame,
False to my passion, fatal to my fame,
Through what mistaken magic dost thou prove
So true to lewdness, so untrue to love?
What oyster-cinder-beggar-common whore
Didst thou e'er fail in all thy life before?
When vice, disease, and scandal led the way,
With what officious haste dost thou obey!
Like a rude, roaring hector in the streets
Who scuffles, cuffs and justles all he meets,
But if his king or country claims his aid,
The rakehell villain shrinks and hides his head;
Ev'n so thy brutal valor is displayed,
Breaks every stew, does each small whore invade,
But when great Love the onset does command,
Base recreant to thy prince, thou dar'st not stand.
Worst part of me, and henceforth hated most,
Through all the town a common fucking post,
On whom each whore relieves her tingling cunt
As hogs on gates do rub themselves and grunt,
Mayst thou to ravenous chancres be a prey,
Or in consuming weepings waste away;
May strangury and stone thy days attend;
May'st thou ne'er piss, who didst refuse to spend
When all my joys did on false thee depend.
And may ten thousand abler pricks agree
To do the wronged Corinna right for thee.

from **"Pretty Judy"**

KEVIN CANTY

There's a popular conception of the teenage male as a kind of hormonal loose cannon, victim to the changes of his body, seeking satisfaction anywhere, anytime. Literary counterexamples to this stereotype are few; when Holden Caulfield says no to the prostitute in *Catcher in the Rye,* we think of him as an exception, not the rule. But male sexual psychology is more complicated than is typically acknowledged. Interspersed with sexual desire are shame, guilt, and confusion; the urge to pounce is quickly replaced with the urge to run, and our first times are often as painful as they are pleasurable.

But nowhere, to my knowledge, are the tortured psychological dynamics of the teenage male drawn more precisely than in Kevin Canty's short story "Pretty Judy" from his collection *A Stranger in This World.* Canty sets up a story line that's a glass incubator for a boy's internal conflict. The plot goes like this: There is a retarded girl who lives on young Paul's block. She's older, maybe high-school aged, but doesn't go to school. She spends her time leaning out her bedroom window, calling out to the neighborhood kids who pass by. Hi Paul. Hi Tommy. Hi Ricky. Paul has heard the rumors, but he's never gone in. One day he notices that Judy's parents' car is gone and, fearfully, he goes up her stairs to find her waiting and available. Each of Canty's lines ups the ante and intensity of their interaction to the point of breakage. But even at the outset you can see the first stage of his thinking, the teenage male's "Oh my god! Oh my god! She's letting me! She's letting me!" that is a function of the early belief that sex is alien to, unwanted, and cordoned off by the very girls with whom we're supposed to be having it. But with Judy, this belief slowly crumbles. Paul realizes that it's he who puts up the barriers, he who brings the limits and restrictions into their world.

Judy can have sex unproblematically; it's what makes her feel pretty. Paul is pierced with guilt and self-loathing, and he's never felt uglier.

For the full effect, you'll have to read the entire story, and I encourage you to do so. "Pretty Judy" is as forceful and immediate as a fist, and it knows where to hit.

●••

They knelt together on the window-seat cushion, touching at the shoulder and the hip . . . Gradually Paul became aware of her body, her warmth and weight. What would she allow him? A red Volvo passed under the window, a black sedan. His hand reached out, he watched it like a movie, and touched her bare forearm below the sleeve of her sweatshirt. Paul himself didn't touch her, only his hand.

Oh, Judy said . . . Oh, she said again, and Oh! As he touched her breast through the layers of fabric, sweatshirt and brassiere . . . It seemed to Paul that she was blind to anything but touch, drunk with it. He lifted her sweatshirt and then put his hand on the hard lace of her brassiere, no resistance, only her soft, lost voice, he rolled her onto her side, reached behind her and fumbled with the little hooks until by some miracle her bra came unsprung and her big, soft breasts tumbled against him. Paul felt drunk with himself, with excitement and with panic. He had fumbled in playrooms before, in cars and in the rough grass of the neighborhood parks, girls from the neighborhood who would negotiate a touch, or on some lucky Saturday allow his blind hand to wander in the darkness of their jeans, but this, this plain revelation, was new to him. She wouldn't stop him, wouldn't stop him from anything . . .

Later he would think of her in animal terms: she mewled like a kitten, bawled and bucked like a hungry calf, and still later—years after—he would decide that this was because there was so little human veneer to her; that sex and awareness were natural enemies, a battle every time between modesty, a sense of order and embarrassment, and the little kindling flame of desire . . .

Don't stop, she said . . .

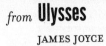

from **Ulysses**

JAMES JOYCE

To eat or not to eat—ass that is.
In Joyce's *Ulysses,* Bloom eats it;
in a story of mine, one of the
characters munches away (I
won't say what this suggests of
me and Joyce—we are fiction
writers after all), yet my vari-
ous unscientific surveys have all indicated the same thing: not many men
that I know eat ass. I was a little surprised to learn this, for, from what I
hear, most women like it—a lot. The body doesn't have many orifices,
after all; you'd think people would want to take advantage of all there
are (think of the improvements of going from two martinis to three). But
the curious truth is that though most men are willing to fuck any part of
a woman's body—the ass, between the breasts, in the armpit, behind
the knee—they still get a little squeamish putting their tongues in the
excretory vacuole.

It's not that I don't understand—shit gets a kind of bad rap, and the
uninformed seem to think that rimming has a lot more to do with feces
than it really does (which, by the by, makes me speculate about the
hygienic habits of the naysayers). But all trepidation and exaggeration
aside, what would one not do to give pleasure? Various Motown hits
have enumerated the deserts one might cross, the mountains one might
climb for the beloved, so I ask, is licking the anus really so taxing?
Anthropology is one long lesson in how one man's abominable is
another's pleasant. What is unthinkable on one side of the globe is commonplace on another (or in between). So, although you might think that
this is a simple sermon on doing all and everything to make your lover
happy (granted, there are some people who are not exactly asking for
the *spécialité du chef* under discussion—yet), I'm really talking about
ethics and perspective. The "inherently" gross is inherent only within a
context, and that context can change—like one's mind. When in Rome,
we are told to do as the Romans. In Southeast Asia, you might well eat

fried termites. And in bed with your true love? Don't count it out.

Eating ass is one thing; writing about it is another. Never have I lingered so long over my clay tablet as when I tried to describe that most curious of tastes (odder still than either the durian fruit or fresh sea urchin). The sad truth is that the excerpt that follows—Joyce's description of Bloom's bum-kissing—dodges the issue slightly. Joyce opts for cadence and mellifluence instead of hard adjectives—he describes the act more than the experience—and it's a shame, for nothing would have given me more pleasure than to see the consummate wordsmith butt up against the aggressively corporeal—in all its ineffability.

●●•

He kissed the plump mellow yellow smellow melons of her rump, on each plump melonous hemisphere, in their mellow yellow furrow, with obscure prolonged provocative melonsmellonous osculation.

The visible signs of postsatisfaction?

A silent contemplation: a tentative velation: a gradual abasement: a solicitous adversion: a proximate erection.

from **The Symposium**

PLATO

Hunchbacked, bad-skinned, defaced, abject, and generally hideous, could you love him for his brain alone? I am not referring to my high school self (though the description is not far off), but to the great ugly duckling of intellectual history, Socrates. Although there is a long tradition of physically repugnant philosophers (Plotinus, for example, was leprous and nosable at some distance), Socrates' physical monstrosity is the most legendary. No real surprise, then, that philosophy has always insisted on a distinction, if not a conflict, between mind and body, for the better part of the guys writing the stuff down would have loved to saw themselves off at the neck.

Yet no matter how hideous Socrates was, the boys continued to line up behind him (or in front, as the case may have been). So what was the draw of this guy who was not only twice their age but unbelievably self-satisfied, condescending, and always on the move? Elementary, my dear Watson, elementary: the brain. Big brain, historical brain, still-respected-after-two-millennia brain. You can imagine how comforting this idea was to a dateless high school pedant, believing that one day he too might woo with cognition alone. Ah, but then few are born with Socrates' brain (even Nietzsche, who was no troglodyte, had a hard time getting lucky). But don't despair, in most cases, brains do prove sexy in time. So for those of you out there who have prayed and hoped, waiting with a candle in the window, I give you this, a parable of the pull of the perspicacious: Alcibiades' account of trying to seduce Socrates.

● ● ·

When I looked at his serious purpose, I saw in him divine and golden images of such fascinating beauty that I was ready to do in a moment whatever Socrates commanded . . . Now I thought that he was seriously enamored of my beauty, and this appeared to be a grand opportunity of hearing him tell what he knew, for I had a wonderful opinion of the attractions of my youth. In the prosecution of this design, when I next went to him, I sent away the attendant who usually accompanied me. Well, he and I were alone together, and I thought that when there was nobody with us, I should hear him speak the language of love as lovers do, and I was delighted. Not a word: he conversed as usual, and spent the day with me and then went away. Afterwards, I challenged him to the palestra; and he wrestled and closed with me several times; I fancied I might succeed in this way. Not a bit. Lastly, as I had failed hitherto, I thought that I must use stronger measures and attack him boldly and not give him up until I saw how the matter stood. So I invited him to supper, just as if he were a fair youth and I a designing lover. He was not easily persuaded to come; he did, however, after a while accept the invitation, and when he came the first time, he wanted to go away at once as soon as supper was over, and I had not the face to detain him. The second time, still in pursuance of my design, after we had supped, I went on conversing far into the night, and when he wanted to go away, I pretended that the hour was late and that he had better remain. So he lay down on the next couch to me, the same on which he had supped, and there was no one else in the apartment.

All this may be told without shame to any one. But what follows I could hardly tell you if I was sober . . . I have felt the pang, and he who has suffered, as they say, is willing to tell his fellow-sufferers only, as they alone will be likely to understand him . . . I have known in my soul or in my heart or in some other part, that worst of pangs, more violent in ingenuous youth than any serpent's tooth, the pang of philosophy . . .

When the lamp was put out and the servants had gone away, I thought that I must be plain with him and have no more ambiguity. So I gave him a shake and said, "Socrates, are you asleep?"

"No," he said . . . and so without waiting to hear more I got up, and throwing my coat about him, crept under his threadbare cloak, as the time of year was winter, and there I lay during the whole night having this wonderful monster in my arms . . . and yet, notwithstanding all this, he was so superior to my solicitations, so contemptuous and derisive and disdainful of my beauty—which really, as I believe, had some attractions—hear, O judges, for judges you shall be of the haughty virtue of Socrates, that in the morning when I awoke (let all the gods and goddesses be my witnesses), I arose from Socrates' couch as from the couch of a father or an elder brother!

—translated by Benjamin Jewett,
modified by Jack Murnighan

from **Justine**

LAWRENCE DURRELL

Although Henry Miller remains part of the constellation of stars in twentieth-century literature, Lawrence Durrell, his close friend, correspondent, occasional editor, and author of the great *Alexandria Quartet*, seems to be on the wane. Perhaps Miller's legend endures because we associate him with brash and raucous sexuality; Durrell, meanwhile, is kinder, gentler, and considerably more modest than old Hank. Yet the two bear strong comparison in both life and work. Both set their principal novels in the sexual humus of squalid foreign cities (Alexandria, Paris); both write in a rambling first-person voice, almost memoir style; both loved and feared women and spent their lives, in Durrell's narrator's words, trying to "know what it really means . . . the whole portentous scrimmage of sex itself." Sex, here, is clearly meant to stand for life, and Durrell and Miller consciously made writing careers on the fruits of that synecdoche.

Written in the late 1950s, the *Quartet* (*Justine, Balthazar, Mountolive, Clea*) is truly a tour de force. The title characters are sculpted impeccably in the contradictions of Greek myth: they are as gods in form and substance, yet have fallen into the banal tragedies of real living. Durrell's treatment is tender and thoughtful in a way Miller's mind would have bulldozed over. Through him we negotiate a series of fantastic infatuations and aggrandized, empty loves to find, at the end, the heart of compassion. Where Miller teaches the irreducible sanctity of the moment, Durrell recites the sermon of long process, of brushing aside romantic delusions and finally embracing what is hard won but true.

The scene that follows is the narrator's first encounter, in the bedroom of his reliable girlfriend, with the mysterious Justine, the femme fatale who, as in many novels if not in life, sets all the relationships in motion. Like Genet, Durrell chronicles the seductive power of the intractable and fierce, of those beyond or incapable of love, hardened, gemlike, in their beauty and resolve. It is hard not to love Justine, but you do so only with regret.

●●·

Across all this, as across the image of someone dearly loved, held in the magnification of a gigantic tear moved the brown harsh body of Justine naked. It would have been blind of me not to notice how deeply her resolution was mixed with sadness. We lay eye to eye for a long time, our bodies touching, hardly communicating more than the animal lassitude of the vanishing afternoon. I could not help thinking then as I held her lightly in the crook of an arm how little we own our bodies . . .

But she had closed her eyes—so soft and lustrous now, as if polished by the silence which lay so densely all around us . . . We turned to each other, closing like the two leaves of a door upon the past, shutting out everything, and I felt her happy spontaneous kisses begin to compose the darkness around us like successive washes of a colour. When we had made love and lay once more awake she said: "I am always so bad the first time, why is it?" . . .

. . . I held her, tasting the warmth and sweetness of her body, salt from the sea—her earlobes tasted of salt. . . .

It was as if the whole city had crashed about my ears . . . I felt . . . in the words of the dying Amr: "as if heaven lay close upon the earth and I between them both, breathing through the eye of a needle."

from "This Condition"

LYDIA DAVIS

Time, the bugger. Oh, how the phrase "Too late!" has haunted the length of my waking days: Born too late; too late to change; too late in the day; it's too late, baby, it's always, invariably, a bit too late. I never seem to get the drift until the drift is gone, the bandwagon I'd jump is ever on the egress and I don't appear capable of figuring out a situation before a new one has come to take its place.

This is how I felt the first time I came across Lydia Davis's short-short story "This Condition." A dear friend read it to me over the phone, and I was livid.

"Damn! Damn! Damn! That would have been perfect for Nerve! I can't believe we didn't get it," I ranted. "Jack," she responded soothingly, "it was published in 1997, a few months before Nerve launched." Alas, too true. The same old condition: born too late.

So even though I'd argue that "This Condition" defines what I was always seeking in Nerve fiction (top shelf writing that's sexy as much for its emotion and wisdom as its erotic content), I didn't get to publish it first. But at least I get to reprint it here in its entirety. For Davis, ever the master of the shortest shorts, manages in this one to create one of the most beautiful, rhythmic, elegant, sexy, Freud thumb-nosing bits of writing you'll ever find. Read it out loud; read it to a friend, a lover, a partner. Davis does more to demarcate desire in 400 choice words than most people do in volumes. She's got an itch; she's got it bad, and we have it right along with her.

●●·

In this condition: stirred not only by men but by women, fat and thin, naked and clothed, by teenagers and children in latency; by animals such as horses and dogs; by certain vegetables such as carrots, zucchinis and cucumbers; by certain fruits such as melons, grapefruits and kiwis; by certain plant parts such as petals, sepals, stamens and pistils, by the bare arm of a wooden chair, a round vase holding flowers, a little hot sunlight, a plate of pudding, a person entering a tunnel in the distance, a puddle of water, a hand alighting on a smooth stone, a hand alighting on a bare shoulder, a naked tree limb; by anything curved, bare and shining, as the limb or bole of a tree; by any touch, as the touch of a stranger handling money; by anything round and freely hanging, as tassels on a curtain, chestnut burrs on a twig in spring, a wet tea bag on its string; by anything glowing, as a hot coal; anything soft or slow, as a cat rising from a chair, anything smooth and dry, as a stone, or warm and glistening; anything sliding, anything sliding back and forth; anything sliding in and out with an oiled surface, as certain machine parts; anything of a certain shape, like the state of Florida; anything pounding, anything stroking, anything bolt upright, anything horizontal and gaping, as a certain sea anemone; anything warm, anything wet, anything wet and red, anything turned red, as the sun at evening; anything wet and pink; anything long and straight with a blunt end, as a pestle; anything coming out of anything else, as a snail from its shell, as a snail's horns from its head; anything opening; any stream of water running, any stream running, any stream spurting, any stream spouting, any cry, any soft cry, any grunt; anything going into anything else, as a hand searching in a purse; anything clutching, anything grasping; anything rising, anything tightening or filling, as a sail; anything dripping, anything hardening, anything softening.

from Pantagruel: Third Book

FRANÇOIS RABELAIS

Each of the major literary languages of medieval Europe had a
comedic author par excellence,
a ribald trickster whose tawdry
wit continues to charm even
today. Italy had Boccaccio,
England Chaucer, and
France the great Rabelais. In five works (four finished, one unfinished
and posthumously published), he tells the supremely satirical tale of
Gargantua and Pantagruel, debauched giants of gluttony, flatulence, and
vulgarity. They drink hogsheads of ale, piss rivers, fart windstorms, flout
armies, and scandalize women. They are, in effect, enormous frat boys
having their way with the theology and politics of sixteenth-century
France. No storyteller has ever taken as many liberties as Rabelais, no
tale has ever been more over-the-top, and, thus, the history of literature
provides few things that are more fun to read. In the excerpt that follows, Rabelais takes a feather from Boccaccio's cap, having a friar tell
an ingenious trick for how to keep a wife faithful. Like Boccaccio (and
Petronius before him), Rabelais knew how to mix sex and riddles,
stimulating the reader both above and below the neck. Here's a prime
example.

● ●·

"I'll teach you one way," said Friar John, "to prevent your wife from
ever making you a cuckold without your knowing about it."

"I beg to you, my friend," said Panurge. "Tell it to me now."

"Use Hans Carvel's ring," said Friar John . . . and went on to
explain. "Hans Carvel was a intelligent and worthy man . . . In his
later years he married . . . a young, attractive, flirtatious girl who

was exceedingly friendly with their neighbors and servants. So after only a few weeks, Hans became jealous as a tiger and suspected that his wife was getting her back end tambourined elsewhere. To try to prevent this from happening, Hans started telling her stories about what misery can arise from adultery and read to her from the Legend of Chaste Women . . . Yet he still found her so resilient and so joyful with the neighbors that he got ever more jealous. Then one night among others, while sleeping beside her, he dreamt he was talking to the devil and explained his concerns. The devil comforted him, and put a ring on his middle finger, and said, 'I will give you this ring. While you wear it on your finger, your wife will not be shared by any man without your consent and knowledge.' Hans thanked the devil . . . and the devil vanished. When Hans awoke, he was pleased to find his finger up the whatchamacallit of his dear wife, who, I forgot to mention, drew back as if to say, 'That's not what you're supposed to put in there!' And she squirmed and squirmed, but he wouldn't let her take off his ring!

"Now isn't that an infallible solution? So take my advice and always keep your wife's ring on your finger!"

—*translated by Jack Murnighan*

from **Voluptuous Sonnets**

PIETRO ARETINO

Pietro Aretino wrote his "Sonetti lussoriosi" in the late 1520s to accompany a series of erotic paintings that he had discovered. Even without seeing the oils, it's not hard to imagine what they depicted. The sonnets are joyous and playful dialogues between lovers, shifting voices (and often positions) even within single lines. Aretino knew he was writing things that hadn't really been seen in Italian, as he points out in the prologue to Book 2 of the Sonetti: "This book is not composed of sonnets, / Nor of chapters, eclogues or songs; / Instead, you'll find . . . people both fucking and fucked-out / Cocks and cunts innumerable; / And many souls lost in the black holes of asses." His little book proved to be the first erotica published with the printing press in Europe and has been reprinted dozens of times since—with good reason.

Aretino's sonnets are marked not only for their ribald wit and consistent polymorphous perversion but also for the full range of loves he and his partner draw into their compass. Despite what we might think of women's expressions of sexuality in ages before ours, Aretino's partner is no less enthusiastic than he, and theirs is a model of balanced gender and sexual relations. Like Chaucer's *Wife of Bath*, the woman in Aretino's sonnets is an outspoken sexual predator. Both characters, however, were written by men, which leads one to wonder: are these women male fantasies, or protofeminist calls for women to embrace their own sexuality? I'd say a little of both.

IV (first book)

Throw your leg up on my shoulder, baby,
And take my cock up in your hand,
And when you want me to push hard or soft,
Whether hard or soft, just dance your ass upon the bed.

And if my cock moves from cunt to ass,
You can call me a rake or a backalley villain;
But I know your lips and I know your holes,
As any good horse knows his mate.

I'll never take my hand from your cock—
Not I, who would never call this way crazy,
And if you don't like it, *Vaya con Dios!*

They say the pleasure behind belongs to you,
And the pleasure in front is made for me,
So just do it right, or I'll make you take a hike!

Rest assured: I would never leave,
Dear woman, from such a sweet assfuck,
Not if it would save the King of France.

XIV (first book)

Give me your tongue, with my feet against the wall,
Tighten my thighs—yes, tight tight together;
Let it go back and forth here in this bed
Where I haven't a care but to be fucked.

Ah, traitor! But my how your cock is hard!
Oh, don't worry! I'll make you whole in my hole;
And one day, you can have me in the other, I promise,
And I vouch I'll leave you a happy man.

I thank you, dearest Lorenzina,
I'll push myself to serve you, but you push too
Push like little Ciabattina knew how to do it.

Come on, come on; I'm pushing, when will you?
Now, I'll do it now! Just give me all that little tonguelet
So I might die. And I, who thirst so for you,

How will you bring me to my conclusion?
Now, now I'm doing it, my good good Lord.
Oh! And now it's done. And I . . . Oh me! O God!

   II (second book)
Madame, your malady is in the lungs;
The remedy is at hand, if you want it.
Lift your thighs a bit higher
To receive in your ass the good medicine.

This works better than waters to the chest,
Dear lady, of this I assure you.
But Sir, if this you want me to believe,
Don't make me wait any longer for my cure.

And voila', my asshole. Oh my! What are you doing?
That's a different shaped hole that you're wrecking;
It's not my pussy you're giving it to there!

Slowly, slow—it's stuffing me to the brim!
But woman, perhaps I should tell you the truth.
That my tool is so enormous.

It'll take the cough right out of your lungs.
Good sir, of my eventual cure I can only hope,
Just don't stop treating me anytime soon.

—*translated by Jack Murnighan*

from **The Starr Report**

KENNETH STARR

It is a curious moment in history
when the steamiest literature
you can get your hands on is a
Congressional investigation, and
the male protagonist is no
Fabio, no stable hand on the
Chatterley estate, but the
President of the United States. For despite what Ken Starr might have
us believe, his Report was written as, and is certainly meant to be read
as, a love story. It has all the components of the pinkest romance novel:
the oblique promise of *l'amour propre* is continually proffered in the
resiliency of Monica's naïve optimism. And bad Bill's responses are
marked by the diffidence and resignation of a man who sees the writing
on the wall. We see him committing the classic error of forgetting that
there was a mind behind the convenient lips, a heart within the heaving
chest, of seeing Monica Lewinsky not as a person but as an appliance.
Thus the abstraction of his responses, as if what was transpiring involved
historical chessmen or universal allegories, not flesh and blood humans.
When she suggested she might tell if he didn't treat her better, he
rejoined, "It is illegal to threaten the president of the United States."
Now this is a phrase I could never imagine saying to a lover (and not only
because I might have inhaled); it confuses self and office, man and sym-
bol. Lovers' quarrels are not resolved by consulting the Constitution. Bill,
stick in hand, was clearly trying to scrape off the unfortunateness he had
stepped into. And Monica, meanwhile, persisted in her hopes, questioning if he really knew her, asking him if he wanted to, only to be silenced
by his kisses. Kisses that said, in effect, "Dear girl, don't you know that
real emotions are not permitted on the stage of a Trauerspiel? Identity is
unimportant here; a hand is moving you. I am that hand . . ."

I myself have come to fear such encounters, where an atavistic urge or
momentary impulse leads me into temptation, or into tempting, a
woman but a decimal of my years. And, like decimals, it is hard to

remember that they are also wholes and harder still to remember that they might see you as larger than life or larger than you are. The easily won, never-asked-for heart is worn like a lodestone, a mantle of lead we try to wriggle out from under. I feel for Clinton because it's hard not to wield power, to not feel and lust for the very act of wielding, and then to shrink beneath the burden of its consequences. Power scripts its own abuse. And thus I feel for Lewinsky too. For it is all too easy to come under its spell. To say, as she did again and again, "Even though he's a big schmuck . . ."

And we, the American people, did we not in the end permit this to pass, murmuring to ourselves the very same sentiment?

●●·

January 7 Sexual Encounter

. . . "[H]e was chewing on a cigar. And then he had the cigar in his hand and he was kind of looking at the cigar in . . . sort of a naughty way. And so . . . I looked at the cigar and I looked at him and I said, we can do that, too, some time."

March 31 Sexual Encounter

According to Ms. Lewinsky, the President telephoned her at her desk and suggested that she come to the Oval Office on the pretext of delivering papers to him. She went to the Oval Office and was admitted by a plainclothes Secret Service agent. In her folder was a gift for the President, a Hugo Boss necktie.

In the hallway by the study, the President and Ms. Lewinsky kissed. On this occasion, according to Ms. Lewinsky, "he focused on me pretty exclusively," kissing her bare breasts and fondling her genitals. At one point, the President inserted a cigar into Ms. Lewinsky's vagina, then put the cigar in his mouth and said: "It tastes good." After they were finished, Ms. Lewinsky left the Oval Office and walked through the Rose Garden.

February 28 Sexual Encounter

According to Ms. Lewinsky, she and the President had a sexual encounter on Thursday, February 28—their first in nearly eleven months . . . [A]ccording to Ms. Lewinsky, the President "started to say something to me and I was pestering him to kiss me, because . . . it had been a long time since we had been alone." The President told her to wait a moment, as he had presents for her. As belated Christmas gifts, he gave her a hat pin and a special edition of Walt Whitman's *Leaves of Grass* . . . [A]fter the President gave her the gifts, they had a sexual encounter: "[W]e went back over by the bathroom in the hallway, and we kissed. We were kissing and he unbuttoned my dress and fondled my breasts with my bra on, and then took them out of my bra and was kissing them and touching them with his hands and with his mouth.

"And then I think I was touching him in his genital area through his pants, and I think I unbuttoned his shirt and was kissing his chest. And then . . . I wanted to perform oral sex on him . . . and so I did. And then . . . I think he heard something, or he heard someone in the office. So, we moved into the bathroom.

"And I continued to perform oral sex and then he pushed me away, kind of as he always did before he came, and then I stood up and I said . . . I care about you so much . . . I don't understand why you won't let me . . . make you come; it's important to me; I mean, it just doesn't feel complete, it doesn't seem right."

Ms. Lewinsky testified that she and the President hugged, and "He said he didn't want to get addicted to me, and he didn't want me to get addicted to him." They looked at each other for a moment. Then, saying that "I don't want to disappoint you," the President consented. For the first time, she performed oral sex through completion.

from **Hell**

HENRI BARBUSSE

The philosophy of aesthetics teaches that art is a function of certain mind-sets adopted by both artist and audience. Photography demonstrates the principle most readily: A photographer must gaze at reality in a particular way, see something photo worthy, click the shutter, capture, print, and frame it. The viewer then must look at it, not as the any old reality that surrounds us but as an isolated fragment put on display for a particular purpose. If these things don't happen, the photo remains a "mere snapshot," and doesn't hold artistic interest. Not only the photographic medium but all of art relies on being designated as such, as Marcel Duchamp tried to indicate when he took a porcelain men's urinal and parodically called it a sculpture. The response he might not have anticipated was that his "Fountain," when placed in a museum context with soft lighting and the requisite mulling students, would elicit an aesthetic response: In that context, the urinal looks almost beautiful. Having been trained how to look at museum pieces, we notice its curvature and form in a way we probably never would have if we were just looking at it in the men's room.

A lot of art benefits from, or even relies upon, this "museum effect." But what about the artist's eye? How do you see the art of the urinal before it's put in a museum? In the first decade of this century (a few years before Duchamp's first exhibitions), Henri Barbusse provided a kind of answer to this dilemma in one of the sexiest philosophical novels ever, *Hell*. Barbusse's contention is that to see art in reality you need to gaze with the eye of the voyeur. Nor does his argument stop there. Reading *Hell*, we ultimately realize that philosophy as well depends on the distance, alienation, detachment, and framing that define the voyeuristic gaze. Philosophy, like art, is all about seeing from the outside the life we live from the inside.

The voyeuristic gaze becomes central in *Hell* when the protagonist, having checked into a boardinghouse, realizes that there is a crack in the wall through which he can see the adjoining room. Never seen, he is nonetheless able to witness a series of people come and go. Soon he finds himself unable to return to his previous life, unable to leave the crack at the wall. He watches a young couple fall in love and an adulterous couple fall out of love, he sees sex and disappointment, lies and heartbreak, and, slowly, he comes to see himself in the steady march of all people toward isolation and death. Though Barbusse's worldview is morose and unrelenting, he is right in saying that one cannot steadily watch the lives of others without eventually becoming a philosopher.

●•·

She was standing now, half-undressed. She had become white. Was it she who was undressing, or he who was divesting her of her things? I could see her broad thighs, her silvery belly in the room like the moon in the night. He was holding her, clasping her as he hung on the divan. His mouth was near the mouth of her sex, and they drew together for a monstrously tender kiss. I saw the dark body kneeling before the pale body, and she was gazing fervently down at him.

Then, in a radiant voice, she murmured: "Take me. Take me again after so many other times. My body belongs to you, and I give it to you . . ."

He stretched her out on his knees. I had the impression that she was naked, though I couldn't make out all the shapes. Her head was thrown back from the window, and I could see her eyes shining, her mouth shining like her eyes, her face starlit with love.

He pulled her to him, the naked man in the darkness. Even in the midst of their mutual consent there was a sort of struggle . . . Pleasure, going beyond the law, beyond even the lover's sincerity, was frantically preparing its final masterpiece. It was such a frenzied, wild, fateful movement that I realized that even God could not stop what was happening . . .

Above the entanglement of their bodies he raised his head and threw it back. There was just enough light left for me to see his face, the mouth open in a broken, sing-song groan, waiting for the approaching pleasure . . . He was grimacing, smiling, dark with blood like a divine martyr . . . He was uttering staccato cries of surprise, as if he was dazzled by something magnificent and unexpected, as if he had not expected it to be so beautiful, as if he were astonished by the prodigies of joy which his body contained.

—translated by Robert Baldrick,
modified by Jack Murnighan

from The Plaint of Nature

ALAIN DE LILLE

There is, sadly, no lack of gay bashing in the history of literature. But the fact that authors have felt the need to attack homosexuality signals that it has always had a certain presence and impact in their cultures. The Pearl poet's fourteenth-century condemnation of same-sex practices (see page 147) is a testament to their prevalence in late medieval England; Alain de Lille's *The Plaint of Nature*, written two centuries before, demonstrates that there was no lack of same-sex sex taking place in twelfth-century France either.

I'm less interested, however, in the fact that Alain's text is conspicuously homophobic and more interested in the manner in which his homophobia is expressed. *The Plaint of Nature* is, to my knowledge, unique among literary texts in being a condemnation of homosexuality as an error of grammar. In Alain's scheme, sex and Latin are made to be analogous, so the sexual practices that Alain doesn't approve of correspond to grammatical errors and irregular Latin forms: male-to-male sex is a confusion of subject for object, masturbation is a reflexive verb that should be transitive, women on top are deponent verbs (passive forms that take active meanings), and gay men are the opposite. So, although the excerpt below isn't sexy per se, it is certainly one of the oddest writings about sex I have ever read, and instructive of the lengths to which authors will go to attempt to denaturalize homosexuality.

● ● ●

By adopting a highly irregular grammar, the human race has fallen from its high estate and inverted the rules of Venus . . .

The plan of Nature gave special attention, as the evidence of the rules of grammar confirms, to two genders, namely, the masculine and feminine (although some men, deprived of the outward sign of sex, could, in my opinion, be classified as of neuter gender) . . . Reproduction demands that the masculine joins the feminine to itself. If irregular combinations among members of the same sex should come into common practice, so that members of the same sex should be mutually connected, those combinations would never be able to gain acceptance . . . For if the masculine gender, by a certain violence of unreasonable logic, should seek one of a gender entirely similar to itself, this bond and union cannot be called a graceful trope or figure of speech but will bear the stain of an outlandish and unpardonable linguistic error.

The regular procedure . . . should assign the role of subadjacent [bottom] to the part characteristic of the female sex and should place that part that is specific to the male sex in the prestigious position of superjacent [top] . . .

In addition to this . . . the conjugations should restrict themselves entirely to . . . the transitive and should not admit intransitive, reflexive or passive forms . . . Furthermore, the active type should not go over to the passive nor should the passive, laying aside its proper character, return to the active or adopt the rule of deponents . . .

With the signs of the discipline of grammar . . . my speech has now inscribed on the tablet of your mind an account of the ruination of Venus . . . In wretchedness and lamentation, I have sung my song of complaint.

—*translated by James J. Sheridan,*
modified by Jack Murnighan

from **Sexus**

HENRY MILLER

Marriage is the death of sex—or so the common wisdom goes. Grim tidings for one who, like me, not only wants to spend the rest of his life with a single person but wants to do it fused at the pelvis. And even though I need both hands to count my parents' marriages, I still believe the institution has something to offer. As an old lover of mine once said, "The difficulty in getting out of a marriage encourages us to try our very best and not run away out of fear or weakness." Backward as this argument may seem, it has a lot of pull. Our eyes stray, our patience tires, our hearts resist breaching, our deepest secrets fear the light: all these things can set us out the door. Marriage gives us pause. It doesn't exactly dead-bolt us in—a good thing, for there are many marriages that should sunder—but it puts a little rust in the old turnstile.

Yet even if the shackle of marriage is a good thing, it does not resolve the problem that the sex might wane. I was thus quite relieved to read Henry Miller's account of an evening he spent back in the arms of his wife, whom he had left so that he could move in with his paramour. Now, granted, Hank never proves to be the model husband, but the scene below details not only the reawakening of the flame that had brought him and his wife together in the first place but, more instructively, his realization that the woman in his arms is quite unlike the person he long thought he knew. Breakdowns in communication had kept her from being as sexually free as she, and he, would have wanted. Finally able to be herself, she's happier than she had ever been, and more appealing. Perhaps, then, we can learn from Miller's experience (though not his method): be open to and open for your spouse and there will always be room for discovery.

She wants to lie down on the floor and put her legs around my neck. "Get it in all the way," she begs. "Don't be afraid of hurting me. I want it. I want you to do everything." I got it in so deep it felt as though I were buried in a bed of mussels. She was quivering and slithering in every ream. I bent over and sucked her breasts; the nipples were taut as nails. Suddenly she pulled my head down and began to bite me wildly—lips, ears, cheeks, neck. "You want it, don't you?" she hissed. "You want it. You want it!" Her lips twisted obscenely. "You want it. You want it!" And she fairly lifted herself off the floor in her abandon. Then a groan, a spasm, a wild tortured look as if her face were under a mirror pounded by a hammer. "Don't take it out yet," she grunted. She lay there, her legs still slung around my neck, and the little flag inside her began twitching and fluttering. "God," she said, "I can't stop it!" My prick was still firm. It hung obedient on her wet lips, as though receiving the sacrament from a lascivious angel. She came again, like an accordion collapsing in a bag of milk . . .

"Oh God," she said, flinging her arms around me, "if only . . ."

"If only what?"

"You know what I mean . . . Was it my fault," she said, "that this never happened before? Was I such a squeamish creature?" She looked at me with such frankness and sincerity I hardly recognized the woman I had lived with all these years.

"I guess we were both to blame . . ."

from **Rabbit Redux**

JOHN UPDIKE

In the film *Strange Days,* set on New Year's Eve 1999, there is a device called the squid deck that can record one person's experience onto a minidisk and then play it back for another. I saw this film in Florence, Italy, and emerged to the cobblestone streets feeling that I had seen a dramatization of the end of subjectivity in the very birthplace of Humanism. What I had always felt made humans human—the inability, ultimately, to communicate the depths of our experience and individuality—would be lost with the advent of this technological bridge. I did not see this as an advancement. For what lends poignancy to the fact of consciousness is the difficulty, the impossibility, in expressing its quiddity. Poetry most conspicuously, but all human interaction really, is constantly butting up against the fact of incommunicability. But the struggle, the exertion and friction of the asymptotic approach, is what has always given literature, and life, its meaning.

I thus imagined that the invention of the squid deck would signal the death of literature. Yet that day has not yet come and might never come. And in the meantime we beat on, aching to express and taking solace in the provisional achievements of others.

It was with this in mind that I read and marveled at John Updike's portrayal of a conflicted wife masturbating alongside her sleeping husband in the second of his famous Rabbit books. Updike enters Janice Angstrom's mind, as Joyce had Molly Bloom's, and returns with the layer-on-layer imbrications of her desire for her husband and her lover, for her free and fixed lives, for her future and her past, all of which rush over as her hand moves between her legs. If the experiences of other people are truly unknowable, Updike has come as close as one can get.

Her body feels tense as a harp. She wants to be touched . . . How sad it was with Harry now, they had become locked rooms to each other . . . She'd been with him so many times she could be quick in coming, sometimes asking him just to pound away and startling herself, coming, herself her toy, how strange to have to learn to play . . .

This is silly. This thinking is going nowhere, there is tomorrow to face . . . at lunch [she] can go over to Charlie's apartment, the light used to embarrass her but she likes it best in the day now, you can see everything, men's bottoms so innocent, even the little hole like a purse drawn tight, the hair downy and dark . . . Determined to bring herself off, Janice returns her hand and opens her eyes to look at Harry sleeping, all huddled into himself, stupid of him to keep her sex locked up all these years, his fault, all his fault, it was there all along, it was his job to call it out, she does everything for Charlie because he asks her, it feels holy, she doesn't care, you have to live, they put you here you have to live, you were made for one thing . . . it feels like a falling, a falling away, a deep eye opening, a coming into the deep you, Harry wouldn't know about that, he never did dare dwell on it, racing ahead, he's too fastidious, hates sex really, she was there all along, there she is, oh: not quite. She knows he knows, she opens her eyes, she sees him lying on the edge of the bed, the edge of a precipice, they are on it together, they are about to fall off, she closes her eyes, she is about to fall off: there. Oh. Oh. The bed complains.

from **Crash**

J. G. BALLARD

Maybe you saw the movie; I hope you didn't. *Crash* the movie is dreck; *Crash* the novel is pure butter. Written in 1973, Ballard's novel traces the psychopathology of a modern world we are still emerging into. It's as if he sat the adolescent version of late-century Western culture on his therapist's couch and flawlessly predicted the neuroses of its adulthood. Through Ballard we see that the merging of technology and eros always involves a prosthetic interface, some augmentation or externalization of the body, be it an automobile or a computer monitor, through which we are forced to cathect in order to feel our own bodies. This is fetish in its true sense: the need for an external trigger, a gateway to the self that exists outside of the self. Desire emerges in a circuit, a passage, a trip, giving extra meaning to the word *drive*. If the threat of technology is that we become ever more onanistic, the greater threat is that we become onanists alienated from the very selves that are meant to give us pleasure.

This is the world already inhabited by the characters of *Crash*. Each is the victim, willing or not, of a series of car wrecks, and their individual and collective libidos grow increasingly dependent on the automobile, and the collision of automobiles, to facilitate their sexual response. In the excerpted scene that follows, in the backseat of a paraplegic crash-victim's specially equipped vehicle, Ballard's protagonist realizes that his old set of erotic triggers have been replaced by a new one. We, meanwhile, get a window on the fallout of a full-bore techno-fetish.

She lifted her left foot so that the leg brace rested against my knee. In the inner surface of her thigh the straps formed marked impressions, troughs of reddened skin hollowed out in the form of buckles and clasps. As I unshackled the left leg brace and ran my fingers along the deep buckle groove, the corrugated skin felt hot and tender, more exciting than the membrane of a vagina. This depraved orifice, the invagination of a sexual organ still in the embryonic stages of its evolution, reminded me of the wounds on my own body, which still carried the contours of the instrument panel and controls. I felt this depression on her thigh, the groove worn below her breast under her right armpit by the spinal brace, the red marking on the inside of her right upper arm—these were the templates for new genital organs, the molds of sexual possibilities yet to be created in a hundred experimental car crashes. Behind my right arm the unfamiliar contours of the seat pressed against my skin as I slipped my hand towards the cleft between her buttocks. The interior of the car was in shadow, concealing Gabrielle's face, and I avoided her mouth as she lay back against the head-rest. I lifted her breast in my palm and began to kiss the cold nipple, from which a sweet odour rose, a blend of my own mucus and some pleasant pharmaceutical compound. I let my tongue rest against the lengthening teat, and then moved away and examined the breast carefully. For some reason I had expected it to be a detachable latex structure, fitted on each morning along with her spinal brace and leg supports, and I felt vaguely disappointed that it should be made of her own flesh. Gabrielle was sitting forward against my shoulder, a forefinger feeling along the inside of my lower lip, her nail against my teeth. The exposed portions of her body were joined together by the loosened braces and straps. I played with her bony pubis, feeling through the scanty hair over her crotch. As she sat passively in my arms, lips moving in minimal response, I realized this bored and crippled young woman found that the nominal junction points of the sexual act—breast and penis, anus and vulva, nipple and clitoris—failed to provide any excitement for us.

Through the fading afternoon light the airliners moved across our heads along the east-west runways of the airport. The pleasant surgical odour from Gabrielle's body, the tang of the mustard leatherette, hung in the air. The chromium controls reared in the shadows like the heads of silver snakes, the fauna of a metal dream. Gabrielle placed a drop of spit on my right nipple and stroked it mechanically, keeping up the small pretence of this nominal sexual link. In return, I stroked her pubis, feeling for the inert nub of her clitoris. Around us the silver controls of the car seemed a tour de force of technology and kinaesthetic systems. Gabrielle's hand moved across my chest. Her fingers found the small scars below my left collar bone, the imprint of the outer quadrant of the instrument binnacle. As she began to explore this circular crevice with her lips I for the first time felt my penis thickening. She took it from my trousers, then began to explore the other wound-scars on my chest and abdomen, running the tip of her tongue into each one. In turn, one by one, she endorsed each of these signatures, inscribed on my body by the dashboard and surfaces of my car. As she stroked my penis I moved my hand from her pubis to the scars on her thighs, feeling the tender causeways driven through her flesh by the hand-brake of the car in which she had crashed. My right arm held her shoulders, feeling the impress of the contoured leather, the meeting points of hemispherical and rectilinear geometries. I explored the scars on her thighs and arms, feeling for the wound areas under her left breast as she in turn explored mine, deciphering together these codes of sexuality made possible by our two car crashes.

My first orgasm, within the deep wound on her thigh, jolted my semen along this channel, irrigating its corrugated ditch. Holding the semen in her hand, she wiped it against the silver controls of the clutch treadle. My mouth was fastened on the scar below her left breast, exploring its sickle-shaped trough. Gabrielle turned in her seat, revolving her body around me, so that I could explore the wounds of her right hip. For the first time I felt no trace of pity for this crippled woman . . .

from The Canterbury Tales

GEOFFREY CHAUCER

Consider this an open challenge: I defy anyone to show me a more raucous, spirited, spicy rant on marriage than the Wife of Bath's monologue in *The Canterbury Tales*. We've had over six hundred years to improve on Chaucer's triumphant creation, but it's never been done. Not even Shakespeare's shrewish Kate (before her taming) can hold a candle to Chaucer's Alison. She's a kind of Mae West of the Middle Ages—loud, lusty, and eminently lovable (though, some might add murderous, as there are suggestions that she killed off her husbands).

In her celebrated *Prologue*, Dame Alison holds forth on how to get the upper hand in marriage, both in and out of the sack. Her philosophy is simple: women should have complete sovereignty over their men. And her tactics are sure-fire: "Until he paid his ransom to me, I wouldn't give him my nicety." Alison's is a manifesto of a certain pro-sex, pro-power, pro-marriage feminism—on her terms, of course—whose wit and enthusiasm more than make up for its sometimes dubious ethics. After reminding men that "with an empty hand, you may no hawks lure," she concludes with a prayer on behalf of women for "husbands meek, young, and fresh in the bed." A final note: I modernized the following passage to remove the difficulties of Chaucer's medieval English, but you should definitely read it in the original and in its entirety. This is but a taste.

Experience, even if it were no authority
In this world is right enough for me
To speak of the woe that is in marriage.
For, gentlemen, since I was twelve years of age
Thank the Lord who in Heaven does live
Husbands at church I've had me five . . .

God bade us to grow and multiply,
And that good teaching well know I! . . .
That wise king Solomon
He had more wives than one
Ah, would that God let me,
Be as oft refreshed as he!
But that gift of God he gave all his wives
Has no man one such that is now alive . . .

To make the perfect student, you must go to many schools,
And to make the perfect work, you must use a lot of tools,
Five husbands later, you know I am no fool!
So bring on the sixth, wherever he may be
For some keep chaste, but they sure are not me! . . .

Though my life you might well want to scold
Well you know that no household
Has every vessel made all of gold.
Some are wood, but have their place,
God loves us all in different ways . . .
So I'll bestow the flower of my age
In the acts and fruit of marriage.
Tell me, to what other conclusion
Were members made of generation?
And so perfectly were they wrought?
It could not all have been for nought . . .

And why in all the books is it said
That the husband must pay his wife in bed?
And what should he use for the payment
If he doesn't use his privy instrument? . . .

In wifehood I will use my instrument
As freely as the Lord it hath me sent.
If I hurt anyone, Lord give me sorrow,
My husband will have it both eve and morrow.
When I find one ready to pay the debt
I'll marry that man, that you can bet.
He'll be my debtor and my slave
And all his suffering he will have
Upon his flesh, while I'm his wife
I have the power for all my life . . .

I say in true, five husbands I had
And three were good, and two were bad.
The three good men were rich and old
But to the bond of marriage could hardly hold
And you know what I mean, without it told!
And help me God, I laugh when I consider,
How much I asked them to deliver! . . .

Now of my fifth husband I will tell
May God never send his soul to Hell,
And yet he was to me most severe
And made me pay a price so dear
That my ribs will feel it till my dying day.
But in our bed he was fresh and gay
And could me so truly understand
That when he wanted my belle chose at hand
Though he beat my every bone to pain
He could win my love again and again . . .

He was, in truth, but twenty years of age
And I was forty, and lust within me raged! . . .
And truly, as my husbands told me,
I had the nicest little thing that ever might be! . . .
So I followed my inclination
By virtue of my constellation
That made me never want to forgo
Giving my chamber of Venus to a good fellow.

—modernized by Jack Murnighan

from Justine

MARQUIS DE SADE

A few years ago, I excerpted from the Marquis de Sade's *Justine* for a *Nerve* article on banned books. Soon thereafter, a reader wrote in to express her concern that Sade "glorifies sexual abuse and rape." I wrote back indicating that I agreed and did not take such issues lightly. Why, then, would I include a passage of literature that glorified these things?

Here I have to admit that I tend to put aesthetic over ethical criteria in the assessment of fiction. If the writing is brilliant I am likely to forgive (if not be intrigued by) portrayals of even the most extreme evil. Cormac McCarthy's novel *Blood Meridian*, for example, contains unspeakable violence, yet is among the greatest novels of the last twenty years. But I would also argue that it is art's responsibility to acknowledge and explore humanity at its best and its worst. Perhaps the foremost of ethical imperatives is honesty, for only the honest and unblinking eye can expose us to the totality of experience and allow us to make the most informed ethical judgments.

My point in excerpting Sade both in the banned-book article and here is to say, Hey, look what literature can do. Books are banned because they affect people, and, to that extent, they show the power that great writing has. Sade, monster that he was, showed more than almost anyone else precisely how disturbing and intense literature can be. That, in my mind, makes his books both great and defensible.

●••

Thérèse, you realize that there is no power which could possibly deliver you out of our hands, and there is neither . . . any sort of means which might . . . prevent you from becoming, in every sense and in every manner, the prey of the libidinous excesses to which we, all four of us, are going to abandon ourselves with you . . .

I fall at Dom Séverino's feet . . . Great God, what's the use? Could I have not known that tears merely enhance the object of libertine's coveting? Everything I attempted in my efforts to sway those savages had the unique effect of arousing them . . .

A circle is formed immediately. I am placed in its center and there, for more than two hours, I am inspected, considered, handled by those four monks who pronounce either encomiums or criticisms.

"Let's to it," says Séverino, whose prodigiously exalted desires will brook no further restraint and who in this dreadful state gives the impression of a tiger about to devour its prey. "Let each of us advance to take his favorite pleasure." Placing me on a couch in the posture expected by his execrable projects and causing me to be held by two of his monks, the infamous man attempts to satisfy himself in that criminal and perverse fashion which makes us to resemble the sex we do not possess while degrading the one we have. But either the shameless creature is too strongly proportioned, or Nature revolts in me at the mere suspicion of these pleasures. Séverino cannot overcome the obstacles. He presents himself, and is repulsed immediately. He spreads, he presses, thrusts, tears; all his efforts are in vain. In his fury the monster lashes out at the altar at which he cannot speak his prayers. He strikes it, he pinches it, he bites it. These brutalities are succeeded by renewed challenges. The chastened flesh yields, the gate cedes, the ram bursts through, terrible screams rise from my throat. The entire mass is swiftly engulfed and darts its venom the next moment. Séverino weeps with rage.

—*translated by Richard Seaver*
and Austryn Wainhouse

from # The Death of the Novel

RONALD SUKENICK

I'm listening to Bob Dylan and reading Ron Sukenick; I think I might be on to something. I'm sure that most of you have listened to Dylan, know how his tuneless gravel eases you back to a kind of stalled moment in time, hovering somewhere about 1974. Some cultural artifacts are so bound in their present that they become preposterous the minute culture shifts. Others somehow distill their moments, giving us access to little anachronistic havens, allowing us to perform the trick of inserting our present selves in the synchrony of events long past. Dylan has always been in this second category for me, and it's one of the reasons I love him so.

Reading Ron Sukenick is having the same effect and evokes pretty much the same time period. My first exposure to Sukenick's consummate sex-and-drug-decade prose was *Long Talking Bad Conditions Blues*, his great unpunctuated po-mo dithyramb. Then came *The Death of the Novel and Other Stories*, an excerpt of which follows. The title story is about Sukenick's teaching a course on the death throes of a genre he worked in, only to find himself smoking dope and having unapologetic sex with his students and various other girls less than half his age. The passage begins with a description of one object of Professor Sukenick's fancy, his student Betty, and ends with them having sex in an East Village pied-à-terre. And although the politically dubious student-teacher fantasy sticks fast in the craw of many of us (especially us former instructors), Sukenick's professor finds the tables of sexual power curiously turned on him by a young lover in a borrowed bed.

● ●●

When I get nervous sometimes I get a little pompous. Especially with students. Especially with students who I want to seduce. The kids at the table smiled at one another indulgently. They liked me. They thought I was hip. For my age. They knew I wanted to make it with Betty. They probably wished me luck . . . their attitude was that it didn't mean that much whether I wanted to fuck Betty, or if I didn't want to fuck Betty, or if in fact I did fuck Betty. That seemed to be pretty much Betty's attitude too. She was a cheerleader type, one of those auburn straight-haired round-cheeked dolls right out of a Coca-Cola ad . . . she was pretty as apples and bland as Uneeda biscuits. Her thighs were like white bread . . . She was America, and I wanted her. In any case she was my smartest student, and I wanted her the way a teacher always wants his smartest student, especially if she's a nice piece of ass. Not that she ever did any work. I gave her A's for her ideas, for her conversation, for her presence maybe, for her pussy, and because getting A's didn't mean a thing to her . . .

Where we going? She asked. I shrugged.

Why don't we go to the city, she said. I know an apartment we can use on the East Side . . .

We walked in and very cool she took off her clothes. Smiling, she lay down on a mattress on the floor and stared up at the ceiling.

I want a drink, I said. She made a face. She never touched alcohol.

There's nothing here, she said. There's some pot in the drawer. I rolled a joint and sat down next to her on the mattress and we smoked it while I caressed her. She stared at the ceiling. I was in a kind of pink revery of which her body was part. I went and pissed, came back, undressed, and lay down next to her. My cock was very impersonal, an animated hose with a life of its own, jumping around between her sensitive and very knowing fingers.

I think of you as Miss America, I said. She smiled. I slid in like a dirigible sliding into a cloud in a beautiful dream. Her body began churning like a bump and grind dancer. She was staring at the ceiling. Suddenly I got the feeling that this was all staged, some kind of routine, a movie maybe, or a cheap story. Her pussy felt like a moist sack of warm membrane, totally physiological. I had something like a sudden Hindenburg disaster. Shit, she said after a while. I flopped out, my penis a dead fish, my heart an empty reservoir.

from Astrophil and Stella, "Sonnet 59"

SIR PHILIP SIDNEY

Sir Philip Sidney was one of the brightest stars of the sixteenth century. Combining raging good looks, innate wit, and a knack for diplomacy, he was the Elizabethan courtier extraordinaire. In 1586, his thirty-second year, Sidney was killed heroically in battle, thereby solidifying his legend. Yet despite his short life, Sidney wrote a number of masterpieces, including the first sonnet sequence in English and the most influential book of literary theory of his century. For over a hundred years following his death, Sidney was considered a finer poet than either Spenser or Shakespeare; most of that fame derives from the *Astrophil and Stella* sonnets, one of which appears in the following excerpt.

The sonnet in question is neither the best nor most famous of the sequence of 108, but it is definitely the bawdiest. Even those unused to reading poetry will have no trouble getting the gist of this one: Sidney is jealous of the attention his desired lover is paying to her lapdog, so he starts enumerating the many advantages he has over her "sour-breath'd mate." Yet this is no ordinary spaniel! To my mischievous eye, the question remains: Is "that lap" of line 10 doing the lapping or being lapped? And where are the "sugar'd lips"? Not that I have a dirty mind or anything, but I suspect that what begins as an innocent poem about a furry little companion seems to develop into a decidedly scurrilous account of Sidney's all-too-successful rival. By the end we find Sidney asking to be lobotomized by love, for as his lover loves only fools, this is the surest way to her heart. No small amount of rancor for fourteen rhyming lines.

Dear, why make you more of a dog than me?
If he do love, I burn, I burn in love;
If he wait well, I never thence would move;
If he be fair, yet but a dog can be.

Little he is, so little worth is he;
He barks, my songs in one voice oft doth prove:
Bidden perhaps he fetcheth thee a glove,
But I unbid, fetch even my soul to thee.

Yet while I languish, him that bosom clips,
That lap doth lap, nay lets in spite of spite
This sour-breath'd mate taste of those sugar'd lips.

Alas, if you grant only such delight
To witless things, then Love I hope (since wit
Becomes a clog) will soon ease me of it.

from **Clit Notes**

HOLLY HUGHES

I don't often go to the theater, but
when I do I usually hold my nose.
Both the predictable lack of
verisimilitude on stage and its
rare opposite, the Brechtian
Verfremdungseffekt, make me
decidedly uncomfortable and
occasionally nauseated. Maybe it's the excessive eyeliner on the players;
maybe it's the way voices take on a vaguely mocking tone when pro-
jected; maybe I just have a deficient gene that tells me I'd rather read
Othello a hundred times than sit through it once in Stratford-on-Avon,
Central Park, or anywhere else.

The upside of this unnatural distaste for theater is that when I do
like a play, I really like it. The first time this happened I was already in
college, seeing a production of Holly Hughes' *The Well of Horniness.*
Having never heard of Hughes, I was utterly unprepared for the hour
and a half of raucous mischief that was to follow. Nymphomaniacal
lesbians from the Lambda Lambda Lambda sorority trying to seduce
even married women into their nefarious ranks: now that's drama! I
finally realized what I had been missing in my theatergoing experiences:
the outspoken, incisive ribaldry of Holly Hughes.

I have only been fortunate enough to see one other Hughes production, *Dress Suits for Hire,* which is perhaps her most beautiful and
enduring play. That's why I was so excited to hear that the scripts
of *The Well of Horniness, Dress Suits,* and three other of Hughes'
plays had been published together under the title *Clit Notes: A Sapphic
Sampler.*

If you were to judge from the cover of *Clit Notes,* where Hughes is
standing full and frontal, clad in nothing but leaves and vines, you'd
think she was some comic portrayal of Ceres, goddess of the harvest, or
maybe a sardonic Primavera, rescued from the clutches of a Botticelli
canvas. And although I know it's just a bit of Hughes' irony, a parody of

the reproductive for a few lambdic laughs, I have to say that the plays contained within do seem to give birth not only to a new theatrical genre (noir lesbian comedy), but to an enviable identity politics based on bald honesty, gentle self-mocking, and the tenacious pursuit of sex.

●••

I've never been what you'd call a morning person.

I'm the kind of person who wakes up so stunned by sleep I can't remember my own name. But now it's starting to become my favorite time of the day.

The difference? It's her.

Now I get to watch her slide out of the sheets into the new day. Her legs—they're always longest in the morning. I've never known anyone who could get so naked before! She's not in any hurry to do anything about that nakedness . . . It's a little present she gives to me, this time. Her standing, back to me, light coming through the palm trees, running over her swimmer's shoulders like river water poured through cupped hands.

That's the moment I remember who I am.

That's the moment I come back to the body I thought I'd lost to my father.

Then she swings around to face me, and Jesus! I'm blinded.

Whatta set of knockers!

Now I know why they call them headlights. Until I started going out with her I never realized: tits can be a source of light!

I know there are people out there who get uneasy when I start talking about my girlfriend's tits. Hooters. Knockers. Winnebagos! I know there are readers who'd be more comfortable if I described my girlfriend's mammalian characteristics as "breastssss."

But I can't do that. She doesn't have breastssss. Thank God! Breastssss are what those ladies have . . . You know who ladies are, don't you?

Ladies are the people who will not let my girlfriend use the public ladies room, thinking she's not a woman. But are they going to let her into the men's room? Nope. Because they don't think she's a man, either.

If she's not a woman and she's not a man, what in the hell is she?

Once I asked my father what fire was, a liquid, a gas, or a solid, and he said it wasn't any of those things. Fire isn't a thing; it's what happens to things. A force of nature. That's what he called it.

Well, maybe that's what she is. A force of nature. I'll tell you something: she is something that happened to me . . .

from **Money**

MARTIN AMIS

There's a game I used to play
with some friends at Cambridge.
Assuming that there was nothing
worse than being an obvious
second best, the point of the
game was to say to one
another, "Hey _____, you're
no _____." Hey Pepsi, you're no Coke. Hey Burger King, you're no
McDonald's, and so on. As the latter component—the truly best—is
meant to be obvious, it shouldn't be necessary to say it. Hey Engels. Hey
Roebuck. Hey Roger Moore. You get the drift. So when I first picked up a
book by Martin Amis, having read a number of books by his extremely
talented father, Kingsley, I had only one thing in my mind: hey Julian
Lennon. I assumed poor Martin's flower was trying to bloom with shal-
low roots in borrowed sunlight. But you know what? I was wrong. Seems
more like he resolved the predictable Oedipal dilemma in the most direct
way possible: kill Pop with his own pen.

Amis the younger is good, real good. The scene that follows is from
his breakthrough novel, *Money*, in which a bloated, bumbling, and fabu-
lously vulgar English commercial director gets bankrolled to make a feature film in Hollywood. Like most of Amis' characters, John Self is a
believable and recognizable caricature, a stock player in the twilight of
the millennium, and we love him through his flaws. Here we find Self at
his best, in a hotel room with the bombshell lead of his film, having done
a "hangman's rope" of a line of cocaine with his fifty-two-inch waist
trousers around his ankles doing what most of us assume we'll never do:
boffing a superstar.

At this moment in time I am doing something that millions of people all over the planet are longing, are aching, are dying to do. Eskimos dream about it. Pygmies beat off about it. You've thought about it, pal, take my word for it. You too, angel, if you're at all that way inclined. The whole world wants to do it. And I'm doing it . . . I am giving Butch Beausoleil one. You don't believe me? But I am! Round from the back, what's more. You get the picture: she's on all fours and clutching the headpiece of her neighing brass bed. If I glance downwards, like so, and retract my gut, I can see her valentine card and the mysterious trail of her cleft, like the inside of a halved apple. Now do you believe me? Wait: here comes her hand, idling slantways down her rump, ten bucks of manicure on each fingertip. Why she seems to be . . . Wow. Selina herself doesn't do that too often. And I bet not even Selina does it on the first date. Well, true sack artists, they adore themselves, every inch . . . I'm in a position to tell you that the camera doesn't lie. I've seen Butch naked before, partially on screen and fully in one of the whack magazines that feature celebrity indiscretions, but that hardly prepared me for all this costly flesh texture and high-tab body tone, not to mention the bunk knowhow on such vivid display . . .

At last: she's making those noises . . . Butch would seem to be girding herself for some kind of apocalyptic jackpot and, yes, I'm along for the ride too, panting and jabbering and holding on for dear life. Now or never. What shall I think about, to help me jump off the train? I'll think about Butch Beausoleil. It's working . . .

from **In Praise of the Stepmother**

MARIO VARGAS LLOSA

If you haven't already read Mario Vargas Llosa's *In Praise of the Stepmother,* you damn well better get cracking. The novel as a whole is remarkable in the scope of its sensuality. Here is a book where we see the unfaded passions of a man of middle years, not only for the armpits, ass, and vulva of his incomparable wife but for the mundane rituals of daily existence: the trimming of nails, cleaning of ears, and, in his estimation, the sublime pleasure of taking a shit. Nor is he the only one in the house with hightened empirical faculties: his prepubescent son Alphonso cloaks some pretty grown-up desire for his heavy-breasted stepmother in the guise of naïve youth. And then there is the stepmother herself, a gloriously crafted character with whom I am still irremediably in love. As to the playing out of their accelerated Oedipal triangle, I won't tip the hand, but I assure you it is not without surprises.

Interspersed in the unfolding of the primary narrative are a number of loosely connected vignettes, occasioned and accompanied by single-page reproductions of great paintings from history. The scene that follows weaves a story behind the image in the great Francis Bacon canvas *Head 1.* It is a minitreatise on the erotics of revulsion, the draw of the horrible, the subcutaneous pull of the abject. The passage is unlike any other in the novel and, I would argue, unlike virtually anything else in literature. Few authors can portray the sexuality of the hideous; fewer still can capture the gravity of its allure.

I have a very highly developed sense of smell and it is by way of my nose that I experience the greatest pleasure and the greatest pain. Ought I to call this gigantic membranous organ that registers all scents, even the most subtle, a nose? I am referring to the grayish shape, covered with white crusts, that begins at my mouth and extends, increasing in size, down to my bull neck. No, it is not a goiter or an acromegalic Adam's apple. It is my nose. I know that it is neither beautiful nor useful, since its excessive sensibility makes it an indescribable torment when a rat is rotting in the vicinity or fetid materials pass through the drainpipes that run through my home. Nonetheless, I revere it and sometimes think that my nose is the seat of my soul.

I have no arms or legs, but my four stumps are nicely healed over and well toughened, so that I can move about easily along the ground and can even run if need be. My enemies have never been able to catch me in any of their roundups thus far. How did I lose my hands and feet? An accident at work, perhaps; or maybe some medicine my mother took so as to have an easy pregnancy (science doesn't come up with the right answers in all cases, unfortunately).

My sex organ is intact. I can make love, on condition that the young fellow or the female acting as my *partenaire* allows me to position myself in such a way that my boils don't rub against his or her body, for if they burst they leak stinking pus and I suffer terrible pain. I like to fornicate, and I would say that, in a certain sense, I am a voluptuary. I often have fiascoes or experience a humiliating premature ejaculation, it is true. But, other times, I have prolonged and repeated orgasms that give me the sensation of being as ethereal and radiant as the Archangel Gabriel. The repulsion I inspire in my lovers turns into attraction, and even into delirium, once they overcome—thanks almost always to alcohol or drugs—their initial prejudices and agree to do amorous battle with me in bed. Women even come to love me, in fact, and become addicted to my ugliness. In the depths of her soul, Beauty was always fascinated by the Beast, as so many fantastic tales and mythologies recount, and it is only in rare cases that the heart of a good-looking youth does not harbor something perverse.

—translated by Helen Lane

from **"To His Coy Mistress"**

ANDREW MARVELL

Anyone who has read seventeenth-century verse knows Andrew Marvell's poem "To His Coy Mistress"; anyone who has lived in this ragtag world of sexual longing knows its sentiment: C'mon, baby, let's get it on. Now no disrespect to Marvin Gaye, but never has the case been better petitioned than by Marvell in his masterpiece. Although most men just whine to their lovers about their robin's-egg-tinted balls, Marvell, he argues. From the oft-quoted opening lines to the final image of the unstoppable sun, Marvell denies love any eternity or stasis. And because it is true that even the hottest flame must burn in sequential time, any second unseized is lost. This is the conceit of Marvell's exquisite bauble, which follows in its entirety. I encourage you to memorize some of its lines; we know all too well how often they'll come in handy.

● ● ●

Had we but world enough, and time,
This coyness, lady, were no crime.
We would sit down and think which way
To walk, and pass our long love's day;
Thou by the Indian Ganges' side
Shouldst rubies find; I by the tide
Of Humber would complain. I would
Love you ten years before the Flood;
And you should, if you please, refuse
Till the conversion of the Jews.
My vegetable love should grow

Vaster than empires, and more slow.
An hundred years should go to praise
Thine eyes, and on thy forehead gaze;
Two hundred to adore each breast,
But thirty thousand to the rest;
An age at least to every part,
And the last age should show your heart.
For, lady, you deserve this state,
Nor would I love at lower rate.

But at my back I always hear
Time's winged chariot hurrying near;
And yonder all before us lie
Deserts of vast eternity.
Thy beauty shall no more be found,
Nor, in thy marble vault, shall sound
My echoing song; then worms shall try
That long preserv'd virginity,
And your quaint honour turn to dust,
And into ashes all my lust.
The grave's a fine and private place,
But none I think do there embrace.

Now therefore, while the youthful hue
Sits on thy skin like morning dew,
And while thy willing soul transpires
At every pore with instant fires,
Now let us sport us while we may;
And now, like am'rous birds of prey,
Rather at once our time devour,
Than languish in his slow-chapp'd power.
Let us roll all our strength, and all
Our sweetness, up into one ball;
And tear our pleasures with rough strife
Thorough the iron gates of life.
Thus, though we cannot make our sun
Stand still, yet we will make him run.

from **"Cleanness"**

THE PEARL POET

The fourteenth-century allitera-
tive poem "Cleanness" (sometimes called "Purity") narrates,
in rather excruciating detail,
the agonies God inflicts on
filthy sinners. Its author is
unknown, though he's
generally referred to as the Pearl or the Gawain poet, after two of his
more popular poems. "Cleanness" didn't catch on quite like the others,
no doubt because it is an example of that oh-so-fun medieval poetic
genre, homiletic verse—didactic sermons thinly veiled in poetry.

Now, although these poems are only as subtle as the Trojan horse,
and about as yummy as cherry cough syrup, they can occasionally make
for good reading. For one thing, you get to learn lots of great stuff, like
how to lace up the armor of chastity, why everything is Eve's fault, and
how to interpret especially sticky Bible passages ("Mom, if Mary
never . . . , then how . . . ?"). All this and alliteration too!

So, much as I'm sure you want to rush out and read some homilies,
maybe you're a little surprised to find one here. Sermons in a sex anthology? Not to worry. Not wanting you to miss out on this vital phase in
medieval letters, I culled one of the raciest passages in the history of the
genre. In it God has caught wind of some male-male sex practices taking
place on Earth, and he's not happy about it. The following excerpt is his
curious response: He condemns sodomy, as the jaded among us would
expect, but not from the reactionary Church position we're used to
hearing today. Instead, he argues that sodomy doesn't make any sense
considering how much fun straight sex can be. Now there's an argument!
And from the mouth of God! So, here it is, an unlikely endorsement from
on high for a particularly tangible form of terrestrial paradise.

The great sound of Sodom sinks in My ears
And the guilt of Gomorrah goads Me to wrath
I shall research that rumor and see for Myself
If they have done as is heard on high.
They have learned a lifestyle that liketh Me ill,
And found in their flesh of faults the foulest,
Each male making mate of men like himself
Fondling the fellows as if they were female.
Yet I designed them a deed and taught them to do it
And deemed it in My dominion the dearest of dances
And set love therein, making such sex the sweetest.
The play of paramours I portrayed Myself,
And made one manner much merrier than all others:
When two who are true tie to one another
Between this male and his mate such mirth may be made
That paradise proper would prove hardly preferable.
They must take to each other in the manner most true
Stealing to a secluded spot, silent and unseen,
And the flame of their love will fire up so free
That all the sorrows of this life will not it slake.

—*modernized by Jack Murnighan*

from Gravity's Rainbow

THOMAS PYNCHON

Thomas Pynchon's *Gravity's Rainbow* is one of the most bizarre and extraordinary novels of the twentieth century. It is gigantic and taxing, and few who begin it finish. I only succeeded in the rush of a forty-eight-hour delirium—boxer-shorted and unshaven in a squalid Parisian *chambre de bonne* with a pot of lentils between my knees. By the book's end I was fully participating in the manic paranoia that fueled its composition, and when I staggered out onto the brightly lit street, I had a very difficult time figuring out what I was supposed to do next.

Gravity's Rainbow is one of those handful of novels, more a world than a book, that overwhelms you with the totality of its vision, immersing you well above the eyeballs. It's also a very difficult novel to pin down: on the one hand an act of extreme dementia, furiously interlarded with layers of conspiracy and machination; on the other, a consummate genre-bender, interchanging moments of *Three Stooges*–like farce with hard science, statistical theory, and meticulous wartime history. It's the kind of book writers probably shouldn't read, considering the effects on the ego of having one's achievements monumentally dwarfed.

But all eulogizing aside, the scene I've excerpted is not for the squeamish. Rarely does a writer of true greatness emerge from the legions of scribblers, rarer still does such a writer address the furthest frontiers of what most people think unthinkable. Here is one of those exceptional moments.

The cell is in semidarkness, with only a scented candle burning back in a corner that seems miles away. She waits for him in a tall Adam chair, white body and black uniform-of-the-night. He drops to his knees.

"Domina Nocturna . . . shining mother and last love . . . your servant Ernest Pudding reporting as ordered."

. . . She is naked now, except for a long sable cape and black boots with court heels. Her only jewelry is a silver ring with an artificial ruby not cut to facets but still in the original boule, an arrogant gout of blood, extended now, waiting his kiss.

His clipped moustache bristles, trembling, across her fingers. She has filed her nails to long points and polished them the same red as her ruby. Their ruby. In this light the nails are almost black. "That's enough. Get ready."

. . . He is on his knees again, bare as a baby. His old man's flesh creeps coarse-grained in the light from the candle. Old scars and new welts group here and there over his skin. His penis stands at present arms. She smiles. At her command, he crawls forward to kiss her boots. He smells wax and leather, and can feel her toes flexing beneath his tongue, through the black skin . . . Some nights she's gagged him with a ceremonial sash, bound him with a gold-tasseled fourragère or his own Sam Browne. But tonight he lies humped on the floor at her feet, his withered ass elevated for the cane, bound by nothing but his need for pain, for something real, something pure. They have taken him so far from his simple nerves. They have stuffed paper illusions and military euphemisms between him and this truth, this rare decency, this moment at her scrupulous feet . . . no it's not guilt here, not so much amazement—that he could have listened to so many years of ministers, scientists, doctors each with his specialized lies to tell, when she was here all the time, sure in her ownership of his failing body, his true body: undisguised by uniform, uncluttered by drugs to keep from him her communiqués of vertigo, nausea and pain . . . Above all, pain. The clearest poetry, the endearment of greatest worth . . .

He struggles to his knees to kiss the instrument. She stands over him now, legs astride, pelvis cocked forward, fur cape held apart on her hips. He dares to gaze up at her cunt, that fearful vortex. Her pubic hair has been dyed black for the occasion. He sighs, and lets escape a small shameful groan.

"Ah . . . yes, I know." She laughs. "Poor mortal Brigadier, I know. It is my last mystery," stroking with fingernails her labia, "you cannot ask a woman to reveal her last mystery, no, can you?"

"Please . . ."

"No. Not tonight. Kneel here and take what I give you."

. . . Her shadow covers his face and upper torso, her leather boots creak softly as thigh and abdominal muscles move, and then in a rush she begins to piss. He opens his mouth to catch the stream, choking, trying to keep swallowing, feeling warm urine dribble out the corners of his mouth and down his neck and shoulders, submerged in the hissing storm. When she's done he licks the last few drops from his lips. More cling, golden clear, to the glossy hairs of her quim. Her face, looming between her bare breasts, is smooth as steel.

She turns. "Hold up my fur." He obeys. "Be careful. Don't touch my skin." Earlier in this game she was nervous, constipated, wondering if this was anything like male impotence. But thoughtful Pointsman, anticipating this, has been sending laxative pills with her meals. Now her intestines whine softly, and she feels shit begin to slide down and out. He kneels with his arms up holding the rich cape. A dark turd appears out the crevice, out of the absolute darkness between her white buttocks. He spreads his knees, awkwardly, until he can feel the leather of her boots. He leans forward to surround the hot turd with his lips, sucking on it tenderly, licking along its lower side . . . The stink of shit floods his nose, gathering him, surrounding. It is the smell of Passchendaele, of the Salient. Mixed with the mud, and the putrefaction of corpses, it was the sovereign smell of their first meeting, and her emblem. The turd slides into his mouth, down to his gullet. He gags, but bravely clamps his teeth shut. Bread that would only have floated in porcelain waters somewhere, unseen, untasted—risen now and backed in the bitter intestinal oven to bread we know, bread that's light as domestic comfort, secret as death in bed . . . Spasms in his throat continue.

The pain is terrible. With his tongue he mashes shit against the roof of his mouth and begins to chew, thickly now, the only sound in the room . . .

There are two more turds, smaller ones, and when he has eaten these, residual shit to lick out of her anus. He prays that she'll let him drop the cape over himself, to be allowed, in the silk-lined darkness, to stay a while longer with his submissive tongue straining upward into her asshole. But she moves away. The fur evaporates from his hands. She orders him to masturbate for her. She has watched Captain Blicero with Gottfried, and has learned the proper style.

The Brigadier comes quickly. The rich smell of semen fills the room like smoke.

"Now go."

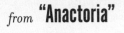

from **"Anactoria"**

SAPPHO

Sappho, a Greek poet who lived over 600 years before the birth of Christ, is the most renowned woman writer of antiquity. Her poems, extant now primarily in fragments, were among the most accomplished of her day. These lyrics (so-called because she accompanied her recitals with a lyre) made her famous in her lifetime—so much so that statues of her were erected, an ancient Greek coin bore her face, and even two centuries after her death, Plato called her the tenth muse.

Today Sappho is still recognized as one of the major contributors to the development of first-person voice in Greek verse. Hers is the voice of the individual, abandoning the standard topic of feuds among the gods to address instead the barebones reality of visceral love and longing, as when she writes "Again desire, / —which loosens limbs and is so bitter and sweet, / makes my body quiver. / You are irresistible." The level of physicality in Sappho's verse suggests an advancement in Greek thinking: that it might not be Fate that dictates the course of human life so much as the exigencies of the emotive self.

Yet Sappho's modern fame is more a result of her association with lesbianism than of her role in the evolution of verse. The term *lesbian* is derived from the name of the Greek isle Lesbos, where Sappho founded a school of women with whom she had sexual relations and to whom she wrote much of her exquisite and sensual verse. Her predilection is summarized in the eminently quotable lines "Lovely girls / for you / my feelings / will never change"; the evidence that she acted on her predilection can be found in lines such as "With the noble oils of flowers / you annointed yourself / and on softest beds fulfilled your desire / for me." Lesbian desire as explicit as this would not be articulated again for centuries.

The poem below demonstrates why Sappho's name is still known to us today. For indeed she was justified when she wrote to one of her lovers, "Take this to heart: In the future / we will be remembered . . ."

●··

He who sits in your presence,
Listening close to your sweet speech and laughter,
Is, in my esteem, yet luckier than the gods.
The thought makes my heart aflutter in my breast.
For even seeing you but briefly,
I lose what words I had;
My tongue finds not a sound;
My eyes fail to see, my ears set to ring;
A fire runs beneath my skin;
Sweat pores from me and a trembling takes my body whole.
I am paler than summer-burned grass, and, in my madness
I fear that I too may die.
And yet, I'll dare it. Just a little more!

—*translated by Henry Thaston Wharton,*
modified by Jack Murnighan

from **Neuromancer**

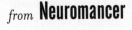

WILLIAM GIBSON

Soon after its 1984 publication, William Gibson's *Neuromancer* emerged as the defining novel of the virtual age not only by coining the term *cyberspace*, but also by generating enormous buzz around the still-nascent cyberculture. Gibson's timing and tack were perfect: using a sci-fi story line in an ultravivid near future, he managed, years before the emergence of the World Wide Web, to crystallize an image of interface technology as a potentially traversable habitat, thus establishing himself as both prophet and pundit of a techno-society in the first throes of a major transformation.

But not only does *Neuromancer* have its thumb on the pulse of late-century Zeitgeist, it is also one of the slickest books of science fiction ever. Winning the triple crown of sci-fi awards (the Hugo, Nebula, and Philip K. Dick), it made Gibson an instant household name. Not bad for a first novel.

The world Gibson creates in *Neuromancer* is an all too convincing dystopia, and not even sex remains unaffected. The steamy scene below involves *Neuromancer*'s two main characters: Case, a burned-out cyber-space hacker, and his bodyguard, Molly the "razorgirl," so-designated for the four-inch retractable blades concealed beneath her fingernails. She's a real bad-ass who beats people up for fun and sports sunglasses surgically inset in her head, but she has a bit of a soft spot for Case (most convenient for film adaptation). The selection is a nice example of Gibson's precision with detail; in a coffin motel in Chiba City we will witness both the pitfalls of sex with cyborgs and a hallucinatory image of the orgasm of the future.

He lay on his stomach, arms stretched forward, tips of his fingers against the walls of the coffin. She settled over the small of his back, kneeling on the temperfoam, the leather jeans cool against his skin. Her fingers brushed his neck.

"How come you're not at the Hilton?"

She answered by reaching back, between his thighs, and gently encircling his scrotum with thumb and forefinger. She rocked there for a minute in the dark, erect above him, her other hand on his neck. The leather of her jeans creaked softly with the movement. Case shifted, feeling himself harden against the temperfoam.

His head throbbed, but the brittleness in his neck seemed to retreat. He raised himself on one elbow, rolled, sank back against the foam, pulling her down, licking her breasts, small hard nipples sliding wet across his cheek. He found the zip on the leather jeans and tugged it down . . . She struggled beside him until she could kick them away. She threw a leg across him and he touched her face. Unexpected hardness of the implanted lenses. "Don't," she said, "fingerprints."

Now she straddled him again, took his hand, and closed it over her, his thumb along the cleft of her buttocks, his fingers spread across the labia. As she began to lower herself, the images came pulsing back, the faces, fragments of neon arriving and receding. She slid down around him and his back arched convulsively. She rode him that way, impaling herself, slipping down on him again and again, until they both had come, his orgasm flaring blue in a timeless space, a vastness like the matrix, where the faces were shredded and blown away down hurricane corridors, and her inner thighs were strong and wet against his hips.

from My Cousin, My Gastroenterologist

MARK LEYNER

Mark Leyner's *My Cousin, My Gastroenterologist*, was one of the favorite books of my now-Mesozoic college days. Although all my friends were striving to develop sophisticated, *New Republic*–y prose styles, I was still lapping up Leyner's playful indulgence as the alpha and omega of good writing. Now, a decade later, as the first grays start to insinuate themselves in my Etonian coif, I occasionally still find myself reading *Gastroenterologist* and doubling over with laughter.

The selection below is classic: it's the one I always read out loud to my friends to turn them on to the book. Now all I have to do is say the opening words, "Hello Mark. This is Elizabeth Hurlick," and I get immediate laughs. As a whole, *My Cousin, My Gastroenterologist* suffers from having too many discontinuous one-liners and not enough glue; in this passage, however, Leyner stays focused and harnesses the full force of his wit. Enjoy, then, this heady shot of Leyner: he's a rush like no other.

●••

Hello Mark. This is Elizabeth Hurlick. I'm one of Trudy's friends from school. Trudy asked me to call and tell you that when she gets home from work she's going to want to make love tout de suite and then eat 'cause she's got an early squash practice so she wants you to . . . put the chicken in the oven . . . run a hot bath . . . and soak in the tub for a while . . . She said that while you're in the tub you should masturbate almost to the point of orgasm and stop and that way you'll have a more copious ejaculation later when you have sex with Trudy because Trudy says you have to propitiate the squash god and the squash god is in the mood for a really super-copious ejaculation, and she said to tell you that . . . she doesn't want you to use any deodorant under your arms because when you're having sex she wants you to smell kind of macho sort of raunchy kind of ruggedly homo sapien kind of rural and she wants you to wait for her wearing the . . . red kimono . . . and when she comes through the door . . . you should nonchalantly let your kimono fall open so your meat sort of pokes out, and then she wants you to lift her skirt up and take her underpants off and rub your knuckles up and down her perineum, if you're writing this down that's p-e-r-i-n-e-u-m . . . I hope you don't mind me leaving this sort of intimate personal message on your answering machine, but I'm a really really good friend of Trudy's and Trudy's told me all about you and I hope we can all get together sometime . . . Trudy says you're creepy in a sort of attractive way and that sounds fun.

from The Book of Margery Kempe

MARGERY KEMPE

Margery Kempe, born around 1373, is among the most famous and important of medieval English mystics. Her *Book* is the first autobiography written in English and one of the earliest works in English by a woman. It recounts her long and variegated life, first as a wife and mother of fourteen children, then as a religious mystic and pilgrim who communed with the Lord, wept uncontrollably, and wore the white habit of a virgin (despite the kids).

The excerpt from Margery's *Book* presents a familiar situation: a wife denying her husband sex, claiming to have no interest when in fact she has a lover on the side who gets all her attention. It's a Hollywood story line, but Margery Kempe's version has a few twists. The first is that the piece was written in the beginning of the fifteenth century; the second is that her paramour is no ordinary man, nor does he use ordinary means for the seduction of the good woman.

The lover, the reader soon discovers, is the Lord, and he's got the moves. It was not uncommon in the Middle Ages for religious mystics to have forms of spiritual union with the Man, but what is particularly interesting about Margery's tale is that God does not simply arrive in a visitation (like Zeus in the golden rain), but speaks to Margery in her soul and gets her to fall for him. But I, for one, can't help feeling for the poor husband—talk about being outmatched!

So, in the Christian spirit of trinity within unity, you should read the piece below for the humor, the sexiness, and to see the Almighty's unique version of the flowers/chocolates/sweet-nothings approach to the age-old art of MacDaddyism. God can definitely make time.

One night, as this creature lay in her bed with her husband, she heard a sound of a melody so sweet and delectable, she thought she had been in Paradise. And then she got out of her bed and said, "Alas that I ever did sin, for it is truly joyous in heaven!" . . . And after this time she never had desire to have sex with her husband, for the debt of matrimony was so abominable to her that she thought she would rather eat or drink the muck in the channel than consent to any fleshly commingling . . .

And so it happened one Friday . . . that her husband asked his wife a question: "Margery, if there came a man with a sword and would smite off my head unless we had sex together as we used to, tell me according to your conscience—for you say you will not lie— whether you would rather my head be cut off or that I play with you like we used to do?" . . .

"Truly I would rather you be slain that we should turn again to our uncleanness"

And he said to her: "You are no good wife."

[Some time later] as this creature was in the Apostles Church in Rome, the Father of Heaven said to her, "Daughter, I am quite pleased with you . . . I will have you wedded to my Godhead, for I shall show you my secrets and my counsels, and you shall live with me without end." . . .

Our lord also gave her a token which endured about sixteen years and increased more and more. That was a flame of fire wonderfully hot and delectable and comfortable, not diminishing but ever increasing, of love, for, though the weather be cold she felt the heat burning in her breast and her heart, as truly as a man would feel the material fire if he put his hand or finger in it. When she felt first the fire of love in her breast, she was afraid of it, and then our Lord answered in her mind and said, "Daughter, be not afraid, for this heat is the heat of the Holy Ghost . . . And therefore you shall have greater cause than ever to love me, and you shall hear what you've never heard, and you shall see what you've never seen, and feel what you've never felt...

[And then the Lord spoke in her soul:] "It is convenient for the wife to be intimate with her husband. No matter how great a lord he is or how poor a woman she is when he weds her, yet they must lie together and rest together in joy and peace. And such it must be between you and me . . . Therefore I must be intimate with you and lie in bed with thee. Daughter, you desire greatly to see me, and you may bodily, when you are in your bed, take me to yourself as your wedded husband, as thy dearest darling, and as thy sweet son, for I will be loved as a son should be loved by the mother and you will love me, daughter, as a good wife ought her husband. And therefore you may bodily take me in the arms of your soul and kiss my mouth, my head and my feet as sweetly as you wish.

—modernized by Jack Murnighan

from **The Thief's Journal**

JEAN GENET

Genet. As if more needs be said.
The *prince noir des lettres* stands
alone, monolithic, iconic, and
synonymous with the idiom he
invented. To include Genet in a
Naughty Bits anthology is like
inducting Babe Ruth into the
Hall of Fame: it confuses the categories of whole and part, for indeed
there is no fame if not Babe's, nothing naughty if not Genet.

Orphan, thief, vagabond, homosexual, prostitute: these, the oft-
mentioned components of Genet's life, get so overromanticized by people who share none of them that, when I catch myself doing it too, I end
up not even wanting to like Genet, not wanting to be another Sartre sitting in the comforts of the rue d'Ulm eulogizing Genet's black-nailed
alterity. Yet the beauty of Genet's prose demands no badge of authentic-
ity, no street scars or bruises, and certainly no saccharine sympathy. We
might try to read Genet as tourists, but we're all too likely to go native,
to feel, alongside our masterful guide, the hard heat of a man's body
pressed against us in a sordid cell, and to suspect that our own scrubbed
experiences blanch in comparison. Reading Genet, I see the safety of my
own life present before my eyes as a blank screen on which he projects
a dance of passionate shadows.

In the scene that follows, Genet sketches, in two paragraphs, the
vicious interlacing of shame, desire, and self-loathing that consume his
male lover as they fuck for the first time. Yet the sad fact is that Genet
seeks out these "queers who hate themselves," finding, perhaps, in their
pained concessions to desire a Dantesque punishment for his own
inescapable self-hatred.

●••

When I buggered this handsome twenty-two-year-old athlete for the first time, he pretended to be sleeping. With his face crushed against the white pillow, he let me slip it in, but when he was stuck, he could not keep from groaning delicately, the way one sighs.

Deeply threaded by my prick, he becomes something other than himself, something other than my lover. He is a strange part of me which still preserves a little of its own life. We form one body, but it has two heads and each of them is involved in experiencing its own pleasure. At the moment of coming, this excrescence of my body which was my lover loses all tenderness, clouds over. In the darkness, I sense his hardness and can feel that a veil of shadow is spreading over his face, which is contracted with pain and pleasure. I know that he knows he derives this pleasure from me, that he awaits it from my hand which is jerking him off, but I feel that the only thing that concerns him now is his coming. Though we are bound together by my prick, all our friendly relations are cut off. Our mouths, which could perhaps re-establish them are unable to meet. He wants only to be more deeply impaled. I cannot see him, for he has murmured "Put out the light," but I feel that he has become someone else, someone strange and remote. It is when I have made him come that I feel him hating me.

—*translated by Bernard Frechtman*

from The Faerie Queene

EDMUND SPENSER

At first glance this selection might not appear terribly promising. It is taken from the longest poem in the history of English literature —Edmund Spenser's sixteenth-century *The Faerie Queene*— which, while once considered among the greatest verse ever written, is now read in its entirety only by the real triathletes of literary studies. Granted, *The Faerie Queene* spans over eleven hundred pages, is written in a faux medieval English, and takes as its theme the allegorical presentation of the moral virtues— hardly Hollywood material. Yet to the attentive (and persevering) reader *The Faerie Queene* proves to be the lushest of semiotic mangroves, extending its endless roots through the swampland of poetic language to generate a complete, self-sustaining ecosystem.

In *The Faerie Queene,* one can find almost anything, including the erotic. The following passage, when read with a discerning eye, is extra-ordinarily sexy. It is part of Spenser's allegorical portrayal of Malbecco, the jealous husband, and Hellenore, his inconstant wife. Malbecco is so jealous that, contrary to medieval courtesy, he never admits errant knights to his castle, no matter what the weather. But the scene takes place during a maelstrom, and the three knights caught in it, Britomart, Paridell, and Satyrane, threaten to burn Malbecco's castle down unless he lets them in. He finally does, and they are taken to meet him at the dinner table. Hellenore soon joins them, and what transpires is a marvel of subtle symbolism in one of the most important and nuanced sign systems in the universe: flirting. So sit back and see how the pros do it.

She came in presence with true comely grace,
And kindly them saluted as became
Herself a gentle courteous dame.

They sat to meat, and Satyrane to Hellenore
Was her before, and Paridell beside.
. . . On her fair face Paridell fed his fill
And sent close messages of love at will.

And ever and anon, when noone was aware,
With speaking looks that secret message bore
He gazed at her, and told his hidden care
With all the art that he had learned of yore.
Nor was she ignorant of that seductive lore,
But in his eye his meaning wisely read,
And with the like answered him evermore:
She sent at him one fiery dart, whose head
Empoisoned was with secret lust and jealous dread.

He from that deadly throw made no defence,
But to the wound his weak heart opened wide.
The wicked engine through false influence
Passed through his eyes and secretly did glide
Into his heart, which it did sorely chide.
But nothing new to him was that same pain,
Nor pain at all; for he so oft had tried
The power thereof, and loved so oft in vain,
That thing of course he counted, love to entertain.

Thenceforth to her he sought to intimate
His inward grief, by means to him well known:
Now Bacchus' fruit out of the silver plate
He on the table dashed, and overthrowed
The cup of fruited liquor overflowed
And by the dancing bubbles did divine
And therein write to let his love be showed;

Which well she read out of the learned line:
A sacrament profane in mystery of wine.

And when so of his hand the pledge had passed
The guilty cup she fained to mistake,
And in her lap did spill her brimming glass
Showing desire her inward flames to slake.
By such close signs they a secret way did make
Unto their wills, and watched for due escape . . .

from Fanny Hill: Memoirs of a Woman of Pleasure

JOHN CLELAND

Fanny, as many of you know, is not what you want to name your daughter. In American slang, it means butt, in English, pussy (making the American fanny pack a rather laughable entity —"Ooh, honey, I really need a good fanny pack!"). That it can mean the backside on one bank of the Atlantic and the front side on the other is one of those vagaries of language that gives me no end of pleasure (like cleave meaning either "to cling or to separate," or egregious meaning "esteemed" until 1700 or so, and "horrible" thereafter). According to the *Oxford English Dictionary,* the first use of "fanny" as something other than a name was in 1879, as a reference to the female genitals. I think it was probably far earlier. The most famous book of English erotica, John Cleland's *Fanny Hill: Memoirs of a Woman of Pleasure,* was published in 1748, and my suspicion is that the book's name (after its fictional protagonist) was a sly joke on the mons veneris (though it is possible, of course, that the slang emerged as a result of the book, even if the OED has no evidence of this happening).

Whether its title is a play on the grassy knoll or not, the oft-banned *Fanny Hill* is a rollicking read. A quarter millennium has passed since its penning, and its language now seems both quaint and charming, but Cleland's masterpiece still makes one wonder: is erotica getting any better? The sizable chunk excerpted here will allow you to decide for yourselves.

● ●·

I was then lying at length upon that very couch . . . in an undress which was with all the art of negligence flowing loose . . . On the other hand, he stood at a little distance, that gave me a full view of a fine featur'd, shapely, healthy country lad, breathing the sweets of fresh blooming youth . . .

I bid him come towards me and give me his letter, at the same time throwing down, carelessly, a book I had in my hands. He colour'd, and came within reach of delivering me the letter, which he held out, aukwardly enough, for me to take, with his eyes riveted on my bosom . . .

I, smiling in his face, took the letter, and immediately catching gently hold of his shirt sleeve, drew him towards me . . . for surely his extreme bashfulness, and utter inexperience, call'd for, at least, all the advances to encourage him . . . carrying his hand to my breasts, I prest it tenderly to them . . . at this, the boy's eyes began to lighten with all the fires of inflam'd nature, and his cheeks flush'd with a deep scarlet . . . his looks, his emotion, sufficiently satisfy'd me that my train had taken, and that I had no disappointment to fear.

My lips, which I threw in his way, so as that he could not escape kissing them, fix'd, fired, and embolden'd him: and now, glancing my eyes towards that part of his dress which cover'd the essential object of enjoyment, I plainly discover'd the swell and commotion there; and as I was now too far advanc'd to stop in so fair a way . . . I stole my hand upon his thighs, down one of which I could both see and feel a stiff hard body, confin'd by his breeches, that my fingers could discover no end to. Curious then, and eager to unfold so alarming a mystery, playing . . . with his buttons, . . . those of his waistband and fore-flap flew open at a touch, when out It started . . . I saw, with wonder and surprise, what? not the plaything of a boy, not the weapon of a man, but a maypole of so enormous a standard, that had proportions been observ'd, it must have belong'd to a young giant . . . It stood an object of terror and delight.

But what was yet more surprising, the owner of this natural curiosity . . . was hitherto an absolute stranger, in practice at least, to the use of all that manhood he was so nobly stock'd with; and it now fell to my lot to stand this first trial of it, if I could resolve to run the risks of its disproportion to that tender part of me, which such an oversiz'd machine was very fit to lay in ruins.

. . . the young fellow, overheated with the present objects, and too high mettled to be longer curb'd in by that modesty and awe which had hitherto restrain'd him, ventur'd . . . under my petti-coats . . . and seizes, gently, the centerspot of his ardours. Oh then! the fiery touch of his fingers determines me, and my fears melting away before the growing intolerable heat, my thighs disclose of themselves, and yield all liberty to his hand: and now, a favourable movement giving my petticoats a toss, the avenue lay too fair, too open to be miss'd. He is now upon me; I had placed myself with a jet under him, as commodious and open as possible to his attempts, which were untoward enough, for his machine, meeting with no inlet, bore and batter'd stiffly against me in random pushes . . . till, burning with impatience from its irritating touches, I guided gen-tly, with my hand, this furious engine to where my young novice was now to be taught his first lesson of pleasure. Thus he nick'd, at length, the warm and insufficient orifice; but he was made to find no breach practicable, and mine, tho' so often enter'd, was still far from wide enough to take him easily in.

By my direction . . . a favourable motion from me met his timely thrust, by which the lips of it, strenuously dilated, gave away to his thus assisted impetuosity, so that we might both feel that he had gain'd a lodgment. Pursuing then his point, he soon, by violent, and, to me, most painful piercing thrusts, wedges himself at length so far in, as to be now tolerably secure of his entrance: here he stuck, and I now felt such a mixture of pleasure and pain, as there is no giving a definition of . . . The sense of pain however prevail-ing . . . made me cry out gently: "Oh! my dear you hurt me!" This was enough to check the tender respectful boy even in his mid-career . . .

But I was, myself, far from being pleas'd with his having too much regarded my tender exclaims . . . I first gave the youth a re-encouraging kiss . . . and soon replac'd myself in a posture to receive, at all risks, the renew'd invasion, which he did not delay an instant . . . Pain'd, however, as I was, with efforts of gaining a complete admission, which he was so regardful as to manage by gentle degrees, I took care not to complain . . . the soft strait passage gradually loosens, yields, and stretch'd to its utmost bearing, by the stiff, thick, indriven engine, . . . let him in about half way, when all the most nervous activity he now exerted, to further his penetration, gain'd him not an inch of his purpose: for, whilst he hesitated there, the crisis of pleasure overtook him, and the close compressure of the warm surrounding fold drew from him the extatic gush, even before mine was ready to meet it . . .

I expected then, but without wishing it, that he would draw, but was pleasantly disappointed: for he was not to be let off so . . . As soon, then, as he had made a short pause, waking, as it were, out of the trance of pleasure, he still kept his post . . . till his stiffness . . . who had not once unsheath'd, he proceeded afresh to cleave and open to himself an entire entry into me . . . made easy to him by the balsamic injection with which he had just plentifully moisten'd the whole internals of the passage . . . And now, with conspiring nature, and my industry, strong to aid him, he pierces, penetrates, and at length, winning his way inch by inch, gets entirely in, and finally a mighty thrust sheathes it up to the guard . . . Thus I lay gasping, panting under him, till his broken breathings, faltering accents, eyes twinkling with humid fires, lunges more furious, and an increased stiffness, gave me to hail the approaches of the second period: it came . . . and the sweet youth, overpower'd with the extasy, died away in my arms, melting in a flood that shot in genial warmth into the innermost recesses of my body; every conduit of which, dedicated to that pleasure, was on flow to mix with it.

from The Exeter Book

ANONYMOUS

They say that Typho, terrible and proud . . .
Conceived . . . the deadly Sphinx, a curse on
the men of Thebes.

—Hesiod

To the Egyptians we owe the wingless sphinx, the sphinx of the desert, the tomb, the sphinx of death; to the Greeks we owe the winged female sphinx, the carnivorous sphinx, the sphinx of the famous riddle. Both are primal, basic symbolic entities, appearing again and again in world literature. Both are mysterious but the Greek even more so. Her riddle (What walks on four legs, on three, and on two?) was the bane of the Thebans —for she devoured all who answered incorrectly—till Oedipus was able to name the answer: man. Four legs in infancy, two in maturity, and three in old age. In a certain sense, then, the riddle of the sphinx is the riddle of all riddles; it doesn't take a sage to realize that all our mysteries point back to ourselves, and we are, ultimately, the end of all our questioning.

Another riddle, then: what is it that humans want, seek, think, and talk about but pretend does not exist? Sex, of course. But if you put the question differently, the answer is not so clear: why is there repression? Many theories abound—none more persuasive than Freud's—yet no answer can quite account for the barbarous tyranny of the superego. What keeps us from sexual freedom? What prevents us from understanding the links between our outer bodies and inner selves? Why, though the forms have varied significantly from culture to culture, century to century, are virtually all human societies founded in and upon some regulation and repression of sexuality, some form of censorship and censoring of desire, some form of denial? The question is so huge it is difficult even to speculate.

And yet. Necessity is the mother of invention, they say; so is privation (the principle behind Raymond Queneau's Oulipo group). In any repressive regime expressions of freedom will find ways of making themselves known. Thus the various outcroppings of sexual literature during the glory days of Christianity (*Le roman de la rose,* Margery Kempe, penitentials, etc.). The key to all these forms, of course, is a superficial layer of orthodoxy, subtended by a racy second meaning. This exoteric-esoteric dynamic (outside-inside layers) is the structure of much of the history of writing on sexuality. Amid prohibition and repression, the poetic capacity to veil meaning finds no greater application than in the writing of sex.

And thus these riddles, composed in Anglo-Saxon in a still somewhat barbarous England (mid-eleventh century), have two answers each. The church-safe interpretations are given at the end; the other possibilities are left to you. Just don't tell the pope.

● ● ·

Riddle 44

A peculiar thing hangs by a man's thigh,
Free beneath the folds. The front is pierced.
It is stiff and hard, quite well-placed.
When a young man raises his cloak
Over his knee, he greets with the head
A familiar hole
That he has frequently filled before
Of the same length
As what dangles there.

Riddle 37

I saw a thing. The belly was behind,
Greatly swollen. Its master, a mighty man, attended to it,
And it had accomplished much
When that which filled it flew through its eye.
It does not continuously die when it has to give
What's within to another, for the treasure returns
To its belly, and the prize is raised.
It produces a son. It is the father of itself.

Riddle 80

I am a man's comrade, a warrior's companion,
Friend to my beloved, a king's retainer.
His blonde woman, an earl's daughter, though she be noble,
Sometimes lays her hand on me.
At times, I have in my stomach what grew in the grove.
Often I ride on a stately steed, at the edge of the grove.
Firm is my tongue. Often I give the poet a reward
When he has sung. Good is my thing
And I myself am sallow. Say what I am called.

Answers: a key, a bellows, a horn

—*translated by Andrew Cole*

from **"Elena"**

ANAÏS NIN

Anaïs Nin never wanted to be an erotica writer. Her diaries indicate quite clearly that she thought erotica was a male-dominated genre in which a woman's sense of the texture and nuance of sexuality could never be expressed. When a "collector" of erotic books commissioned first her friend Henry Miller and later Nin to write for a dollar a page, she was defiant: the "poetry" of sex would be lost if she was to write sex on command. Yet eventually she decided to try, and the results would later be published together under the title *Delta of Venus*. And though Nin felt that her diaries were her true explorations into sex as a woman, she eventually conceded that her voice also emerged in her erotica, despite the conventions of the genre.

Now, a half century later, the situation is rather different. Erotica is no longer a male stronghold, and much of the femininity that Nin was at pains to express has become the stuff of erotic cliché. Reading Nin is like reading a primer in the genre, though a very good one at that. Nin's project was to inject humanity into writings on sex; contemporary erotica should try to pick up where she left off.

● ●•

When she was about to come and could no longer defend herself against her pleasure, Leila stopped kissing her, leaving Bijou halfway on the peak of an excruciating sensation, half-crazed. Elena had stopped at the same moment.

Uncontrollable now, like some magnificent maniac, Bijou threw herself over Elena's body, parted her legs, placed herself between them, glued her sex to Elena's, and moved, moved with desperation. Like a man now, she thumped against Elena, to fell the two sexes meeting, soldering. Then as she felt her pleasure coming she stopped herself, to prolong it, fell backwards and opened her mouth to Leila's breast, to burning nipples that were seeking to be caressed.

Elena was now also in the frenzy before orgasm. She felt a hand under her, a hand she could rub against. She wanted to throw herself on this hand until it made her come, but she also wanted to prolong her pleasure. And she ceased moving. The hand pursued her. She stood up, and the hand again traveled towards her sex . . . Leila's pointed nails buried in the softest part of Elena's shoulder, between her breast and her underarm, hurting, a delicious pain, the tigress taking hold of her, mangling her. Elena's body so burning hot that she feared one more touch would set off the - explosion . . .

Elena and Leila together attacked Bijou, intent on drawing from her the ultimate sensation. Bijou was surrounded, enveloped, covered, licked, kissed, bitten, rolled again on the fur rug, tormented with a million hands and tongues. She was begging now to be satisfied, spread her legs, sought to satisfy herself by friction against the other's bodies. They would not let her. With tongues and fingers they pried into her, back and front, sometimes stopping to touch each other's tongue . . . Bijou raised herself to receive a kiss that would end her suspense . . . She almost cried to have it end.

Classicists and Fellini fans will already be familiar with Petronius's first-century chronicle of the decadence of Nero's Roman Empire, the great *Satyricon*. I was never a big fan of Fellini's film adaptation; it's dark and vulgar and lacks the mischief that a Pasolini would have given it. In fact, *The Satyricon* would have been a perfect Pasolini springboard: bawdy, sardonic, and class-conscious, recounting the adventures of Encolpius, a wayward thief, as he is passed from one set of probing, poking aristocratic fingers (both male and female) to another. Along the way our poor hero (whose name means "embraced") gets assaulted by a sex-crazed hag, continually loses his boy lover Giton to a variety of competitors, manages to offend Priapus (the god of erections) who then punishes him with chronic technical difficulties, and finally goes to be "cured" by another old hag who rams a leather dildo "rubbed with oil, ground pepper and crushed nettle seed" up his anus. There's a cure for impotence!

So as you can probably tell, *The Satyricon* makes a damn good read. The only problem is that four-fifths of the original text is lost, and often you'll be set up for a really naughty bit only for the narrative to break off and start again in a different place. Talk about a tease! But the parts that remain not only chronicle the indulgence and excess that marked the declining phase of the Roman Empire but create a literary precedent for my favorite satyric and ribald tales of the Middle Ages. Without Petronius, there might have been no Boccaccio, no Chaucer, no Rabelais. With this in mind, I chose a particularly Boccaccian excerpt that details a trick for getting what you want from a reluctant lover.

"When I went to Asia . . . I lodged in a house at Pergamus, which I found very much to my taste, not only on account of the neatness of the apartments, but still more for the great beauty of my host's son; and this was the method I devised that I might not be suspected by the father as a seducer. Whenever any mention happened to be made at table of the abuse of handsome boys, I affected such keen indignation, I protested with such an air of austere morality against the violence done to my ears by such obscene discourse, that the mother especially looked upon me as one of the seven sages. Already then I began to conduct the youth to the gymnasium; it was I who had the regulation of his studies, who acted as his monitor, and took care above all that no one should enter the house who might debauch him.

"It happened once that we lay down to sleep in the dining room (for it was a holiday; the school had closed early; and our prolonged festivity had made us too lazy to retire to our chamber). About midnight I perceived that my pupil was awake, so with a timid voice I murmured this prayer: 'O sovereign Venus, if I may steal a kiss from this boy, and he not know it, I will make him a present tomorrow of a pair of turtle doves.'

"Hearing the price offered for the favor, he began to snore, and I, approaching the pretended sleeper, stole two or three kisses. Content with this beginning, I rose early in the morning, brought him, as he expected, a choice pair of doves, and so acquitted myself of my vow.

"The next night, finding the same opportunity, I changed my petition: 'If I may pass my wanton hand over this boy,' I said, 'and he not perceive it, I will give him for his silence a pair of most pugnacious fighting cocks.' At this promise the lad moved toward me of his own accord, and was afraid, I verily believe, lest he should find me asleep. I quieted his uneasiness on that score, and moved my hands over his entire body with all the desire that drove me. Then when daylight came, I made him happy with what I had promised him.

"The third night, being again free to venture, I leaned over his wakeful ear and said: 'Immortal gods, if, while he is sleeping, I should be able to make the fullest and best love to him, in return I will tomorrow give the boy a fine horse, a cross between the Asturian and the Macedonian breed—so long as he never wakes.' Never had the lad slept more soundly. First I took his lovely chest fully in my hands, then I breathed kisses from his mouth, and finally all my longings were brought to one climax. Next morning he remained sitting in his room, expecting my present as usual. It is much easier, you know, to buy turtle doves and fighting cocks than an Asturian horse, and besides, I was afraid lest so considerable a present should render the motives of my liberality suspected. So after walking about for some hours, I returned to my lodgings, and gave the boy nothing but a kiss. He looked about him on all sides, then throwing his arms round my neck said, 'I say, master, where is the Asturian?'"

—*adapted by Jack Murnighan from a*
nineteenth-century translation

from The Name of the Rose

UMBERTO ECO

Not long ago, I got to meet Umberto Eco. I had waited a long time for the opportunity, but it proved to be a rather anticlimactic affair. Television cameras were descending on him, and, before he was mobbed, I only managed to get out one sentence: "Fredric Jameson says hello." His response: "Oh, really." I had wanted to say so much more, to blurt out, "Caro Umberto, we've lived parallel lives. I'm a semiotician and a medievalist too! And now we're both writers!" But there are two types of writers in the world: those that television cameramen mob and those that television cameramen shove out of the way.

Although I started reading Eco in college, it wasn't until graduate school that meeting him became a possibility. One day when I was in Jameson's office (he was my thesis adviser) discussing—what else—medieval literature and semiotics, he asked me "Do you know Eco?" I said, "Sure, I've read almost all his books." But Jameson meant did I know him personally, had we met. No, we hadn't. "Oh, but you must. We used to vacation together. When you go back to Italy, you should pay him a visit."

I did go back to Italy but was always too afraid to look Eco up. The conventional thought is that we all want to befriend or date or reproduce versions of ourselves and are drawn to them like Narcissus to his own image. I'm not so sure this is the case. Perhaps the truly similar allow us to see ourselves in a way that Narcissus was never able to—he didn't realize he was looking at his own image—whereas with the doppelgänger, you are aware of what it is—a mirroring of yourself, open to your view. I was afraid to meet Eco perhaps because I feared how I would see myself in his eyes. He would truly be a jury of my peers, and it wasn't clear that I'd live up. Was my Italian good enough, my Latin? Had I read enough books? In my everyday life, these things don't come up;

with Eco, I knew I would be in the audience of someone who had done the same things as I had in life and who had probably done them better. The doppelgänger scared off Narcissus.

I can take some comfort that, at last report, Eco wasn't editing a magazine like *Nerve*. Perhaps I've got him there. But he does write a damn good sex scene, as in the following excerpt from *The Name of the Rose*. I just hope he doesn't apply for my job.

●••

Saint Michael Archangel protect me, because for the edification of future readers and the flaying of my guilt I want now to tell how a young man can succumb to the snares of the Devil, that they may be known and evident, so anyone encountering them in the future may defeat them.

So, it was a woman. Or, rather, a girl. Having had until then (and since then, God be thanked) little intimacy with creatures of that sex, I cannot say what her age may have been. I know she was young, almost adolescent, perhaps she had past sixteen or eighteen springs, or perhaps twenty . . .

I knew her vernacular very slightly; it was different from the bit I had learned in Pisa, but I realized from her tone that she was saying sweet words to me, and she seemed to be saying something like "You are young, you are handsome . . ." It is rare for a novice who has spent his whole life in a monastery to hear declarations of his beauty; indeed we are regularly admonished that physical beauty is fleeting and must be considered base . . . The girl, in saying this, had extended her hand until the tips of her fingers grazed my cheek, then quite beardless. I felt a kind of delirium, but at that moment I was unable to sense any hint of sin in my heart.

Suddenly the girl appeared to me as the black but comely virgin of whom the Song of Songs speaks. She wore a threadbare little dress of rough cloth that opened in a fairly immodest fashion over her bosom, and around her neck was a necklace made of little colored stones, very commonplace, I believe.

Then the creature came still closer to me . . . and she raised her hand to stroke my face, and repeated the words I had already heard.

And while I did not know whether to flee from her or move even closer, while my head was throbbing as if the trumpets of Joshua were about to bring down the walls of Jericho, as I yearned and at once feared to touch her, she smiled with great joy, emitted the stifled moan of a pleased she-goat, and undid the strings that closed her dress over her bosom, slipped the dress from her body like a tunic, and stood before me as Eve must have appeared to Adam in the garden of Eden . . . whether what I felt was a snare of the Enemy or a gift of heaven, I was now powerless against the impulse that moved me . . . I was in her arms, and we fell together onto the bare floor of the kitchen, and whether on my own initiative or through her wiles, I found myself free of my novice's habit and we felt no shame at our bodies and cuncta erant bona . . .

Who was she, who was she who rose like the dawn, fair as the moon, clear as the sun, terrible as an army with banners?

—*translated by William Weaver*

from The Life I Lead

KEITH BANNER

It must have been in the seventh grade when I was given the dubious honor of taking a speech class with a man whose teeth were small billboards advertising the deleterious effects of coffee and cigarettes. His breath, not benevolent, was itself an argument for having him speak to large audiences—if only to prevent the face to face. Yet it was in his classroom that I learned early and important lessons not only in oratory and argumentation, but in the harsh truths of Realpolitik—and of love. There was one Asian American girl in the class, and my feelings toward her alternated between jealousy and infatuation. I wanted to be the best, most persuasive speaker in speech class, but I was not, and she most surely was. I still remember my reaction to her most triumphant speech —the topic eludes me, I believe it had something to do with the environment or global politics—and as she concluded, I blurted out: "But she's too persuasive! Her facts are all wrong, but you'll believe her anyway!" And the cess-mouthed teacher, though he remained silent, must have been thinking, Yes, son, and ain't it the way of the world.

Almost twenty years have passed, and these days I don't put much stock in what are called facts. My personal politics reflect this epistemological crisis and are based on trying not to tell anybody what I think they should believe (other than friends, lovers, and family, of course). The truth is, I think I'm still smarting from the lesson of that girl's speech, from watching someone twist what I held to be the truth into something that no one in their right mind would subscribe to.

The Greeks called verbal alacrity of this kind rhetoric, and they took the discipline very seriously. During the Renaissance, people were terrified of the power of language, and feared that a good speaker could, like Shakespeare's *Richard III*, get anybody to do anything he wanted. We think we are less gullible today—were it not for politics and advertising, it might even seem like rhetoric was a dying art. But of course, it's not, nor will it be as long as anybody cares about money or power or sex. Rhetoric and persuasion are manipulating us all the time, but we can't always see the classmate working us over without our being able to do anything about it.

That is one of the reasons why I was both fascinated and troubled by Keith Banner's recent novel, *The Life I Lead*. Its protagonist is a pedophile, yet I, like many readers, continually found myself sympathetic to him. To my continued horror, the understated rhetorical strength of Banner's portrayal kept sucking me in, making me feel the full weight of this man's humanity and his tragedy. Banner's pedophile didn't ask for his predilections, and if you keep reading you can't but feel for him. Banner captures the compassion behind the crime as he puts before your eyes the terrifying range of human possibility.

N.B.: The excerpt that follows is not an endorsement of sexual relations with minors. It is a fictionalization and is reprinted for the purpose of exploring a component of human sexuality.

/●●·

The boy is walking toward the locker room, and there I am close to the front. He has got a cut on his foot. I am seeing him bleed. I thought that I was a ghost then, brought back into real life by the smell of his blood. But then again I was always with him, even when he did not know it. I was following him, walking through walls to get to him.

Me in church clothes standing there. He looks up at me. I stare down at his foot.

I say, "Oh my gosh. You've cut yourself, Bud. Oh no." I was slowing down my voice to prove to him that he meant something to me.

"I know," he says, slow-voiced too.

"What happened?" I say, people screaming and splashing in the background.

He looks at me and then gets it, that I really want to know. Nobody else wants to but me. So he takes me over to this broken bottle in the grass by the fence, on the other side of the pool.

"That's what did it," he says, all cute and serious.

Little thing just walking in the grass because the cement part was too hot and his feet were burning off. So he cut his foot on that glass bottle there, shining in the sun. Little drops of blood on the concrete.

"I'm going to take you and get that fixed up, Bud."

Even though he seemed scared by me, the boy smiled and allowed me to lift him up. For all anybody knew at the pool, I was his dad. First I stop off in the locker room with him and put toilet paper on his foot. The blood glows through the white toilet paper. I carry him out to the car. This is the justice of stopping myself, for when I stop myself I can give up and get what I want: him, with a cut foot, in the car with me. This is why I tell myself to stop, so I can give in eventually.

The car starts, like it knows if it doesn't I might crack wide open, my blood turning automatically into fire.

I go to the Super X drugstore and buy peroxide and cotton and bandages. I smile at the old guy cashier with a beard. I think he thinks of me as a sweet man buying clean things. Then there is the lady at the Motel 6, looking at me like I am a dope pusher or a sex fiend. She has a baseball cap on, spider legs for eyelashes. She takes my credit card, saying something about luggage. Any luggage? I don't know what I say in return. But I leave with a key.

The boy waits in the car while I do all this, then I drive back to where the room is and then I carry him into the motel room in secret.

I take him into the green and white bathroom first off. Begin to wash his feet, especially the cut one. I wash the cut one very carefully. I wash the cut and his toes with soapy water in the white light, him standing on the sink, dipping his toes toward me. There we are in the mirror, it is not weird at all.

This is a painting of us in a museum. I think he likes what I am doing very much, in fact. I am just careful enough to let him like it. I realize too the Jesus aspect in this. I work the soap into a lather. The boy is quiet. Quieter than a cloud or than clothes-pins or a car dashboard in winter.

"Yeah," I keep saying. "Oh yeah. We'll get you fixed up."

The peroxide, after I pour a little on, bubbles around his cut, bubbles and bubbles. I am so hard I feel like I could cut myself off from it and it would land soft on a pillow, its own dreamy thing. I cannot let him touch it.

I call him honey several times. Once inside the motel room, I start calling him that, instead of Bud. It just comes out natural. Honey this and honey that. Out in the bedroom, the TV happens to be on. Something on HBO with Sylvester Stallone. I keep the room dark, but it is not hellish, no.

I bandage his cut, and he is still in his swim trunks. One last time I look at him in the mirror after I dry off his feet. His face is serene, his black hair still a little damp, his skin glowing half red and half brown from being out in the sun.

Me and him walk out, and we sit together on the edge of the bed.

"My name is Dave," I whisper, as we watch people get shot.

"Nathan," he says.

"Nathan," I say. "Now that is a name."

I am not touching him. At all. Nathan is the sweetest name. It's almost the same when spelled backwards, and this goes through my head several times: "Nathan" and "Nahtan." It is so easy just sitting in the AC, hanging out with him, quiet, the movie going, me re-spelling his name until it spells my name in a way, like "Nathan" spelled backwards is my name spelled forwards. We sit there and watch explosions. I think of how me and Troy used to sit and watch TV all the time.

"What did you buy with the ten?" I say.

"I got an Uzi water gun," he says, not taking his eyes away from the screen.

"Wow," I say, laughing a little and crying. "You shoot people with that?"

"Just water," he says.

"How's your foot, honey?" I ask.

"Fine," he tells me. He keeps it propped up kind of cute.

The credits are rolling, right after a big building blows up. Standing, I am crying but smiling. The crying scares him a little. Adults only cry on TV in his world. It reminds him, I bet, how serious situations like this totally are. But again, "serious" isn't something this is about. This is supposed to be fun, supposed to be about him and me getting to know each other, the end.

I say, standing there in front of him, "Honey, I want you to stand up on the bed like a big boy."

Seeing him, his ribs glowing through his skin, sitting there like he is in a library with no lights on, so well behaved, his foot Band-Aided, it is perfect. Even though I cry silent like that, my voice is still low-pitched. I think I was pretending to be a veteran baseball player. I don't know. But then as soon as I ask, he moves. Just like my puppet. He stands up on the bed.

"Yes," I say, like an exhale of breath that I had kept in all day.

The room goes all dark as I have reached backward and shut the TV down. I stand back and ask him nice if he would not mind pulling down his swim trunks.

Nathan says, "Why?" His face does not change. He just wants a straight answer on that.

This sends something through me. My heart shrinks up into a very small stone. I look at him in the dark, his face glowing, like cobwebs lit by a flashlight.

"I don't know," I say. And I didn't know why, I did not, or I did but it could not at that time be put into real words. So I look at Nathan's face, and he looks at mine. My crying stops. He has a small nose and thick eyebrows and he seems not to like being here anymore.

I laugh, to take away from the seriousness.

"Don't do it," I say.

I start laughing harder and harder. Get a hold of yourself, Dave. But I feel like the voice in my head is only joking with me and that kind of joking hurts me, like I am tricking myself over and over, endless: torturing myself with my own voice. Can you keep mocking yourself this way and stay sane?

"Don't you dare do it," I say.

What did my laughing do to him? I don't know. I guess it scared him, I guess it made him think of how laughing and crying can often go together in a crazy world. I remember how Troy used to not cry in front of me out in the garage, but sort of hum, on his knees, like he was praying to the god of bees, and the humming turned gut-sounding after a while, like the sound of his voice was actually the sound of the blood going through his veins.

I pick Nathan up then and hold him up like a little baby, my arms sort of hurting.

"You," I say, laughing more.

Then I put him down on his feet on the floor. He looks up at me.

"I wanna go," he says.

"Well, I don't blame you for that," I say. "Not at all, honey."

I go over and smooth the bedspread from where he had been standing up on it. Smooth it with both my hands, closing my eyes. The material is like satin, but has many snags from hangnails. He goes and turns the TV back on, sits down on the other side of the bed. I open my eyes then and stop smoothing out the spread, looking at the silhouette of Nathan's face in the TV light. I think of what is inside that head, and how I am some man in the dark of his mind walking around smoothing out his footprints behind him. It is like he'll never know where he has been because I am doing that.

"Well, honey, you just wanna stay and watch some TV?"

I laugh then. Softer. Sit down beside him. He looks up at me, his lips parting slowly.

"No," he says, but also it is like he is trying to be nice, 'cause he does not move. I slowly take his hand in mine. We hold hands for a short while, watching HBO.

Soon after that, I take him out of the room. On the way back, we are both very quiet. Nathan just sits next to me, and then this is when I have the realization that I can do whatever I want to this little kid. Anything I please. It scares me deep down knowing how much power I could have, scares me where you have the fear of rats and snakes and high places and drowning in deepest water.

from **Breakfast of Champions**

KURT VONNEGUT

There is little doubt that the names for genitalia leave something to be desired. Penises are better off than vaginas in this department; breasts and testicles do quite well, but the poor clitoris really suffers. Some friends and I, aware of these lexical shortcomings, set about inventing our own terminology for the most anatomical of anatomical parts, hoping to lend some sanity to the madness. Penises should, we concluded, be divided according to whether or not they are erect. The erect penis, so in need of a better moniker than Woody or Hard-On, much less Boner, we opted to call a Slinder—and we encourage you to draw out the "L" sound for maximum effect. The sad, floppy, wrinkly, shell-less sea creature of a thing that is the unerect penis we refer to simply as a Zirt. And we remind you that, like books to their covers, you can't judge a man by his Zirt.

The vagina, meanwhile, has made a great cultural comeback, though its appertaining terminology has been slower to evolve. Having concluded that the stretching, resilient, emotive, involuted, self-dewing masterpiece needed more joyous names than those beginning with T, C or P, we agreed unanimously on *Voorheeee!* (always in italics, always with the exclamation point) as the official name, which can be shortened to "my *V*" for practicality. We realize that this abbreviation could lead the uninitiated to believe we were adopting the traditional medical term referred to at the beginning of this paragraph, but no endeavor as ambitious as ours is free of all risk.

Balls are fine, though we prefer to call them Motchies, as in "Hey, no teeth on the Motchies!" whereas breasts can now be referred to either with the Middle English "paps" or our new-and-improved "Sha-Shas." The anus, long neglected, so-called hole of either bung or ass, is now the Feep, a name we hope will not remain obscured in darkness. Finally, for that great idiomatic oversight, the clitoris, so mysterious to most men (and some women) that it has barely evoked any nonclinical sobriquets (the ludicrous "love button" and the most ironic "little man in the boat" notwithstanding), we offer Stalgon the Imperial or the Twee, depending on your mood. We sincerely hope these new designations serve all your conversational and interrogative needs.

N.B.: The excerpt that follows, from Kurt Vonnegut's classic *Breakfast of Champions*, concerns itself with female anatomy and its popular slang. We provide it as a point of cultural reference.

A wide-open beaver was a photograph of a woman not wearing underpants, and with her legs far apart, so that the mouth of her vagina could be seen. The expression was first used by news photographers, who often got to see up women's skirts at accidents and sporting events and from underneath fire escapes and so on. They needed a code word to yell to other newsmen and friendly policemen and firemen and so on, to let them know what could be seen, in case they wanted to see it. The word was this: "Beaver!"

A beaver was actually a large rodent. It loved water, so it built dams. It looked like this: The sort of beaver which excited news photographers so much looked like this:

This was where babies came from.

from **The Kama Sutra**

VATSYAYANA

The *Kama Sutra* is the greatest
sex manual ever written. Com-
piled in the fourth century from
texts dating back to 800 B.C.,
its depth and breadth are
staggering. With chapters
on, among other things, scratching, biting, squeezing, caressing, screwing, fellating, relaxing, seducing, meeting your wife, meeting other men's
wives, pandering, prostituting, breaking up, making up, making better,
and making bigger, it covers all the sexual bases, plus a few you might
not have known about—for example, can you name the eight different
types of marks that can be left with fingernails?

The diversity of sexual practices in the *Kama Sutra* reflects the
great number of Indian subcultures from which its compiler drew his
information. In some regions cunnilingus and fellatio are common, in
others forbidden. In some places men dress as women and work as
prostitutes; in other places there aren't prostitutes at all. Sodomy tends
only to take place in the south, whereas in the north the women don't
even like to kiss. Finally, "in country villages" and in Koshala (a matriar-
chal society), women like violent sex and dildos and often hide a multi-
tude of young men in their quarters to "satiate [their] desires, either one
by one, or as a group." Is that what they mean by the wisdom of the
ancients?

Among my favorite sections is the one on penis enlargement. The
surest technique seems to be that of taking the hairs of the shuka insect,
mixing them with oil, and then rubbing them on the penis for ten consecutive nights. When the penis swells, its owner should sleep face
downward on a wooden bed with a hole to let the perturbed member
hang through. Various cooling mixtures are then employed to ease the
accompanying pain, and once the man feels okay again the swelling
endures for life. Sounds good, right? But before you run off to depilate

your backyard shukas, take note: the *Kama Sutra* advises that all techniques for increasing penis size be learned from an expert.

The excerpt that follows is taken from the section on the stimulation of erotic desire. It divides all potential players into six categories, depending on the size of their equipment. What's marked is the attention given to the pleasure of the woman as well as the man—a concern we don't expect to find in centuries prior to our own. But the *Kama Sutra* is just as much for her as for him, and even cites a source as saying that a woman needs to have an orgasm in order to be impregnated. I think the continued propagation of the species during the Victorian period in England disproves the theory, but hey, you can't knock its intention.

●••

Man is divided into three classes, viz. the hare man, the bull man, and the horse man, according to the size of his lingam [penis]. Woman also, according to the depth of her yoni [vagina], is either a female deer, a mare, or a female elephant. There are thus three equal unions between persons of corresponding dimensions, and there are six unequal unions, when the dimensions do not correspond, or nine in all . . .

There are also nine kinds of union according to the force of passion or carnal desire, as follows: A man is called a man of small passion whose desire at the time of sexual union is not great, whose semen is scanty, and who cannot bear the warm embraces of the female. Those who differ from this temperament are called men of middling passion, while those of intense passion are full of desire. In the same way, women are supposed to have the three degrees of feeling as specified above. Lastly, according to time there are three kinds of men and women, the short-timed, the moderate-timed, and the long-timed; and of these, as in the previous statements, there are nine kinds of union.

But on this last head there is a difference of opinion about the female, which should be stated. Auddalika says, "Females do not emit as males do. The males simply remove their desire, while the females, from their consciousness of desire, feel a certain kind of pleasure, which gives them satisfaction, but it is impossible for them to tell you what kind of pleasure they feel. The fact from which this becomes evident is, that males, when engaged in coition, cease of themselves after emission, and are satisfied, but it is not so with females."

This opinion is however objected to on the grounds that, if a male be a long-timed, the female loves him the more, but if he be short-timed, she is dissatisfied with him. And this circumstance, some say, would prove that the female emits also.

But this opinion does not hold good, for if it takes a long time to allay a woman's desire, and during this time she is enjoying great pleasure, it is quite natural then that she should wish for its continuation. And on this subject there is a verse as follows: "By union with men the lust, desire, or passion of women is satisfied, and the pleasure derived from the consciousness of it is called their satisfaction."

The followers of Babhravya, however, say that the semen of women continues to fall from the beginning of the sexual union to its end, and it is right that it should be so, for if they had no semen there would be no embryo.

To this there is an objection. In the beginning of coition the passion of the woman is middling, and she cannot bear the vigorous thrusts of her lover, but by degrees her passion increases until she ceases to think about her body, and then finally she wishes to stop from further coition.

This objection, however, does not hold good, for even in ordinary things that revolve with great force, such as a potter's wheel, or a top, we find that the motion at first is slow, but by degrees it becomes very rapid. In the same way the passion of the woman having gradually increased, she has a desire to discontinue coition, when all the semen has fallen away. And there is a verse with regard to this as follows: "The fall of the semen of the man takes place only at the end of coition, while the semen of the woman falls continually, and after the semen of both has all fallen away then they wish for the discontinuance of coition."

Lastly, Vatsyayana is of opinion that the semen of the female falls in the same way as that of the male.

—translated by Sir Richard F. Burton

from **Fear of Flying**

ERICA JONG

When *Fear of Flying* first came
out in the early '70s, it articulated
a growing sense among women
that the popular conception of
female sexuality—demure, delicate, deferential—didn't cover
all the bases. Women were
recognizing and embracing their own sexual power as never before, and
Jong's best-seller gave a voice to the transformation.

A generation later, *Fear of Flying* would continue to inspire women at
certain stages of their sexual development; it also, from my own experience, helped them communicate to the boys around them just what was
going on. I was given a copy in the early weeks of a relationship in my
sophomore year of college; little did I know at the time that she intended
it to be a textbook, and I was a remedial student. Its famous concept—
the zipless fuck—is a metaphor for sex without context, without com-
plication, between preferably unacquainted individuals who share no
language but touch, get to the business, and then get out of each other's
lives. No fuss, no muss. But my girlfriend of the time wasn't trying to get
me to bonk her and get lost; she saw the greater implication in the book
that, at times, sex should be able to be a purely in-body experience (with
all the psychology that implies), devoid of any intellectualizing or prob-
lematizing. She didn't want to separate the emotions out of our coupling;
she just wanted me to shut up and get to it.

The reason the zipless fuck is so appealing, of course, is that most
fucks are pretty damn zip-full. Very few women I know—or men even—
would want anonymous sex all the time. The foibles and bumbling
around zippers and socks and condoms and all their metaphorical equiv-
alents in the psyche are what make sex more than just a release of fluids.
Sex can make us weak, and weakness can make us beautiful. But of all
good things we can sometimes get enough—even of care and compas-

sion. The zipless fuck was a call for un-PC sex—but un-PC sex dictated on a woman's terms, not in the conventional way men had been having it for millennia.

So what I learned most from my girlfriend of sophomore year was how sexy an assertive woman could be. From that point on I realized that assertiveness and sexual self-awareness normally went hand in hand. I will never forget the first time we went to my dorm room. I had "decorated" it with a chaos of "found art" oddities of every shape and form; upon opening the door, her first and only words were, "I could never, ever, have an orgasm here." *Fear of Flying* had left its mark: dome feminism, 1; Jack décor, 0.

●••

A grimy European train compartment (Second Class) . . . In the window seat a pretty young widow in a heavy black veil and tight black dress which reveals her voluptuous figure. She is sweating profusely . . . The train screeches to a halt in a town called (perhaps) Corleone. A tall languid-looking soldier, unshaven, but with a beautiful mop of hair, a cleft chin and somewhat devilish, lazy eyes enters the compartment . . . He is sweaty and disheveled but basically a gorgeous hunk of flesh, only slightly rancid from the heat. The train screeches out of the station.

Then we become aware of the bouncing of the train and the rhythmic way the soldier's thighs are rubbing against the thighs of the widow . . . He is watching the large gold cross between the widow's breasts swing back and forth in her deep cleavage. Bump. Pause. Bump. It hits one moist breast and then the other. It seems to hesitate in between as if paralyzed between two repelling magnets. He is hypnotized. She stares out the window, looking at each olive tree as if she had never seen olive trees before . . . He rests his left hand on the seat between his thigh and hers and begins to wind rubber fingers around and under the soft flesh of her thighs. She continues staring at each olive tree as if she were God and had just made them and were wondering what to call them . . .

Then the fingers are sliding between her thighs and they are parting her thighs, and they are moving upward into the fleshy gap between her heavy black stockings and her garters and they are sliding up under her garters into the damp unpantied place between her legs.

The train enters a galleria, or tunnel, and in the semi-darkness the symbolism is consummated. There is the soldier's boot in the air and the dark walls of the tunnel and the hypnotic rocking of the train and the long high whistle as it finally emerges.

Wordlessly, she gets off at a town called, perhaps, Bivona.

from **The Art of Love**

OVID

Knowing my penchant for long-
deceased authors and moldering
books, I am occasionally asked
who I would like to have been
and what I would most like to
have written. Few authors of
truly great works lived envi-
able lives: Who would want to be Milton, the supremely cantankerous
self-proclaimed "church of one," or the miasmic Plotinus, rotting publicly
from the inside out, or, even worse, to be burned at the stake, like Julian
of Norwich when she dared suggest that God's love was universal? It's a
commonplace that authors live meager and brutish lives, so much so that
one wonders if it's worth it to be a Dostoevsky in order to write a
Brothers K.

But then there is that lucky group of writers whose lives were as
extraordinary as their work. Rimbaud set poetry on its heels before he
was twenty, then got bored and started running guns in North Africa.
Marlowe was the jewel of the pre-Shakespearean stage and his generation's preeminent rake and ladies' man. The earl of Rochester was so
charming and handsome that for more than a century after his death
popular drama in England was still modeling characters after him.

It is not, however, from among these fortunates that I would pick my
dream life. No, without a moment's hesitation, I would choose to be
Ovid, the Roman poet born forty years before Christ, author of, among
other works, the *Metamorphoses* and the *Ars amatoria* (The Art of
Love). These two texts bespeak the glory of both the literary and personal halves of Ovid's life, set in perfect harmony. The former work is
one of the great acts of imagination in the history of literature and has
been a deserved best-seller for two millennia. The latter is a raucous love
manual from someone who clearly knew women, loved women and
spent his life figuring out how to snare them. Though predominantly for

men, *The Art of Love* concludes with a section for the ladies, on how to behave when caught. Elsewhere Ovid gives makeup tips and rules of conduct, but here he advises on the vagaries of bedroom performance in what reads like a head-on challenge to Cynthia Heimel.

●••

We must come to the heart of the matter, so that my weary keel reaches the haven at last . . . In our last lesson we deal with matters peculiarly secret; Venus reminds us that here lies her most intimate care. What a girl ought to know is herself, adapting her method, taking advantage of the methods nature has equipped her to use. Lie on your back if your face and all your features are pretty; if your posterior is cute, better be seen from behind. Milanion used to bear Atalanta's legs on his shoulders; if you have beautiful legs, let them be lifted like hers. Little girls do all right if they sit on top, riding horseback; Hector's Andromache knew she could not do this: too tall! Press the couch with your knees and bend your neck backward a little if your view, full-length, seems what a lover should crave. If the breasts and the thighs are youthful and lovely to look at, let the man stand and the girl lie on a slant on the bed. Let your hair come down, in the Laodamian fashion. If your belly is lined, better be seen from behind. There are a thousand ways: a simple one, never too tiring, is to lie on your back, turning a bit to the right. My muse can give you the truth, more truth than Apollo or Ammon; take it from me, what I know took many lessons to learn.

Let the woman feel the act of love to her marrow, let the performance bring equal delight to the two. Coax and flatter and tease, with inarticulate murmurs, even with sexual words, in the excitement of play, and if nature, alas, denies you the final sensation cry out as if you had come, do your best to pretend. Really I pity the girl whose place, let us say, cannot give her pleasure it gives to the man, pleasure she ought to enjoy. So, if you have to pretend, be sure the pretense is effective, do your best to convince, prove it by rolling your eyes, prove by your motions, your moans, your sighs, what a pleasure it gives you.

So our sport has an end: our swans are tired of their harness. Time for their labors to rest, time to step down from our car. As the young men did, now let the girls, my disciples, write on the votive spoil, "Ovid showed us the way."

—*translated by Rolfe Humphries*

from The Romance of the Rose

JEAN DE MEUN

The Romance of the Rose was the most popular literary work of the 1200s. Reading this excerpt, I think you'll understand why. It was started in the first half of the century by a relatively conservative Frenchman, Guillaume de Lorris, who died having written only four thousand lines. Forty years later, the poem was taken up again by a saucy wisecrack, Jean de Meun, who employed Lorris' Christian allegorical frame and added eighteen thousand more lines to sneak in some seriously scandalous content. The crazy thing is: he got away with it. A hundred years later, when Christine de Pisan, France's first professional woman writer, started a letter campaign to complain about the *Romance*'s explicit discussions of male genitalia, she was attacked by the top religious figures of the century. Somehow the *Romance* was accepted, and copies of it spread around Europe, influencing the greatest writers of the day (Chaucer translated it, Dante adapted it, and everybody stole from it).

The passage that follows is from the end, when the main character, the Good Lover, finally gets the chance to pluck the allegorical rose he's been after for the whole book. Now a case might be made that the *Romance*'s rose is no ordinary rose, and that the Lover's staff and sack are not just for walking and carrying, but if you, with your lascivious leanings, detect any sexual innuendo in the following scene (gasp!), I need only remind you that it is meant to represent the heart of a good Christian embracing the true teaching of the Church. And naughty you if you think otherwise!

After that, I made my way like a loyal lover
Toward the beautiful aperture,
The goal of all my pilgrimage.

With all my effort, I brought with me
A scrip and a staff, so stiff and sturdy...
Quite well-made, of supple skin without a seam.
Nor was it empty. Nature, who gave it to me,
Had placed with great care two hammers therein . . .

I tell you truly, I love my scrip and hammers
Better even than my lute and harp;
I was honored that Nature gave me such fine ones,
And learned to use them wise and well.
Nature also gave me my staff
And I learned to polish it before I could even read . . .
It makes me happy to gaze on it, and, feeling so,
I thank Nature for her present.
It has comforted me in many places; I always carry it,
And it always serves me well.
Do you know what I do?
When I am on a journey
And happen upon a hidden place,
I thrust my staff into dark ditches,
Or test the depth of deep fords.
Some I find so deep,
Or with banks so far apart,
That it would be less trouble to swim two miles
In the sea . . .

Now let us leave such wide roads
To those who like to travel them,
And let those of us who prefer footpaths to cart roads
Follow those more joyously . . .

I had a great desire to touch the relics,
And with my staff unsheathed,
I, a happy, vigorous lad,
Knelt between the two pillars,
For I had great desire to adore
With devout and pious heart,
The beautiful statue, so worthy of devotion . . .

I lifted the curtain a bit
That covered the relics,
Wishing to approach the statuary
That I knew was close to the relics.
I wanted to kiss it devoutly,
And to push within its sheath,
And place myself there with full assurance;
Entering with my staff with the sack hanging behind.
I thought I'd be able to poke in easily,
But when I tried, it popped back out.
I tried again, but to no avail. It always popped back.
There was no way I could get it in,
For, I soon discovered, there was an inner barrier,
That I felt but could not see . . .

I had to attack it vigorously . . .
But finally found a narrow passage
That I might enter. With my staff,
I battered the barrier, hoping to make my way in,
But I couldn't even get half way.
I was frustrated that I could make no headway,
Nor find a way to go any further . . .
It was clear I was the first to try to pass,
It was not so well known as yet to collect tolls from other travelers.
I don't know if anyone else has enjoyed it as much since,
But for me I loved it so much I could scarcely believe it . . .

At last, I spurted a little seed on the bud, having
Touched it to play with the petals . . .
All the seed got so mixed together,
And that's how I made the tender rosebush widen.

—*translated by Jack Murnighan*

from Autumn of the Patriarch

GABRIEL GARCÍA MÁRQUEZ

Gabriel García Márquez is primarily known, in this country at least, for his monumental *One Hundred Years of Solitude* (Bill Clinton's favorite book), yet I believe his subsequent work, *El Otono del Patriarca (The Autumn of the Patriarch)*, to be an even finer literary achievement. For a long time I read nothing but *Autumn;* it seemed so complete, so lyrical and poignant, so exquisitely sad and oceanic that I would finish and, instead of starting something new, I'd just pick it up and read it again.

My respect for him is so great, it halts my pen. I feel like I'm one of those proverbial monkeys given typewriters and eternity, who looks up from his own page of garble and sees Hamlet emerging from his neighbor's keys. Both *One Hundred Years of Solitude* and *Autumn of the Patriarch* are so far beyond what virtually any other contemporary writer has written you wonder if he didn't find some manuscripts in a crashed UFO. Reading García Márquez at his finest gives you the impression that there is nothing more important in this god-lost world than writing, but he's so good he makes you never want to write again yourself.

But alas, we beat on. For even the master himself has not been himself in the last twenty-five years. No surprise, perhaps, for the reaction to the 1974 release of *Autumn* was probably a major disappointment to the writer at the height of his powers. Though at least as ambitious, the book was nowhere near as well received as *One Hundred Years* (released seven years prior). *Autumn* is a masterpiece, but it's a difficult read, and the three-page sentences and fifty-page paragraphs try the patience of many readers. Consequently even today it lingers in partial recognition.

The following passage, however, is not only wonderfully sexy and evocative, but demonstrates in miniature the snowfall rhythm and complexity of the novel, which, rereading it now, tempts me again never to read anything else.

●•·

I couldn't conceive of the world without the man who made me happy at the age of twelve as no other man was ever to do again since those afternoons when after school he would be lying in wait for the girls in blue uniforms with sailors' collars, he would call to us, entice us with candy, they all ran off frightened, all except me, when no one was watching I tried to reach the candy and he grabbed me by the wrists with a gentle tiger's claw and lifted me painlessly up into the air with such care that not a pleat in my dress was wrinkled and he laid me down on the urine-scented hay, he was more frightened than I, you could see his heart beating under his jacket, he was pale, his eyes were full of tears, he touched me in silence with a tenderness I never found again, he made my little buds stand out on my breasts, he put his fingers underneath the edge of my panties, he smelled his fingers, he told me, it's your smell, I didn't need the candy any more to climb through the stable skylight to find him waiting for me with his bag of things to eat, he used bread to soak up my first adolescent sauce, he would put things there before eating them, he gave them to me to eat, he put asparagus stalks into me to eat them marinated with the brine of my inner humors, delicious, he told me, you taste like a port . . . he left me to boil in the incandescent fleeting mallow sunsets of our love with no future telling me that not even he himself knew who he was. . . .

—*translated by Gregory Rabassa,*
modified by Jack Murnighan

from **"Libido"**

RUPERT BROOKE

I always feel a certain amount of guilt and queasiness writing about people who died early deaths, especially if, at the time I'm putting pen to paper, I'm already older than they were ever to be. Stranger still if they were authors or artists, and strangest of all if they accomplished in their abbreviated lives more than I am likely to achieve in mine, even if I live to 100.

Rupert Brooke was one such brief, bright flame. His one score and eight-year life was as though scripted for a BBC biography: born in England in 1887, with considerable erudition and Galahad good looks, he entered Cambridge in 1913, wrote a few dozen exquisite poems, joined the Royal Navy to go off to the Great War in 1914 and died in the Aegean seven months later. The artist/soldier is a kind of hero that has not been present in cultures on either side of the Atlantic in decades, but World War I vaunted and cut down many. Brooke, Wilfred Owen, Isaac Rosenberg, Alan Seeger: all dead, all in their prime.

And though Brooke remains famous primarily for his war poems, he wrote a number of love poems as well. The sonnet "Libido" is his most elegant; its theme is a burning bed—inspired midnight visit to a sleeping paramour. There is little more beautiful than the image of a milky Adonis leaving his tangled sheets to slip into his lady's bedroom and wake her with a kiss, until we recall Brooke's fate, and know that only the embracing arms of war awaited him on his final night.

●••

How should I know? The enormous wheels of will
Drove me cold-eyed on tired and sleepless feet.
Night was void arms and you a phantom still,
And day your far light swaying down the street.
As never fool for love, I starved for you;
My throat was dry and my eyes hot to see.
Your mouth so lying was most heaven in view,
And your remembered smell most agony.

Love wakens love! I felt your hot wrist shiver
And suddenly the mad victory I planned
Flashed real, in your burning bending head . . .
My conqueror's blood was cool as a deep river
In shadow; and my heart beneath your hand
Quieter than a dead man on a bed.

Good advice is hard to come by. And yet, every blue moon or so in my lusty wanderings among the deepest darkest library stacks, I stumble upon a poem or snippet from the classics that can be readily applied to life's tough situations. In various parts of the book, I have argued that Rabelais gives good advice for keeping your partner faithful, that flirting lessons can be learned from Spenser's *The Faerie Queene,* that Goethe shows you how to balance ambition and eros, and that Andrew Marvell's "To His Coy Mistress" was a more convincing version of "Let's Get It On" than even Marvin Gaye's. Who's to say that High Art and Self-Help have to be at opposite ends of the shelf?

This excerpt has it both ways. Taken from one of the crown jewels of the Arabic tradition, the incomparable *Arabian Nights,* it provides a useful stratagem for convincing your lover to let you take the road less traveled. Few people read Scheherazade's tale in its entirety; most often because it comes in expurgated editions, bowdlerized by its translators and editors. Not so in Sir Richard Burton's original, nineteenth-century rendition, which is as licentious and brilliant as Burton himself. The great British ambassador, who spent much of his life sampling the pleasures, peculiarities, and perversions of Arabic cultures, was a superman if there ever was one. He spoke more than twenty languages, was among the first English translators of the *Kama Sutra, The Arabian Nights,* and countless other Eastern classics, and he lived a life of highest adventure and eroticism. Like the anthropologist Tobias Schneebaum, Burton made no separation between sexual and cultural exploration. As a result, he probably achieved as great a synthesis of learning and loving as anyone in history. I modified his translation a bit to remove some obscurities and infelicities, but what remains is a rhetoric for encouraging what's sometimes called The Catholic Girl's Compromise. Who would have guessed at the incidental benefits of population control?

●●·

"My soul thy sacrifice! I choose thee out
Who are not menstrous or oviparous:
Should I with women mell, I'd beget
Brats till the wide world grew straight for us.
"She respondeth (sore hurt in sense most acute
For she had proffered what did not besuit):
"Unless thou stroke as man should swive his dear,
Blame me not when horns on thy brow appear.
Thy wand seems waxen, to a limpness grown,
And more I palm it, softer grows the clown!"
And I to her: "If thy coynte I do reject
There might be elsewhere we could connect."
And yet, she showed again her tender coynte,
And I was forced to cry: "I will not roger thee!"
She drew back saying, "From the faith
He turns, who's turned by Heaven's decree!
And front-wise futters, both night and day,
Most times in ceaseless persistency."
Then swung she the round and shining rump
Like silvern lump she showed me.
I cried: "Well done, O mistress mine!
No more am I in pain for thee!
O thou of all that Allah oped
Showest me fairest victory!"

—*translated by Sir Richard Burton*

from An Unseemly Man

LARRY FLYNT WITH KENNETH ROSS

It takes a bold man to confess to having had sex with a chicken. And bold is certainly an appropriate word to describe Larry Flynt, publisher of *Hustler* magazine, subject of the biopic film *The People vs. Larry Flynt,* who had enough gall (and, from some perspectives, sense of humor) to put a woman coming out of a meat grinder on the cover of his magazine and to confess in his autobiography to having done it with Ms. Little. And then having killed her.

As someone who has never wrung the neck of my coital partner in that slow-down time normally reserved for a cigarette, I can say that I was a bit taken aback by Flynt's confession. I figure the least a chicken deserves having (counter to the usual meaning of the word) just been boned is a handful of corn kernels or a pat on the back. I once had the grave misfortune of looking after a chicken coop. The first night I was sitting, two dogs broke in and offed half my flock. I shed no tears. Chickens are nasty, pathetic, heinously filthy creatures whose brains are as small and hard as their beaks. After the massacre, one chicken was left wounded and unable to walk; when I put food next to it, the other chickens would come take it away, even though they had plenty for themselves. In an act of grim mercy, I eventually had to kill the poor bird with the back of a shovel, though the truth is I would have liked to have barbecued the lot.

The thought, then, of putting my privy member into the rump or whatever it is of a chicken could not be more anathema. But leave it to Flynt, who certainly has done more than almost anyone else to propagate the relatively grody aspects of the male libido, to lead the charge. Such noble campaigns as Freedom of Speech and Right to Sexual Expression often have unlikely heros; Flynt, in all his tasteless glory, is not least among them.

I have always had a voracious appetite for sex. I usually describe my sexual proclivities as pedestrian, and although my sexual behavior has ranged over the years from the bizarre to the heroic, only one of my early experiences could actually be considered "deviant." This was the occasion when, at age nine, I had sex with a chicken. Yes, this is what the old preachers called bestiality. In the hollows of eastern Kentucky it wasn't all that unusual. Sexual relations with animals — particularly cows, sheep, and horses — were common. Some of the older boys in the area told me that a chicken was as good as a girl — that its egg bag was "hot as a girl's pussy" and "chickens wiggled around a lot more." In fact, they added, it was better in some ways because you could just grab the first chicken that came by — no wooing, no waiting. Anxious to experiment, I caught one of my grandmother's hens out behind the barn, managed to insert my penis into its egg bag, and thrust away. When I let the chicken go, it started toward the main house, staggering, squawking, and bleeding. Fearing that my grandmother would see the hen and want to know what had happened, I caught it and wrung its neck, then threw the bird in the creek. I decided that I liked girls better.

from The Kisses

JOHANNES SECUNDUS

For most of my adult life I've been obsessed with the issue of devotion—about commitment and our deep desire to have it shown. In one of my Nerve.com columns, I tried to get across how difficult it is to express the true goodness of our hearts, how much love we have inside but how little of it gets out and how, even when it does emerge, it's often misconstrued or unseen. Not a happy thought, but I think a true one. This time I want to talk about those times when we do find a way, when the necklace really fits, when the words come out right, when the shoulder is there to receive the tears, when we arrive with blooms in hand (and not just to make up). The human heart, like an under-prepared tourist, is not terribly good with the language, but sometimes finds ways of making itself heard.

Those expressions can range from the comic to the sublime, and either type can be effective. To try to prove the point, I have chosen excerpts that exemplify each end of the spectrum. On the sublime side, there's an absolutely delicious section of the small, soft, deft, witty and incomparably romantic sixteenth-century book *The Kisses* by Johannes Secundus. But first, on the comic side, I thought I might as well share a relic of my misspent youth: a list of anagrams I made of my then-girlfriend's name. (Bear in mind this is only an excerpt: in my devotion, or dementia, I drew out fifty full variations.) True, penning a Petrarchan sonnet would have been a more recognizably amorous act, but we do what we can. As with most things in life, it doesn't matter so much what one does to show one's love, only how.

Is a polish to his nail
Is a nail to his polish
His all, his pain too
I hop on a thin lil' ass
I halt, I splash in, oo . . .
Hail hot lip, ass, loin
Alias: hot loin/hips
Ha, I top his stallion!
Ah! ah! spill it in soon!

Kiss V

When you, Neaera, clasp me in your gentle arms, and hang upon my
shoulder, leaning over me with your whole neck and bosom, and
lascivious face; when putting your lips to mine, you bite me and
complain of being bitten again; and dart your tremulous tongue
here and there, and sip with your querulous tongue here and there,
breathing on me delicious breath, dulcet sounding, moist, the sus-
tenance of my poor life, Neaera when you suck away my languid
breath, my burning, parched breath, parched by the heat that rages
in my bosom, and extinguish the flames that consume me, exhausting their heat by your inhalations; then I exclaim, "Love is the god
of gods and no god is greater than Love; but if there be any one
greater than Love, you, you alone, Neaera, are in my eyes that
greater one."

—*translated by Walter Kelly*

from **"Lucky Pierre"**

GUILLAUME IX

Guillaume IX, a now little known poet of eleventh-century France, is the earliest of the traveling troubadours who survives on the page, and thus, in a certain sense, could be called the first love poet in medieval Europe. As both the count of Poitiers and the duke of Aquitane, Guillaume was a true philosopher king—but not exactly the kind Plato had in mind. No, instead of forging reason and wisdom into a perfect alloy, Guillaume neglected his civic duties in favor of versifying and skirt chasing, concerning himself less with the laws of state as what he calls the "leis de con" (the laws of pussy). Writing in Old Provençal, Guillaume is widely considered the father of the courtly love lyric. And although in later hands these lyrics would become ornately stylized jewels on the nobility of love and the sanctity of the emotive heart, Guillaume's prototypes are ribald, raunchy, and brazen. In one, he asks to outlive the war so he can get his hands beneath his neighbor's mantle; in another, he can't pick between his two steeds (you know what kind); in a third, he sums up his life philosophy with the words:

I don't like women who put guards on their quim,
And I don't like ponds that don't have fish to swim,
And I don't like braggarts with their "Me, me, me"
For when you look at what they've done, there isn't much to see.

But despite his dislike of boasting, Guillaume isn't shy about proclaiming his bedroom artistry. He says he's called the "Sure Master" for "so well have I learned the sweet game / that I'm a hand up on all other men." But apparently things don't always go his way, despite his skills. Pussy's law, as it turns out, is that, unlike most things, it gains from being detracted from, like a forest, where if you cut down one tree three grow back. Leave your lover alone and she'll replace you with three others.

My favorite of his poems is a tale of how he tricks his way into a threesome with two married women. Like Petronius before him, and Boccaccio and Rabelais after, it's another case of brains winning beauty but, in this case, not without a few scrapes.

●●·

In Auvergne, just out of Limousin,
I was walking all alone
When I came upon the lady Garin
Strolling beside the lady Bernard
Both of whom said meek hellos
In the name of Saint Leonard.

And this is how I answered that day,
I didn't say "yeah" or "nay,"
Nor one word of sense did they hear me say,
Just: "Babariol, Babariol,
Babariay."

Then Agnes says to Ermessen:
"We've found what it was we sought.
Sister, by God, let's take him in
For he is mute
And so he'll never dispute
Or tell what we do with him."

"But Sister, this man is ingenious
He stopped speaking simply for us;
So let's go fetch a cat,
Who'll claw down his back,
And we'll see if the show's made for us."

So we ate and drank—it was quite a feast,
Till Agnes came back, holding the beast.
Then she took off my shirt
And to make sure it hurt
Dragged it from my back to my knees.

Though the pain I did repent
My crafty ruse did not relent,
And, convinced, they set a bath to run.
I knew I had gone
Into a carnal oven
And eight days passed 'fore we were done.

And boy did I fuck them, as you will hear,
One hundred and eighty-eight times!
So much I did fear
I would break all my gear,
I can't tell you the pain I was in.
No, I can't tell you the pain I was in.

—*translated by Jack Murnighan*

from **A Man for the Asking**

CATHERINE BREILLAT

Most semisentient people will tell you that there's something wrong with being able to watch porn or be sent to war at age eighteen but not being able to order a beer until you're twenty-one years old. It's a standard complaint in high school and college, but it does reflect some serious problems with our culture's understanding of personal development. If I got to choose (and I'm sure the president will be calling me any day now), the age-responsibility breakdown would look something like this:

If you're age . . .	You're old enough to . . .
9	play doctor with your neighbor
10	realize truth is arbitrary
11	buy fireworks
12	smoke first cigarette (so yucky you don't smoke again till college)
13	read *Nerve*
14	get a part-time job
15	drive
16	go to R-rated movies
17	drink
18	have sex (with gentle, older partner)
19	watch porn
22	have sex with someone younger than you
24	enter college (work and read till then so you know what interests you)
28	get married
29	watch *The Exorcist* by yourself

30	be a parent
31	read the classics
37	write first novel
43	try writing poetry
50	pick a religion (or opt for none)
99	be drafted

I admit that some of these rules could be broken without adverse consequences, but the prohibitions against writing before a certain age are the ones I take most seriously. And though there are historical examples that go against my breakdowns—both Keats and Rimbaud wrote world-class poems in their teens and early twenties—there are plenty of examples that prove the rule. The cavemanlike poems that I wrote on the walls of my college dormitory attest to the fact that I should have paused before penning; Ethan Hawke might have let a few more wrinkles set in before beckoning the muses; and the *Jugendschriften* of even such greats as Marx, Nietzsche, and Freud are better left unopened.

An interesting case study is Catherine Breillat's first novel, *A Man for the Asking,* published in 1968 when the author was only sixteen. Few novels are as badly written, yet few contain so much explicit sexuality. And coming from a milky-skinned, ember-eyed *lycéenne* (a close-up of Breillat graces the English cover and frontispiece), the book becomes more of an anthropological document than a work of literature. Breillat, who scandalized America again two years ago with her supposedly racy (but really rather prudish) film, *Romance,* set Europe on its ear at the close of the 1960s with *A Man for the Asking*'s accounts of infidelity, indiscriminate fucking, bondage, and anal sex. You can be assured it sold well.

Curiously, there's a definite continuity between the portrayal of sex in *A Man for the Asking* and that in *Romance.* Both are extremely graphic yet amazingly detached, even judgmental, as if Breillat has spent her life having oodles of sex she never really enjoyed. Perhaps that is the case. And perhaps, then, her book is an argument for not starting so young; if you're only sixteen and you're already sexually jaded, something is very, very wrong.

●••

He will raise her leg right up to his shoulder where he will hold her foot in his two hands so she won't fall, in fact he also places on it his face, his mouth from which there flows a continuous stream of saliva on this foot as cold and soft as an ivory which does not keep him from looking exclusively at the geometric locus of his arc: equidistant between the two spread legs a first drop of blood is beginning to form, L. moans and the spreading goes further as he arches backward, dazzled by the birth of this double peony, that Japanese flower with two linked petals whose stem she conceals entirely within herself.

L. is a vase, a porcelain in which a tuberose can be made out losing its breath, a violent anemone for she has not said that she was submarine and carnivorous, voracious flowers, into which he must go down as far as

—L. is bent over and taut as the wood of the bow she is as well as the target palpitating like a beckoning blinker. He cannot miss he who is vibrating like a bowstring and with one hand adjusting the drugged arrow, for he is dazzled and this dazzlement, far from being fatal, makes his back stiffen and his entire overcome body go down, he finds himself inside her while she thinks her final dizzying hour has come and she begins to beg.

—"Do it again," L. says, but nothing will ever be the same again, violence can be played out only once, already too much blood has rushed to her head, she is too heavy, too moist, he has hurt her, harassed her, bareassed her and L. has derived an amazed enjoyment from it, the same violence will never have the same effect.

—translated by Harold J. Salemson,
modified by Jack Murnighan

from **Adam Bede**

GEORGE ELIOT

Greek mythology and the Christian Bible make one thing clear: there are times when you shouldn't look back. Orpheus went to retrieve his beloved Eurydice in Hell and lost her when he turned around; Lot's wife was allowed to flee Sodom but was turned to a pillar of salt when she gazed back to watch the city's destruction. Most of us have had life experiences that have taught us the same lesson: Don't light up "just one more" Chesterfield, don't have martinis with your ex, don't go to your tenth-year reunion, don't try to remake your kids in your image and don't ever get a face-lift. The past is the past, and you're better off leaving it behind.

Yes, it's a lesson we all know, but we tend only to learn it the hard way (that's probably why my New Year's resolutions have been the same for the last eleven years). In the fabulous excerpt below from George Eliot's *Adam Bede,* we see man at his most invertebrate. Squire Arthur Donnithorne had resolved to stop leading on the impressionable farm girl Hetty. They had been at a dinner, he found himself flirting with her, immediately regretted it and realized he had to nip things in the bud. But can Donnithorne stick to his guns? Can he resist the tear-dewed cheeks of the ravishing rube? Take a wild guess . . .

● ●·

She would have wanted to put on her hat earlier than usual; only she had told Captain Donnithorne that she usually set out about eight o'clock and if he should go to the Grove again expecting to see her and she should be gone! Would he come? Her little butterfly soul fluttered incessantly between memory and dubious expectation. At last the minute hand of the old-fashioned brazen-faced time-piece was on the last quarter to eight, and there was every reason for its being time to get ready for departure. Even Mrs. Pomfret's preoccupied mind did not prevent her from noticing what looked like a new flush of beauty in the little thing as she tied on her hat before the looking-glass . . .

How relieved she was when she had got safely under the oaks and among the fern of the Chase! Even then she was as ready to be startled as the deer that leaped away at her approach. She thought nothing of the evening light that lay gently in the grassy alleys between the fern, and made the beauty of their living green more visible than it had been in the overpowering flood of noon; she thought of nothing that was present. She only saw something that was possible: Mr. Arthur Donnithorne coming to meet her again along the Fir-tree Grove. That was the foreground of Hetty's picture; behind it lay a bright hazy something—days that were not to be as the other days of her life had been. It was as if she had been wooed by a river-god, who might any time take her to his wondrous halls below a watery heaven. There was no knowing what would come since this strange entrancing delight had come. If a chest full of lace and satin and jewels had been sent her from some unknown source, how could she but have thought that her whole lot was going to change, and that tomorrow some still more bewildering joy would befall her? Hetty had never read a novel: if she had ever seen one, I think the words would have been too hard for her: how then could she find a shape for her expectations? They were as formless as the sweet languid colors of the garden at the Chase, which had floated past her as she walked by the gate.

She is at another gate now—that leading into Fir-tree Grove. She enters the wood, where it is already twilight, and at every step she takes the fear at her heart becomes colder. If he should not come! O how dreary it was—the thought of going out at the other end of the wood, into the unsheltered road, without having seen him. She reaches the first turning towards the Hermitage, walking slowly—he is not there. She hates the leveret that runs across the path: she hates everything that is not what she longs for. She walks on, happy whenever she is coming to a bend in the road, for perhaps he is behind it. No. She is beginning to cry: her heart has swelled so, the tears stand in her eyes; she gives one great sob, while the corners of her mouth quiver, and the tears roll down.

She doesn't know that there is another turning to the Hermitage, that she is close against it, and that Arthur Donnithorne is only a few yards from her, full of one thought, and a thought of which she only is the object. He is going to see Hetty again—that is the longing which has been growing through the last three hours to a feverish thirst. Not, of course, to speak in the caressing way into which he had unguardedly fallen before dinner, but to set things right with her by a kindness which would have the air of friendly civility, and prevent her from running away with wrong notions about their mutual relation.

If Hetty had known he was there, she would not have cried; and it would have been better; for then Arthur would perhaps have behaved as wisely as he had intended. As it was, she started when he appeared at the end of the side-alley, and looked up at him with two great-drops rolling down her cheeks. What else could he do but speak to her in a soft, soothing tone, as if she were a bright-eyed spaniel with a thorn in her foot?

"Has something frightened you, Hetty? Have you seen anything in the wood? Don't be frightened—I'll take care of you now."

Hetty was blushing so, she didn't know whether she was happy or miserable. To be crying again—what did gentlemen think of girls who cried in that way? She felt unable even to say "no," but could only look away from him, and wipe the tears from her cheek. Not before a great drop had fallen on her rose-colored strings: she knew that quite well.

"Come, be cheerful again. Smile at me, and tell me what's the matter. Come, tell me."

Hetty turned her head towards him, whispered, "I thought you wouldn't come," and slowly got courage to lift her eyes to him. That look was too much: he must have had eyes of Egyptian granite not to look too lovingly in return.

"You little frightened bird! Little tearful rose! Silly pet! You won't cry again, now I'm with you, will you?"

Ah, he doesn't know in the least what he is saying. This is not what he meant to say. His arm is stealing round the waist again, it is tightening its clasp; he is bending his face nearer and nearer to the round cheek, his lips are meeting those pouting child-lips, and for a long moment time has vanished. He may be a shepherd in Arcadia for aught he knows, he may be the first youth kissing the first maiden, he may be Eros himself, sipping the lips of Psyche—it is all one.

from **J**

KENZABURO OE

How much would you risk, what would you sacrifice to sip from the deepest well of human experience? The question usually comes up regarding murder: Would you kill a person just to know what it feels like? To know what it means to rob someone of their life? To push the knife blade till it breaks the skin, then turn it in the spurting artery? Most of us, thankfully, are not born to become disaffected, murderous Patrick Batemans of *American Psycho*, the upper-class kids in *Rope*, or the randomly shooting "model Surrealists" of André Breton's *Second Manifesto*. We live quiet, contained lives, for the most part as morally as we can, and only infrequently wonder what we might be missing. The film *Fight Club* challenged this ethos in a particularly poignant way: would you hit rock bottom to know what that meant, to know you would survive, to allow yourself the understanding of absolute abjection? As in Cormac McCarthy's *Blood Meridian* or René Girard's analysis of ritual, violence is an age-old gateway to enlightenment. Would you?

When the question is taken from extreme violence to extreme sex, it loses none of its intrigue. Most of us have indulged, at least in the safety of our own minds, in outlandish sexual behavior and felt the icy burn of its appeal. Much of the porn industry is based on precisely this instinct for sexual tourism. But what if the objective is not mere arousal but a kind of philosophical redefinition of the *Fight Club* kind? What if there was a kind of sexual abjection that you could pass through in order to emerge in nirvana, enlightenment, or at least outside the straitjacket of quotidian boredom?

This is the question raised when the protagonist of Kenzaburo Oe's 1963 novel *J* decides to become a *chikan*—a groper of women on commuter trains. Oe, a Nobel Prize winner, crafts the philosophical birthing of a pervert with incredible nuance. This excerpt, where J has his first encounter, is one of my favorite passages of erotic prose in the entire history of literature. There are things one can only know through experience; it is up to us to decide whether we dare to do them.

 ● ●·

Standing immediately in front of him was a woman of about his age. She was at a right angle to him, and their bodies were pressed together, with her chest, stomach, and thighs fitted to his. J caressed the woman. His right hand moved into the space between her buttocks, while his left hand traveled down her belly toward the space between her thighs. His erect penis was touching the outside of her leg. He and the woman were about the same height. His heavy breath stirred the down on her flushed earlobes. At first J trembled with fear and his breathing was irregular. Was the woman not going to cry out? . . . When his fear was at its peak, J's penis was hardest. Now it was pressed tight against the woman's thigh. He shook with profound fear as he stared straight at her chiseled profile . . . If the girl cried out in disgust or fear, he would have an orgasm. He held on to this fantasy like fear, like desire. But she didn't cry out. She kept her lips firmly closed. Suddenly her eyes closed tightly, like a curtain with its ropes cut falling to the stage. At that instant the restraining pressure of her buttocks and thighs relaxed. Descending, J's right hand reached the depths of her now-soft cheeks. His left hand went to the hollow between her outspread thighs.

J lost his fear and, at the same time, his desire weakened. Already his penis was beginning to wilt.

—translated by Luk Van Haute

from **Child of God**

CORMAC MCCARTHY

It's a longstanding philosophical
(and religious) question what we
humans do from choice, and what
we are fated—or programmed
—to do. I've never been a big
believer in predetermination or
destiny, and even Noam
Chomsky's claim that we are all hardwired for language has always
seemed rather implausible to me. When the argument turns to sex, however, I find myself much more available to the idea that we are all born
with some basic blueprint—and perhaps even with our particular tastes.

Whether we are natured or nurtured is not an idle question by any
means, and the implications change depending on what specific sex
practice or predilection you're talking about. Most people tend to think
that sexual extremists, like pedophiles, are born with their leanings
(though it is also argued that abuse or child porn encourages them
along). With other sex offenders, it's not so clear. Is one born a rapist, is
one led to rape, or is it, in some measure, a matter of choice? It's hard
not to think that it's a combination of all of the above. Sexual orientation
is another tricky issue. It is often thought of as something we're born
with, though there are arguments both ways (thus the Christian Right's
"deprogramming" centers for homosexuals). Atypical tastes, like fetishes
or S/M, raise questions of their own. Sadomasochistic play has become
quite mainstream, but still I wonder if there aren't serious players who
would say that S/M is not an option but a necessity. Is that necessity
inborn or acculturated? Hard to say.

Cormac McCarthy's haunting early novel, *Child of God,* brings these
questions to a head in its portrayal of the mental disintegration of
adolescent protagonist Lester Ballard. Lester starts out a little weird,
then moves off into the woods by himself and slowly begins to lose it.
His relations with the fairer sex don't go particularly well—to say the
least—and he soon learns, at first by accident, that the newly dead are

not as hard to deal with as the living, breathing, and resisting. Was Lester born a necrophiliac, or did his disastrous encounters with women and slipping mental health turn him into one? In the scene that follows, Lester comes upon a car where a young, copulating couple have mysteriously died. The possibilities dawn on him gradually but irrevocably. Was he destined?

● ●·

He knelt there staring at the two bodies. Them sons of bitches is deader'n hell, he said.

He could see one of the girl's breasts. Her blouse was open and her brassiere was pushed up around her neck. Ballard stared for a long time. Finally he reached across the dead man's back and touched the breast. It was soft and cool. He stroked the full brown nipple with the ball of his thumb . . . Leaning over the seat he took hold of the man and tried to pull him off the girl. The body sprawled heavily, the head lolled . . . He could see the girl better now. He reached and stroked her other breast. He did this for a while and then he pushed her eyes shut with his thumb. She was young and very pretty . . . [She] lay with her eyes closed and her breasts peeking from her open blouse and her pale thighs spread. Ballard climbed over the seat.

The dead man was watching him from the floor of the car. Ballard kicked his feet out of the way and picked the girl's panties up from the floor and sniffed at them and put them in his pocket. He looked out the rear window and he listened. Kneeling there between the girl's legs he undid his buckle and lowered his trousers.

A crazed gymnast laboring over a cold corpse. He poured into that waxen ear everything he'd ever thought of saying to a woman. Who could say she did not hear him?

from **The Old Testament**

I think it was Umberto Eco who said that he dreaded reading the Bible as a teenager, until he discovered how much sex was in it. He had a point. As early as 2 Genesis, God says, "It is not good for a man to be alone" (a belief I've long subscribed to), and he makes first the animals, then Eve. I'd rather not comment on the order of these events—the implications are clear to those who want them to be clear. I'd rather point out that Adam gets a partner in Eden faster than most of us would at a sex addict's convention.

And such is the nature of the Bible as a whole: couplings are common, incest omnipresent, and innuendo aplenty. The Good Book does not lack for good parts, especially the Old Testament—you just have to sift through endless lists of progeny and litanies of the scourges inflicted on the Israelites to get to them.

Take the story of Abraham and Sarah (originally Abram and Sarai), the second sexually active couple in Genesis. In the course of a few chapters, Sarah, while pretending to be Abraham's sister to protect him, gets abducted into Pharaoh's harem (bad Pharaoh, bad Pharaoh), proves herself to be Abraham's half sister, gets released, then gets taken into Abimelech's harem (who is warned by God not to go near her), gets released, convinces Abraham to have a baby (Ishmael) with the maid Hagar, and eventually has a baby with him herself (Isaac). So much happens so fast in the Bible, that reading it for naughty bits is like trying to distinguish body parts in scrambled adult channels on TV. If your attention wavers for even an instant, you risk missing the enchilada.

Amid all the wham-bam sex tales in the early books of the Old Testament, the most interesting involve Lot and his daughters. Lot, you'll remember, was the one man in Sodom that the Lord decided to save from the fire and brimstone. So he sends two angels to Lot's house to warn him of the destruction and give him instructions for getting himself and his family out of Dodge. Now the inhabitants of Sodom were not called Sodomites for nothing, so when they see the two male angels—certified hotties—going into Lot's house, they want a piece of the action. "Both old and young, all the people from every quarter" circle around Lot's house, banging on his door, calling, "Where are the men which came in to thee this night? Bring them to us that we may know them." Among the fabulous euphemisms for sex in the King James translation, "to know" is one of my favorites. I envision a mob of sex fiends hemmed in around Antonio Sabato Jr., screaming, "We want to know you, we just want to know you." You get the point.

Lot realizes he has a difficult situation on his hands. So he goes out to the throng, locking the door behind him, and says: "I pray you, brethren, do not so wickedly. Behold now, I have two daughters which have not known man; let me, I pray you, bring them out unto you, and do ye to them as is good in your eyes: only unto these men do nothing; for therefore came they under the shadow of my roof." Here is a good example of what can transpire in the course of a few biblical words. You scan the line, scan it again, and say to yourself, In place of the angels, did Lot just offer the crowd his virgin daughters to do with what they will? I mean, being a good host is nice and all, but that seems a bit extreme. The mind reels—not unproductively—at what would befall the innocents if they were cast to the awaiting wolves.

Thankfully, the angels intervene. They pull Lot back into the house and blind the Sodomites pressing against the door. Then they facilitate Lot's exit, with wife and daughters in tow, but, in their flight across the plain, Lot's wife makes the mortal mistake of looking back (like many of us toward old relationships) and is turned into a pillar of salt.

Yet the saga of Lot and his daughters is not over. Having fled to the town of Zoar, he eventually becomes afraid and moves himself and his daughters to the mountains. Apparently it's a little underpopulated up there, and his daughters begin to despair of ever getting nookie. The older says to the younger, "Our father is old, and there is not a man in the earth to come in unto us after the manner of all the earth. Come, let us make our father drink wine, and we will lie with him, that we may preserve the seed of the father." Ah, the old Get Dad Drunk and Have Him Impregnate Us trick—pretty sneaky, Sis! So on consecutive nights the daughters get Lot schnookered and go lie with him (again, a nice euphemism, though not as good as "come in unto"). Lot, the sod, doesn't seem to notice either time. Eventually each of his daughters gives birth to a son.

Now, mind you, all this has happened in the first twenty pages of the

Bible (at least in my edition). This is some kind of book. By comparison, the first twenty pages of *Best American Erotica 2000* contain nowhere near as much sex and only a fraction of the scandal. True, conventional erotica tends to have more adjective-heavy descriptions of sex than one finds in the Holy Book (the Song of Solomon is the exception, as we will see), but for sheer quantity of nudge nudge, the Bible is up there.

By and large, the Old Testament is a very weird document, full of bizarre and rather unsavory tidbits that the New Testament tried to smooth over. Even God himself had to be rendered kinder and gentler the second time around, for in the Hebrew books he was forever casting plagues and famines down on the people, and insisting on himself as a "consuming fire" and a "jealous God." In Isaiah 3:16–17, for example, the "haughty" daughters of Zion with their "wanton eyes, walking and mincing as they go and making a tinkling with their feet" will be smote down by the Lord, and he will discover their "secret parts." Ooh. Best take off those bangles before it's too late.

But my favorite Old Testament oddity occurs in Deuteronomy 23:1, where, in a list of all those who will not make it to Heaven, it is written: "He that is wounded in the stones, or hath his privy member cut off, shall not enter into the congregation of the Lord." Rum thing, not only do you have to go through this life without the priviest of privies, but the gates of Paradise are closed to you to boot (and the fact that you can sing a decent falsetto is pretty minor recompense). Yet the intrigue of this passage doesn't end there: why, in fact, are the memberless or the crushed-testicled not welcome into the New Jerusalem? Interesting question. There are numerous medieval theological debates about whether angels eat and drink, piss, and shit (and where it goes if they do), but I've never heard anyone ask if they screw. Yet here is evidence that the celestial nightclub serves up more than just juice and cookies. Perhaps this is not the venue to reinscribe us in thirteenth-century scholastic arguments, but the point is still intriguing: if it was just sex the elect were after, the penis would be enough. But if the balls are also necessary, this suggests a certain import to the physical male orgasm itself. To my mind this complicates Aquinas's notion that the postprandial material discharge of angels is only a vapor (but not a flatulence, mind you); for even if we agree that angel excretion is but gas, what are we to do with angel jizz? I'm sure Aquinas would have said it was some kind of noumenal hand lotion.

Even in the briefest of introductions to sex in the Old Testament, no account can ignore one of the most erotic, exquisite texts not just in the Bible but in the whole history of Western literature: the Song of Solomon. In all the reams of biblical interpretation, this is the text that has received the most treatment. The reasons are twofold: the Song of Solomon is sufficiently explicit to be embarrassing to the antisensuality of the later Christian Church, and thus required extensive backpedaling. This is the obvious, confessed reason so many monks spilled their ink on its pages. The other, only slightly less obvious, is that it is very fun to read, and decidedly arousing, especially if the only other thing you're reading is Samuel and Jeremiah's accounts of the punishments visited upon the wicked.

In effect, the Song of Solomon is generally agreed to be a dialogue between two lovers (although I, for one, detect more than two total speakers, but that truly is a debate outside our scope), one called Solomon (not necessarily the famous king who appears elsewhere in the Old Testament), the other his unnamed lover, who, by some accounts, may have written the piece. Orthodox Christian interpretations attempt to downplay the hot and heavy eroticism in the Song by saying that the female lover is the Church, Solomon is Christ, and their love is the spiritual union of the material Christian apparatus with the higher spiritual forces.

Yeah right. The Song begins: "The song of songs, which is Solomon's. Let him kiss me with the kisses of his mouth: for thy love is better than wine." If the point here was supposed to be that the Church wants to merge itself with the love of Christ the Savior, there would have been considerably less distracting ways of saying it. No—the Song of Solomon is a love poem, and the love is a very corporeal one. That it made it into the foundational book of Christianity is a mystery beyond my comprehension. But, like the Psalms, here is a part of the Bible that can be read purely for the love of its poetry.

I'm touched all the more by the Song for the occasional odd chord it strikes. Such compliments as "thy neck is like the tower David builded for an armory" or "thy hair is as a flock of goats, that appear from mount Gilead" have perhaps lost some of their charm in the last few thousand years (a modern adaptation might be: thy hair is like dark-suited businessmen, leaping out of skyscrapers on Black Monday). And there are moments that seem downright overdone: "My beloved put in his hand by the hole of the door, and my bowels were moved for him."

For the most part, though, the poem's imagery is most pleasantly evocative. A few highlights: the lover says that her beloved "feeds among the lilies" and that her hands, when she rises up to him, are "dropped with myrrh." And Solomon, meanwhile, says to her, "Thy lips, O my spouse, drop as honeycomb: honey and milk are under thy tongue." And she back to him: "Blow on my garden, that the spices thereof may flow out. Let my beloved come into his garden, and eat the pleasant fruits." Heart be stilled!

Fan though I am, I hadn't read much of the Bible until I went to graduate school and, on a rather prolonged lark, decided to become a medievalist. As a result, I found myself a late twenty-something pagan having to read the whole of the Good Book. I did it straight through— not quickly, mind you, but steadily. What I discovered between the now worn-off covers of my red-letter edition corresponded so minimally to what I had anticipated I wondered if I had the right religion. The sex and sexual oddities were only some of the Bible's unforeseen pleasures (others include the almost James Bond—like coolness of Christ, the beauty of Paul's prose, the phenomenal stories of Job and Ruth, the bombast of Ezekiel, etc.). Having now read the entire Bible multiple times over, I am still a pagan, but I'm all for placing copies in every hotel room. It's the most influential book in Western culture, and it's a lot better than TV.

Acknowledgments

First off, I'd like to thank the friends and readers who pointed me toward their favorite bits—without you, I would have been in the unenviable position of having to rely exclusively on my own knowledge. Mike Moore deserves special mention for often reminding me of the actual facts of history (quite opposed to what I am wont to believe) and for catching my all-too-frequent typos. I also received enormous technical help from the *Nerve* gang, especially Isabella, permissions queen, my fabulous assistant, Jessica, and my editors, Genevieve, Susan, and Emily. Thanks also to my editor at Crown, Rachel Kahan, who let me keep many of the nerdy bits, despite the sales team's admonishments. More than anyone, I have the founders of *Nerve*, Rufus and Genevieve (again), to thank, not only for letting me get away with the column in the first place, but for tolerating such iconoclastic indulgences as Naughty Pushkin Month and Burn Victim Week. It is a rare privilege for a writer to be able to invent his genre as he goes along; I thank them for having sufficient faith in me to let me loose. One of my advisors in graduate school once told me that you're only as good as your colleagues; in my years at *Nerve*, I can only hope that that was true.

Credits

From *Money* by Martin Amis, copyright © 1984 by Martin Amis. Published in the U.S. by Viking Penguin and in the U.K. by Jonathan Cape. Used by permission of Viking Penguin, a division of Penguin Putnam Inc. and the Random House Group, Ltd.

From *Giovanni's Room* by James Baldwin, copyright © 1956 by James Baldwin. Used by permission of Doubleday, a division of Random House, Inc.

Excerpt from *Crash* by J.G. Ballard. Copyright © 1973 by J.G. Ballard. Reprinted by Permission of Farrar, Strauss, and Giroux, LLC.

From *Vox* by Nicholson Baker. Copyright © 1992 by Nicholson Baker. Reprinted by permission of Random House, Inc.

From *The Life I Lead* by Keith Banner. Reprinted by permission of the author.

From *Hell* by Henri Barbusse, copyright © 1995. Reprinted by permission of Turtle Point Press.

From *The Floating Opera* by John Barth, copyright © 1967, 1968 by John Barth. Used by permission of Doubleday, a division of Random House, Inc.

From *A Stranger in this World* by Kevin Canty, copyright © 1994 by Kevin Canty. Used by permission of Doubleday, a division of Random House, Inc.

From *Falconer* by John Cheever. Copyright © 1975, 1977 by John Cheever. Reprinted by permission of Alfred A. Knopf, a division of Random House, Inc.

The Exeter Book, translated by Andrew Cole. Reprinted by permission of Andrew Cole.

"This Condition" from *Almost No Memory* by Lydia Davis. Copyright © 1997. Used by permission of Salt Hill, a division of Syracuse University Press.

Excerpts from *The Name of the Rose* by Umberto Eco, copyright © 1980 by Gruppo Editoriale Fabri-Bompiani, Sozogno, Etas S.p.A., English translation copyright © 1983 by Harcourt Inc. and Martin Secker & Warburg Limited, reprinted by permission of Harcourt, Inc.

From *Serve It Forth* by M.F.K. Fisher. Copyright © 1937, 1954, 1989 by M.F.K. Fisher.

From *The Thief's Journal* by Jean Genet, 1965 edition. Reprinted by permission of Grove Press.

About the Author

JACK MURNIGHAN received a Ph.D. in literature from Duke University in 1999 while editor-in-chief of Nerve.com, the website that pioneered "literary smut." At Nerve he coedited (with Genevieve Field) the short story collection *Full Frontal Fiction* (Three Rivers Press, 2000). He now writes essays and fiction full-time. His stories have been chosen for *The Best American Erotica* in 1999, 2000, and 2001.

Want More?

You'll find it in: